Praise for *Betrayed*

"An adrenaline-p... ... ...and humor. Corporate ... ...ty, kidnapping, murd... ... an intriguing story tha... ...put down."

—*Romance Junkies*

"A high-speed adventure… You can't help but be caught up in the fast-paced, action-packed, explosive scenes."

—*Tome Tender*

"Such an intense and wild ride…Engaging and heart-warming…The story is intense, filled with passion…and full of adventure and love. A mesmerizing combination of action and swiftly moving plot. Brilliantly done!"

—*Addicted to Romance*

"Rebecca York does it again with another exciting romantic suspense that will keep you turning the pages."

—*The Reading Cafe*

"Well done! The characters are enduring, engaging, and captivating. The storyline is intriguing and suspenseful. I can hardly wait for the next installment."

—*My Book Addiction and More*

"The author keeps the reader guessing with lots of twists and turns and draws the reader deeper into the story with the captivating men of Rockfort Security. I was completely engrossed from the very beginning."

—*Literary Addicts*

Praise for *Bad Nights*

"Tense and intriguing, the first of York's Rockfort Security books is an action-packed read that promises much for the series to come…a suspenseful, visceral reading experience."

—*RT Book Reviews*

"A heart-in-throat thriller and a soul-satisfying romance—a fantastic read!"

—*Long and Short Reviews*

"Filled with action, adventure, and a steamy love story… entertaining romantic suspense with complex characters and a thrilling plot."

—*Book Lover and Procrastinator*

"This is a guns blazing, fast-paced, suspense-filled story. The premise was outstanding."

—*Tome Tender*

"Fast-paced, riveting, and loaded with tension."

—*The Royal Reviews*

"[Rebecca York] did an excellent job with the suspense element… She turned the tables in a brilliant stroke of genius. It's a page turner for sure."

—*Night Owl Reviews,* Reviewer Top Pick

"Filled with danger and sizzling passion."

—*Single Titles*

PRIVATE AFFAIR

REBECCA YORK

sourcebooks
casablanca

Published by Sourcebooks Casablanca, an imprint of Sourcebooks, Inc.
P.O. Box 4410, Naperville, Illinois 60567-4410
(630) 961-3900
Fax: (630) 961-2168
www.sourcebooks.com

Printed and bound in Canada.
MBP 10 9 8 7 6 5 4 3 2 1

To my husband, Norman, who has supported my career every step of the way.

Chapter 1

A SUDDEN JOLT OF UNEASE MADE THE HAIRS ON THE back of Angela's neck prickle. She might have stopped and looked around. Instead, she quickened her pace, hurrying toward the car. She'd parked behind her shop when she'd arrived early that morning. She put in long hours, but it was worth it because she was building her business and her reputation as a local fashion maven.

Her sedan had an automatic lock that opened when she reached for the door handle, and she breathed out a sigh of relief as she slipped behind the wheel and locked the doors. Usually she didn't mind walking to her vehicle after hours. It was only a few steps from the back door of her boutique, after all, and the area was well lit. Which was good, because lately she'd had the feeling that someone was lurking in the darkness, watching her. She glanced up at the car's dome light and tried to turn it on. But it seemed to be on the fritz. And did the car smell funny? She twisted around, looking in the backseat, but saw nothing.

Then she shook her head, trying to dispel her unease. Was she getting paranoid? Or was she tempting fate with her success in the fashion world?

Her shop was on Main Street in Ellicott City, a 250-year-old mill town built into a river valley. The old stone townhouses that lined the narrow thoroughfare were now full of antique shops, restaurants, boutiques,

and other retail outlets that catered to tourists and
affluent locals. As you drove down the hill toward
the Patapsco River, the shops on the left backed right
into a massive stone cliff. In fact, the living stone was
sometimes part of the back wall. On the right side of the
street, there was room in the rear for parking. Some shop
owners lived above their stores or rented out the space.
Angela preferred to get out of the crowded downtown
area when she wasn't working.

Her boutique, called What She Wants, sold trendy
women's clothing. It was doing so well that she was
thinking about expanding. The store next door had been
vacant for a few months, and she was probably going to
ask the owner if she could expand into the extra space.
That way she could have twice the display area and
be able to add the line of slinky underwear she'd been
thinking about. Plus, she could have a bigger lounge in
the back where customers could relax with a cup of tea
while they modeled clothing for each other. That was
part of the charm of her shop—the unhurried atmosphere. Destination shopping.

She smiled to herself as she pictured doubling her
domain. Maybe she wasn't as big a success as the
former class star, Olivia Winters. Olivia was a big deal
in the New York fashion scene. A jet-setter who was the
envy of half the country's female population. And a sex
object for the guys. Was that the bad part? Because there
had to be a bad part, didn't there?

But Angela could deal with Olivia's fame and fortune.
And she was sure the two of them would have a lot to talk
about at the upcoming Donley High ten-year reunion.
She was already working on plans for some of the events,

and if she couldn't get Olivia onto the planning committee, she was at least hoping to get her best friend from
high school down to Maryland for the reunion.

Her mind turned from her fears of being stalked to
the reunion plans. She was on the committee, and she
was going to make sure that this was the best ten-year
reunion Donley had ever seen.

For just a moment, a painful memory from her high
school days zinged into her mind. Quickly she pushed it
away. All of that was over and done with. You couldn't
dwell on the past. You had to keep moving forward if
you wanted to be a success in life.

With a firm shake of her head, she nosed the car away
from the downtown area into the subdivision where she'd
bought a comfortable townhouse after her divorce from
Chip. She'd met him at a young singles mixer a couple
of years after she'd graduated from high school. He'd
seemed like a good guy—ambitious and personable, with
a college degree in hospitality and a good job at a national
hotel chain. But he'd turned out to be one of the few major
mistakes she'd made. She'd gotten rid of him as soon as
she'd realized he wasn't about to let his wife have a career
that might eclipse his importance as the man of the house.

She'd bought her end unit at a good price after the
housing bubble crash. In the driveway, she clicked the
remote, waited for the garage door to open, then drove
in and closed the door behind her.

She was hungry. Maybe she should have stopped
at that new French carryout on the way home instead
of having to fix something. Well, it would have to be
something quick, like a can of the low-cal soup she had
in the pantry.

Before she could get out of the car, someone grabbed her from behind—someone who must have been in the car all the way home from the shop.

She cried out in shock and disbelief, but the cry turned into a gasp as the person behind her grabbed her shoulder to anchor her in place while they slipped something around her neck.

In desperation, she kicked out her legs and bucked her body, writhing in her seat as she tried to free herself from the stranglehold. But the hand held her fast as the cord tightened and tightened.

Did she hear words whispered in her ear? Hateful words about what a slut she'd been in high school—and how she'd broken her word.

No, she wanted to scream. It wasn't true. She'd kept her vow of silence. But the person with the rope around her neck kept whispering, telling her she wasn't going to get the chance to blab about her past at the reunion—or anyone else's past.

The awful voice kept talking, filling her mind like boiling syrup in a pot bubbling on the stove, and she knew who it was. Someone dangerous. Someone she'd avoided for years.

"You little slut. You thought you were a big deal. You thought you could hide your true colors, didn't you?"

Again she tried to scream that it wasn't true. It had never been true. And no matter what she had been in high school, she was a different person now. Then she'd been unsure of herself. Eager to fit in. Now she knew she didn't have to conform to anyone's standards but her own. She was put together. Successful, and on her way to bigger and better things.

But there was no breath in her lungs for those pro-
tests, or for anything else. She was slipping from consciousness. She tried to focus on her shop. On her big
plans. But black dots danced in front of her eyes. Then
the blackness overwhelmed her.

Chapter 2

OLIVIA WINTERS GLANCED AT THE MAN BESIDE HER IN the driver's seat of the comfortable SUV. They'd had things to discuss the whole way over here, but as he pulled into a parking space in front of the old stable that had been turned into a restaurant called the Ironwood Grill, they fell silent. This was the second meeting of the Donley High School ten-year reunion committee. Olivia had deliberately missed the first get-together, and she hadn't intended to make this one. But now everything had changed, and here she was.

She felt a shiver like a cold ocean wave travel over her skin as she thought about why she was here. When she'd first gotten the email about the reunion, she'd had the sudden sensation of being in an elevator dropping out of control down a dark shaft. No way had she ever considered deliberately going back and mingling with these people again. Yet here she was, returning to the scene of... What was it? The most miserable years of her life? She had vowed to stay as far away from the reunion as she could. What was she going to say to these people after all these years? But the death of her friend, Angela Dawson, had turned her resolve upside down. She and Angela had been best friends in high school, and they had kept in touch after Olivia had moved to New York. Now Angela was gone, and Olivia was about to join the group planning the reunion—with Max Lyon beside her. He'd gone to Donley, too, a couple of years ahead of her class.

She gave him a quick glance, hoping she was concealing her raw nerves. "Showtime," she whispered.

"Yeah. Just remember what we talked about," he said in his deep, masculine voice. It had made her uncomfortable at first. Then she'd admitted that she liked it. His voice helped steady her—that and the private-detective wisdom he'd shared.

"Uh-huh," she answered, knowing she was focusing on the easy part of the equation, a set of rules, rather than her churning emotions. There were so many reasons to be on edge, starting with her uncertainty about seeing her former classmates again.

When he cut the engine, she felt a sense of finality. Too late to back out now.

It wasn't quite six thirty, and because they were well into spring, there was still a little natural light lingering in the parking lot. Given her choice, she would have elected to arrive under cover of darkness, but that would have brought its own perils—making her and Max late to the party so that all eyes would be on them when they entered the room.

To her right, a car door slammed and she jumped. Max put a hand on her shoulder, and her body stiffened even more. She knew that personal contact with him had to be part of the deal, but she was having trouble adjusting to the way his touch made her feel. Maybe because she was attracted to him and didn't want to be. Really, the chemistry between them only got in the way.

"Relax," he said, and she took a couple of breaths, doing her best to comply, trying to pretend that her nerves weren't tingling like a bunch of live electric wires twisting inside her.

"Is this worse than being on the runway?" he asked.

"No contest."

"Why?"

She hated when he asked probing questions that she'd rather not answer. Revealing her insecurities wasn't supposed to be part of the deal, but this was a bad time to start an argument with him. Even if he was the arguing type, which didn't seem to be true.

"Because I never liked playing charades," she answered, struggling to keep her voice even.

"Don't you play a part every time you put on a designer outfit? Or when you do a TV commercial?"

"That's different," she shot back.

"How?"

"For one thing, when I'm working, I'm separated from the audience. For another thing, I don't have to get emotionally involved with my work," she snapped, then wondered if she'd given away too much.

When he made a snorting sound, she added, "And because of Angela. Someone coming to this meeting could be the one who..." She swallowed. "Who killed her..." As her voice trailed off, she raised one shoulder.

"Yeah," he answered. "That's the main reason we're here."

He glanced at her as she pressed the back of her skull against the firm support of the headrest, feeling the solid barrier through her thick hair. It was long so she could wear it up if she needed a high-society look, or she could keep it down and appear to be barely out of her teens. But neither of those were the part she was currently playing. Tonight her hair was a sexy blond mane flowing around her slender shoulders. And her makeup was runway perfect, as always. At least her looks were something she could be confident about, which had basically always been true.

"You know your lines. Everything's going to be fine," Max murmured.

Impossible. It wasn't going to be fine. She'd known that well enough from the beginning. But she'd come up with the plan because it was a quick way to pick up some useful information. When she started to nervously twist the strap of her purse, Max reached out and stilled her hand.

The pressure of his warm fingers on hers made her go very still. Through her lashes she glanced up at him and saw something she hadn't noticed earlier. The rigid look on his face told her his emotions were as conflicted as hers.

This was the only time she'd seen him look jumpy, and she didn't know whether to be glad or worried that he was reacting, too.

Just then, movement on the other side of the car window caught her eye, and she seized the opportunity to shift her attention away from the man who had pressed his hand over hers. As she looked past Max's shoulder, she saw a group of people she recognized crossing the parking lot. The first one to register was the large bulky form of Tommy Larson, former Donley star quarterback. He was still well-muscled, with shoulders as broad as North Dakota. She remembered he'd married Bunny Raymond, former captain of the cheerleading squad. But he wasn't with her now. Instead he had another woman on his arm, someone even more stunning than Bunny.

Olivia had heard that they'd gotten married a couple of years out of school. She'd been surprised that two people with such swelled heads could live in the same house. Apparently it hadn't worked out. And now Tommy was going the same route with another beauty?

He glanced in her direction, stopped and squinted, then did a double take as he apparently recognized her— and maybe Max as well. Obviously he hadn't expected to see either one of them here today. But she'd gone to considerable trouble to make the meeting—with Max at her side.

Instinctively, she slid closer to him, and he slung his arm possessively around her shoulder as he followed the direction of her gaze and saw her react to the approaching couple.

He turned so that his warm breath fanned her ear, like he was getting ready to nuzzle her in a sexy move. Nice thought, but instead he was sticking to business. "That's Tommy Larson," he said, either remembering the former football player from the way he'd strode around the halls of Donley High or recognizing him from the yearbook and Web pictures he'd studied.

"Yes," she managed, goose bumps rising on her arms—and not just from seeing her former classmates. She was reacting to Max, and she didn't want to. Not now. And not ever.

Two newcomers emerged from the darkness farther down the parking lot and joined the man and woman looking in their direction. Mark Tate and Sue Harrison. Again, Olivia couldn't stop herself from making a quick evaluation. Mark looked kind of stressed out, his face aged more than the ten years that had passed since she'd seen him, and his dark hair was thinning. Sue had put on a few pounds and was wearing a knit shirt that did nothing to hide the ripples of fat around her middle.

She knew she was making judgments about her former classmates in an effort to calm herself. And as the foursome stared in her direction, she sat as still as a statue, staring back calmly while her heart was pounding inside her chest like it was doing a Calypso number on *Dancing with the Stars*.

Maybe she was fooling the people outside the car, but not the man sitting beside her. "You've got more going than any of them," Max whispered.

Maybe now. And perhaps it was true if you were talking in terms of worldly success. But here, in this place, it didn't matter what she had transformed herself into. She was back in a world where you could be laughed at for wearing the wrong color blouse on the wrong day or for having the wrong socks.

She heard herself saying, "They probably think I'm a snob who forgot where she came from. I mean, I've hardly been back here since I left for New York."

"You've been busy. But you'll convince them you're just a good old Donley girl."

She laughed. "Yeah, right." She'd wanted that so badly back in high school that she'd done some things and gotten into some situations that made her cringe now. Of course, she'd run with the in crowd, by virtue of her looks, she supposed. And maybe her lack of interest in making the honor roll was because everybody figured it was only for kids who related better to books than people. But she'd never really felt like she belonged. The popular kids mostly came from upscale developments in Columbia and Ellicott City. She'd lived on a farm, and she'd gone to Donley because her father had grown up with the guy who'd become superintendent of schools and had gotten her special permission to go to the best high school in the county.

Max broke into her thoughts of the past. "You've got me in your corner—your man who's going to make it very clear to the jerks out there that if anybody gives you a hard time, they'll have to answer to him."

She liked the way he said that with absolute conviction, as if he weren't just playing a role. Still, you could argue that it was true. Watching out for her was part of his job.

Absorbing the words, she allowed herself to lean into him, comforted by the feel of his solid body against hers. Unlike most guys, he was taller than she was. And in fighting shape. He made her feel protected, and she fought the impulse to close her eyes, shut out the world, and stay right here in the car. But they had business to attend to.

They sat together for long seconds, until he reminded her of reality. Straightening, he said, "We'd better get in there while the getting's good."

"Right," she answered, then opened the car door and joined him in the parking lot.

—◇◇◇—

Max slid a glance at the tall, slender blond walking beside him. From her expression, he knew she was wondering what the hell she was doing here, dredging up memories and feelings from long ago. He had similar doubts about his own past. The only good thing about tonight that he could focus on was that the meeting wasn't being held at Donley High School. If he never set foot in that place again, it would be just fine with him.

They were halfway across the parking lot when Max felt Olivia stumble on an uneven patch in the sidewalk. Automatically, his arm shot out to steady her.

As she had in the car, she leaned against him, and he cradled her slender body protectively against his.

"What happened?"

"I guess I'm too out of it to pay attention to where I'm walking. My foot caught on something."

"Okay," he answered, thinking that she had plenty of experience walking gracefully—in front of very critical audiences. But tonight, not so much. She'd confessed she was nervous before they'd left home, and in the car she'd been jittery. Still, he hadn't realized how much this was getting to her, maybe because he'd made assumptions based on her successful career.

"Are you okay?" he asked, sensing the tension rippling through her body and wondering if she could really pull off this performance. It had seemed like a good idea in the planning stages. Now he was thinking they should have considered a plan B.

"I'll be fine," she said in a voice that sounded far from fine. "Just give me a minute to center myself."

Truth be told, he hadn't wanted this assignment. But Olivia Winters had come to the Rockfort Security Agency for help, and he was the only member of the team who could in good conscience handle the job. Not because of any special skills he possessed, but because the other guys in the agency had obviously ruled themselves out.

As he stood with Olivia, he used the opportunity to take in the details of the area, pretending he was watching for new arrivals to the meeting.

Still with his arm around her, he turned his back on the open area and pulled his cell phone out of his pocket, hiding his action from view with his body. Punching in a number, he waited until Shane Gallagher, one of his partners, picked up. He and Jack Brandt were nearby, stationed where they had a good view of the restaurant—from two different angles.

"See anything we should watch out for?" he asked.

"As far as we can tell the area's clear."

"Okay. Thanks," he answered, hoping their reassurance was solid. Or maybe the person who had killed Angela Dawson would come sneaking up on the meeting, and Shane and Jack would grab them before anything else bad could happen to former members of the graduating class.

Max, Shane, and Jack had pooled their resources to start Rockfort Security more than two years ago. Unlikely as it sounded, they'd met in a Miami jail—which was an excellent instant evaluation of their strengths and weaknesses. When they'd found they had a lot in common—including being from the DC-Baltimore area—they'd kicked around the idea of starting the agency. Since they'd opened their doors, Rockfort's reputation had spread through recommendations from satisfied clients. Now he was the point man on this case, and his two partners were his backup.

"Your phone's on vibrate?" Jack asked.

"Yeah."

"We'll signal if we see anything you need to know about."

Max signed off, wondering who else might be out there. In his mind, he hadn't called the perp "him." In some ways, being a woman would be an advantage for the killer. A woman would have an easier time hiding in small spaces or pretending to be a customer at Angela's boutique.

When he put away the phone, Olivia gave him an anxious look. "Anything wrong?"

"No. I was just checking with Jack and Shane."

"And?"

"Nothing suspicious."

"Good." The four of them had gotten together for several planning sessions, and she was more or less comfortable with his partners. Maybe more comfortable than with him, because they could keep a professional distance, like backstage crew members. With her, he didn't have that luxury.

"Were you expecting trouble?" she asked in a voice she couldn't quite hold steady.

"No. It would be stupid to attack this meeting. But you could say it was stupid to attack Angela so blatantly. I have to be prepared for trouble now."

"Or—to put it another way, for the killer to be a nutcase," she whispered.

"Yeah."

He dragged in a breath and let it out, switching his focus to his role in this drama. He was going to mingle with a whole bunch of people from his high school days. If they remembered him, it would be by his bad boy reputation. And he might even remember some of them, although he certainly hadn't run with their crowd back in the day. But it had been difficult not to notice the school celebs parading their status through the halls of Donley

High. It was different with Olivia. She'd gone to classes and partied with them. But he'd made up for the lack of personal knowledge by studying the backgrounds of everybody who was on the reunion committee—and a lot of the other people in the class as well. He'd also discussed most of them with Olivia, getting her take, although sometimes her answers made him wonder if she was being entirely honest.

Like had she been intimate with some of the boys back in high school? Under ordinary circumstances, he could have said that was none of his business. Now any intimate relationships would have given him more insight into the dynamics of the group. But he wasn't going to ask her about it.

They started for the restaurant again, and when they stepped through the door into the air-conditioned atmosphere, Max took a moment to orient himself. Although the exterior was an old barn, the interior had been completely remodeled into an upscale grill, converted after he'd left Howard County with a parquet floor, dark wood booths along the walls, and tables in the middle of the room. There were diners at many of the tables in groups of two or four. Nothing that looked like any kind of meeting. But that probably wouldn't be in the main room.

As he stood taking in the scene, a redheaded hostess wearing three-inch heels and a strappy green sundress approached them.

"Can I help you?"

"The Donley reunion committee meeting?"

"Oh, that's in our party room. Just down the hall." She gave Olivia a studied look, then gestured toward a corridor on their left.

"Thank you," he answered, wondering if the hostess recognized Olivia from some of the commercials she'd done. Or perhaps her pale skin just stood out against the darkened interior of the restaurant. He knew she didn't want to be here, and he would have handled this part of the assignment on his own, if that had been possible. But she was his ticket into the group, his best opportunity to meet them in a casual way.

When she'd first come to the Rockfort Agency with her suspicions, Max and his partners had been skeptical. They'd thought she was overreacting to the murder of her high school friend, Angela Dawson, and to the lack of leads in the case. When she'd told them someone was murdering people from her high school class, they hadn't seen any evidence of a serial murderer. But she'd asked a couple of questions that had gotten them at least considering her supposition.

"What if someone wants a bunch of my classmates dead? And what if they want it to look like the murders aren't connected? So they do it in different ways to make it seem like random events."

The theory had been intriguing—especially since Olivia had brought them newspaper clippings and Web accounts of three deaths among her classmates. One was Angela. One was a guy named Gary Anderson, and the third was Patrick Morris. The problem was they hadn't come up with a motive. The best they could do was that all of the victims had been part of the "in crowd" back in high school.

The Rockfort men had discussed the case with Olivia, and she hadn't been able to give them a reason for the murders, but Max was pretty sure she wasn't telling them everything she knew. Since the two of them were spending a lot of time together, he had the chance to get it out of her—if he used the right approach. Unfortunately, he still wasn't sure what that would be, but he sensed that he'd need to tread cautiously. Maybe her reactions to the people on the committee—and their reactions to her—would give him a clue. Then he'd have a better idea of questions to ask after the meeting.

—◦◦◦—

As they walked down the corridor lined with photos of local scenes that must have been taken in the '20s and '30s, Olivia felt Max reach for her hand and knit his fingers with hers. If she were honest, it felt comforting to hold onto him. He was a physically imposing man, tall and well-muscled. And her talks with him had convinced her that he was a top investigator. Of course, some of the questions he'd asked her had made her uncomfortable. Like, for example, did she think she was a target of the killer, and why? She'd said she didn't know, and she'd wondered how much she was going to have to say about her past.

She stopped worrying about that as they approached the Oak Room, where the meeting was being held, her professional training kicked in. Her head rose. Her shoulders straightened, and she took several breaths of the stale, refrigerated air. Max noticed the change in her immediately. Turning his head he murmured, "That's my girl."

His girl. She didn't want to react, but she felt the warmth of those words spreading through her overcharged system, even though she was sure he had only meant them as a figure of speech. Or as part of the roles they were playing.

Before she could worry any more about the implications, they reached their destination.

Olivia took in the scene in one quick sweep. Small tables had been pushed together to make one long conference-type table. Around the room were about twenty people, some sitting in captain's chairs, some loading small plates from a snack buffet, and some standing in informal knots talking. Included in the latter group were the people she'd seen in the parking lot—plus a bunch of others she remembered from her high school days. Was one of them a predator? Or were they all potential prey? Or was she wrong about this whole thing? That could be true, but her gut told her that the previous deaths were connected, and more people would die if she and Max didn't figure out who wanted her classmates dead.

As her gaze swung to Tommy Larson and his date, Olivia had the feeling that they'd rushed inside to tell everyone she was going to be walking through the door with a hunky-looking guy, because it felt like everyone had been waiting for their arrival. Now all eyes turned toward them.

For a moment her facial muscles felt frozen, like the first time she'd stepped out onto a runway and known that her life was about to change for the better—if she didn't screw up. The weight of that knowledge had almost choked off her breath, but somehow she'd managed to walk out there without falling on her face—or fainting. Back then she'd felt so unsure of herself. But since then she'd had years of experience playing the part that was expected of her. She swallowed hard and forced a smile that she knew didn't meet her eyes.

"Hi, everyone. I'm so glad to be back in Howard County for a while. I'd like you to meet my fiancé, Max Lyon," she said. "Max, these are some of the people I've been telling you about from my high school class."

Chapter 3

OLIVIA COULD HARDLY BELIEVE SHE'D SPOKEN THOSE words. And it looked like a lot of the people in the room were having a similar moment of confusion. She stood in the doorway, taking in the varying reactions to the short speech. Some eyes widened. One or two of her former classmates shook their heads. And a minority at least made an attempt to look as if they welcomed her and her new fiancé at the meeting.

Linda Unger, who had sent out the letters inviting people to the event, crossed the room to greet her. Linda had always seemed like her head was screwed on straight. When Olivia had looked her up, she'd found out that Linda had been married to a guy she'd met in college, but he had been killed in an automobile accident a few years ago. They had no children. The revelation had saddened Olivia. Linda had been a good kid, and Olivia had hoped her life had turned out well. Of course, it still could. Like it still could for Olivia herself.

"It's good to see you after so long. We thought you were in New York."

"I was. But Max and I are treating ourselves to a little break," she answered. As the lie left her lips, her grip tightened on Max's hand. "I, uh, heard about your husband. That must have been so hard," she added, shifting the focus away from herself.

"It was," Linda answered.

Back in high school, Olivia and Angela Dawson had been sort of friends with Linda, although there had been some rivalries between them. Like that Linda had been one of the girls who'd vied with her for starring roles in the drama club productions. But that was ten years ago. Did any of what had happened in high school matter now? Apparently it mattered to someone. At least that was how she was interpreting the deaths of her classmates. And Max wouldn't be here with her if he hadn't subscribed to her theory.

To her vast relief, Olivia didn't have to say anything else, because Max took over, reaching out to shake Linda's hand like a long-lost friend, explaining in his deep, warm voice that he and Olivia had gotten engaged recently and that he'd considered the reunion committee a perfect way to meet her former classmates. Plus, it meant that she wasn't going to leave him home alone while she went out.

Brian Cannon, one of the former big men on campus, walked up to them, studying Max. Seeing him and the other guys in the class was a test for her, and she gave him her best smile. But his focus was on Max.

"I've seen you before. But not recently," he mused. "Hmm. Didn't you go to Donley?"

"Yeah. I was a couple classes ahead of you," he said, making it clear from the tone of his voice that he didn't want to talk about his high school years.

But Brian didn't let it go, and Olivia remembered that he'd often been pushy back in high school. "Strange that the two of you ended up together," he said, raising his voice to carry around the room.

"Both of us are different from the high school kids we were," Olivia said, hoping it was true for her. She knew for sure Max had changed. The confident detective standing next to her was nothing like the defiant boy she remembered from the bad old days. Or probably he had some of the same traits, but he was using them differently. For herself, mingling with these people again was having a strange effect on her—as if she were slipping back into the role she'd played at Donley.

"Did you know each other then?" Brian asked.

"Not really," Olivia clipped out. They'd met, but she wasn't going to explain that to Brian.

"Of course I'd noticed her," Max interjected. "Who didn't?"

"So where did you meet—officially?" Linda asked.

"I was on a business trip to New York," he answered easily. "And a friend who thought we'd like each other introduced us." He flashed a grin. "He was right."

"Why haven't we heard anything about your engagement?" Brian asked. "You'd think it would be on one of those celebrity gossip shows."

"We're keeping it a secret for the time being," Max said. "And we'd appreciate it if you helped us out with that, by not talking to the press or anything. We're still enjoying our privacy."

Olivia watched the group's reactions. Some nodded. Others murmured agreement, but she wondered if that many people could really keep quiet about the engagement of a former classmate who was a minor celebrity.

"How come you aren't off in the Caribbean or somewhere exciting?" Linda asked.

Max slung his arm around Olivia and pulled her close. "We'll do that later. Right now, we can make our own excitement."

Olivia flushed. And she was almost relieved when

one of the men in the back focused on Max. Almost—
because any questions would mean he was going to be
telling the tall tales they'd agreed on.

"You said you were on a business trip to New York.
What business?" one of the men in the back demanded in a
challenging voice. It was Troy Masters, the most successful
member of the reunion committee. Olivia knew that Troy
had graduated from Princeton and used his connections to
become a rich money market manager. She also knew that
he liked being thought of as the guy who'd made it big.

"Financial advisor," Max answered, using the cover
story that the Rockfort men had worked out for him.
They had also quickly constructed an online background
for him that would substantiate the claim.

"I might be able to use your services," Mark Tate allowed.

"We can make an appointment in a few weeks," Max
answered easily. "Olivia and I are both taking some time
off to look for a place to live."

"In New York?"

"No. A place where we can get away."

Within minutes, Max had introduced himself to
everybody in the room. And as five more people arrived,
Linda told them who he was. As Olivia watched him
interact, it was obvious he knew how to work a crowd,
how to get people to like him. The women were practically eating out of his hand as she watched them flirt
with the handsome new fiancé of their former classmate.
But despite the female attention, he was able to quickly
make friends with the guys, too.

Even Perry Palmer. Olivia had always considered him
a space cadet. A few minutes ago she'd heard him telling
Linda that he had his PhD and was doing research at the

Johns Hopkins Applied Physics Lab. Well, good for him, she thought before her attention switched back to Max.

She watched the people's expressions close up a bit when he steered the conversation down a less pleasant avenue—the one that had brought her down from New York. "I guess you all heard about what happened to Angela Dawson," he said when the noise level in the room dropped a little. "Pretty scary."

The rest of the conversations stopped dead. The sound of Ben Campbell crunching on a potato chip was the only noise in the room.

The guy Max was talking to, Joe Gibson, filled the sudden quiet. Tall and thin with a shock of thick sandy hair, Joe had been the president of the business club. Now an insurance agent in Ellicott City, he appeared to have combed his hair to the side to conceal a rapidly retreating hairline.

"Yeah, I read about it in the *Baltimore Sun*. It's a damn shame. She had such potential."

"You were friends with her?" Max asked.

He gave a little shake of his head. "She was more the all-work-and-no-play type. At least after high school."

Olivia gave Joe an assessing look. Back in high school, he hadn't had much respect for women. She suspected that hadn't changed.

As some of the classmates lowered their voices and speculated about the murder, Olivia watched Max observing the members of the group without appearing to be particularly watchful. Again he used a natural opportunity to widen the discussion. "You remember Gary Anderson?" he inquired.

"Wasn't he found in a drainage ditch?" Jill Cole

asked with a little shudder. She had been heavy in high school. Olivia noticed that she'd slimmed down considerably. Good for her.

Max nodded.

"What does that have to do with Angela?" Tommy Larson asked in the aggressive voice she remembered from ten years ago. "It was in winter on a freezing day. Gary's car crapped out on him… He was walking to get help and slipped."

"You know a lot about it," Max observed drily.

"I knew him. Not well. And the only thing I know about the accident was what I read in the paper—or what people were saying at the funeral," Tommy added quickly.

Max kept his expression open. "I saw both their names in your yearbook when I was looking to see who might be at the meeting tonight. Isn't that a little strange, for two people in your class to, uh, end up dead under questionable circumstances?" He shrugged casually, but Olivia knew he was carefully cataloging everyone's reaction. She also noticed that he hadn't mentioned Patrick Morris, who had died in his house from carbon monoxide poisoning. It was probably because Max didn't want to make it look like he was focused on deaths in the reunion class.

Still, she knew he'd already done that when Brian Cannon demanded, "Are you trying to make something of that?" His chilled voice cut through the previously friendly atmosphere.

"Uh, no," Max answered. "But I was thinking that maybe you all ought to stay aware of your surroundings."

Some of the people in the room looked like they didn't want to hear that advice.

"Noted," Tommy clipped out.

Did that mean he knew for certain he was in no danger because he was the perp? Or was he just putting up a macho front to maintain his image?

Tommy kept his gaze on Max, then went into aggressor mode. "What are you doing here exactly? You're not part of our class. The invitation only went out to class members." That was something else she remembered, the quarterback often going on the offensive.

"Olivia and I are spending as much time together as possible. She asked if I'd like to come to the meeting, and I said I would."

Tommy folded his arms across his chest. "I thought it was only for class members. You weren't in our class."

"Then why did you bring a date?" Olivia asked.

"That's different."

"How?"

"She's staying in the background."

Like women are supposed to, Olivia thought, but didn't voice the comment.

Linda jumped in. "Of course Olivia's fiancé is welcome if he wants to help out. There's a lot to do, and we can use all the worker bees we can get."

There were some murmurs around the room. Then the general conversation picked up, most people sticking with deliberately cheerful subjects like children, the purchase of new homes, and the remodeling of old ones.

It was all pretty casual in a one-upmanship sort of way, with everybody trying to make it clear how successful they were. Olivia found herself trying to fight off a headache. It was so strange being back here. She admitted to herself that she'd been intimidated by these people when she was in high school. Now she didn't have to prove anything to them.

Before they got too far into the small talk, Linda banged a spoon against a glass, getting everybody's attention and saying that they should get the meeting started.

Max rejoined Olivia from where he'd been standing with a group of guys and took the chair next to hers as the rest of her former classmates arranged themselves around the table.

When everybody was seated, Linda passed out sheets of paper with her agenda. Max read his rapidly, then leaned back in his chair, looking totally relaxed and interested in the proceedings, even making a suggestion for a place where the barbecue could be held.

He even got out a ballpoint pen and little notebook and began taking notes.

Olivia was relieved that the meeting settled down to an easy give and take. Most of the attention shifted away from her and Max, although she caught some of the others around the table eyeing him. When Linda asked her if she was willing to work on the committee sending out promotional materials, she agreed to help, thinking that she could always back out later.

"I want to kick-start this ten-year anniversary celebration," Linda said as the meeting drew to a close. "So I think we should meet again in two weeks to see what progress everybody has made."

There was general agreement, and with the official business concluded, Olivia wanted to duck out. But Max seemed to be in no hurry to leave. Apparently he was still taking the opportunity to observe everybody.

People drifted into little groups to chat or congregate

around the snack table. A few people came up to Olivia, but the conversations were stiff. She had been away for almost ten years. Most of the other people at the meeting had stuck around the area and probably got together from time to time.

She watched Max help himself to a buffalo wing, then turn and smile as Laura Jordan came gliding up to him. Laura was a curvy brunette who had been considered sophisticated back in high school. Ten years had only accentuated her charms. She and Max were on the other side of the room, but Olivia could tell from the bombshell's body language that Laura had no compunctions about coming on to another woman's fiancé.

As Olivia watched Laura move in on Max, a jolt of primitive emotion shot through her, taking her by surprise. When she realized it was jealousy, she sternly reminded herself that she had no right to be possessive of Max Lyon. He wasn't really her fiancé. He was only here with her on an undercover assignment, and the engagement had been the best way to give him access to the group. Still, when he glanced in her direction and caught her watching him, he looked a bit uncomfortable. Excusing himself, he crossed the room to where she was still sitting.

"Maybe it's time to go home, sweetheart," he said, his voice loud enough to carry around the room, his hand cupping possessively over her shoulder.

Knowing that he was just playing a part, Olivia flushed. But she stood obediently and leaned into him as he slung his arm around her waist.

Still strung tight as a rubber band about to snap, Olivia looked up to see that Laura had followed Max and was studying Olivia with a little smirk on her face.

Olivia couldn't help wondering if the other woman was comparing their bodies. Olivia was model thin. Laura had a lot more for a man to grab on to.

With a smirk, she asked, "So how did you two get together anyway? Was it a case of opposites attract?"

Olivia's mouth went dry as cotton.

But Max smoothly repeated the response he'd given to some of the others earlier, about their meeting at a party and starting to talk about finances.

"But you trust him with your money as well as… uh…everything else," Laura observed sweetly.

"Yes," Olivia managed, thinking that the evening had gone pretty well until now.

"Is marriage going to interfere with your career?"

"No."

"But you aren't planning to get pregnant?"

"These days, that's not a deterrent," Olivia said. "Several of the Victoria's Secret models had babies and continued to work. I could name a lot of them, like Heidi Klum, Adriana Lima…"

"But for now, I think we know how to avoid that," Max added.

"You're both living in New York?"

The questions were coming fast, too fast for Olivia to think. She'd held herself together through the meeting, but it had suddenly become difficult to maintain her cool.

Prickles of tension gnawed at her, and the headache she'd pushed to the background was suddenly pounding in her temples like a stereo speaker with the bass jacked up too high.

Chapter 4

RESCUE CAME FROM THE MAN WITH HIS ARM AROUND her. "It's been a fun meeting, but it's past our bedtime," Max said in a loud voice.

Beside him, Olivia blinked, knowing he'd chosen those words and the loud tone for a very specific purpose—to make it seem like they were anxious to get home and jump each other's bones.

She flushed as her pretend fiancé steered her out of the room. She walked stiffly beside him down the hall, neither one of them speaking, because they were both aware that the wrong people might be listening. Was anyone watching them from the doorway? The loving couple, who in reality barely knew each other.

Max held on to her all the way down the hall. It had still been light when they'd walked into the restaurant. As they stepped outside, Olivia saw it was dark. The air had cooled off, and she shivered as they headed for Max's vehicle.

As they walked, he pulled out his phone and pressed the redial button, which meant he must be checking in with his partners.

"Nothing?" he asked.

When the man on the other end of the line agreed, he put the phone back in his pocket.

They didn't speak to each other until they had climbed into the car. Turning to her, he said in a voice that helped dispel the chill she'd been feeling, "You did well."

"So did you. Thanks."

He nodded as he started the engine, pulled out of the parking space, and headed for her house. Well, to the house where she had grown up. Her parents were both gone now. Mom had passed while Olivia was still in high school, and Dad followed a few years after she'd left home. In fact, it was the money Mom had left her that had made it possible for her to pick up and go to New York. When Dad had died, she'd thought about selling the farm property.

But her financial advisor had told her to hang on to the house and surrounding acreage because the land was only going to go up in value. Since she hadn't wanted to simply leave the house to deteriorate and she could afford to keep it up, she'd had workmen come in over the years to make sure everything was in good repair. And she didn't have to feel guilty that valuable farmland was simply sitting idle. The guy who owned the next property over leased the land to grow corn and tomatoes.

With the house still in the family, she had a base of operations here. She'd paid a company to come in and give it a thorough cleaning before she'd arrived—with her new fiancé in tow. She fought a grimace. What was everyone going to think when they found out the whole marriage deal had been just a ruse to give Max the freedom he needed to investigate the incidents? Because deep down she was sure they had been murder.

"What?" Max asked, and she knew he'd seen her reaction. That was something she found hard to deal with. He picked up on everything. Well, she amended, it was a good thing—as long as he wasn't focused on her.

"I was just thinking about the people at the meeting," she fibbed.

"Are they the way you remember them?"

"Pretty much. Older versions of the kids who were in school with me. Well, Jill Cole slimmed down a lot," she said, then glanced at Max. "You think I'm too concerned with people's looks?"

"Naw. It's part of your training."

She was relieved he hadn't thought less of her for that. Then she was annoyed with herself for caring. She'd hired him to do a job, and his opinion of her wasn't relevant. Or it shouldn't be. Changing the subject as they headed for the western part of the county, she asked, "Did anyone seem suspicious?"

"You mean, did I think any of them was the killer?"

"I guess it would be a little hard to tell."

"There was no aha moment, if that's what you mean. Of course, I did get a reaction when I mentioned two of your deceased classmates in the same breath."

She nodded. Trying to figure out how the deaths were tied together was one of the first things Max had done—as opposed to the local police who didn't even think that Gary and Patrick had been murdered, as far as she could tell. That was one of the reasons she'd contacted Rockfort Security. When she'd spoken to the local cops, they'd assured her they were investigating Angela's death. But she had been frustrated by their lack of progress and their inability to tie together what had happened to Angela, Gary, and Patrick. Of course, to be fair, if Gary and Patrick had been murdered, someone had gone to a lot of trouble to make their deaths look like accidents. And then there was the problem of motive. Why them? And why Angela?

When she'd gotten the news about Gary and Patrick,

Olivia had been in the midst of grueling shooting schedules—one for a new designer line of evening wear and the other for swimsuits. She hadn't been able to come down for either funeral. But when Angela had turned up murdered, the news had sent a chill up Olivia's spine. Patrick's death really could have been an accident. So could Gary's for that matter. But her gut had told her otherwise, and she'd been seized by the conviction that she had to take action—before someone else died.

She wasn't sure why she *knew* there was going to be a next time. But the anticipation had gnawed at her, and she'd started investigating local detective agencies. She'd gotten some good recommendations for Rockfort Security, and they had felt right. But had she made a hasty decision by teaming up with Max? She hoped not. In almost every way, he was perfect for the job. That he'd gone to Donley was a plus. But Olivia hadn't counted on the simmering sexual dynamic she sensed between them. She thought the attraction was mutual and wondered if they would struggle to keep the relationship on a strictly professional level.

She shifted her gaze toward Max. "You still think it could be a woman?"

"I don't want to discount it."

"But what's the motive?"

"What's the motive if it's a man?" he countered.

They'd been over this several times, and Max had been digging into the backgrounds of the victims. So far, he hadn't come up with anything that connected them besides being in the same graduating class and sharing some classes and activities. Olivia knew he was hoping she could supply a connection—if she thought back about the relationships. Or if she was honest with him about her high school years. But wasn't that asking too much? Who wanted to look back at the fears and insecurities of high school?

They drove in silence toward her parents' house, past a couple of small, well-lit shopping centers that hadn't been in existence when she'd lived in the county.

"The area's changed," she murmured, voicing her thoughts aloud as she took in the signs of civilization encroaching on what had been open fields.

"For better or worse?" Max asked.

"Depends on whether you think strip malls and housing developments are better than farms."

He nodded. "But there are some advantages to civilization. You can run out for a pizza without driving twenty minutes each way."

"Right. You can even have that pizza delivered," she agreed, thinking that when she'd been little, the county services out here had been minimal. They didn't even have garbage collection back then. Mom would carefully gather the vegetable scraps at the sink, then take them outside and toss them over one of the fields near the house. The health department probably would cite you for doing something like that now. You had to use an approved composting container.

There was no light at the end of the entrance road, and Max slowed as he looked for the driveway.

"There's a redbud tree next to the mailbox," Olivia said.

"Sorry. I guess I never got into tree identification."

"The ones with the gorgeous little pink flowers in spring. Two weeks of eye-popping glory. Then just big leaves shaped like shields."

"Okay. Yeah. I think I know what they look like when they're blooming. They're all over the woods, right?"

"Yes."

"But I never noticed the leaves."

He spotted the tree and turned at the lane that led to her old house. As he bumped up the gravel road, a couple of floodlights went on, and she took a good look at the house where she'd grown up. It was vintage farm property like a thousand others in this part of Maryland. The hundred-year-old house was dwarfed by the barn that stood thirty yards to the right. Generations of Winterses had lived here, and she understood why Dad had stayed on, even when he'd gotten too old to farm. The thought of breaking her ties with this place made her chest tighten. She might have struggled hard to escape her background, but it seemed it would always be in her soul.

They got out of the car, and she waited a moment before climbing the two steps to the sagging porch, aware of Max behind her. They'd been here only a couple of days, and already she was uncomfortable with the living arrangements. If she could have fixed him up a place in the barn, she would have done it, but of course that was impossible—for a lot of reasons. She had hired him for this job, and she could hardly be so ungracious as to kick him out of the house. And then there was the demanding newly engaged couple act that they had to pull off.

When she started to unlock the door, Max put his hand on her arm. "Remember the alarm?"

Her jangled nerves made her mutter an unladylike curse under her breath. "No. Sorry."

Early in the morning, the three Rockfort men had done a hurry-up job of installing an alarm system in the house. If anyone opened a door or a downstairs window without punching in the code, a siren would go off right away. If they opened a door, there was a two-minute delay to give you time to enter the code. In any case, if the alarm went off, the system would also send a signal to the Rockfort offices. Max had punched in the arming code when they'd left, and she'd been so focused on the upcoming meeting that she hadn't thought about it now.

"But you remember the numbers?"

"Yes."

She turned the key and opened the door, then heard it chime before a series of beeps started, reminding her she had two minutes to press in the code.

In the kitchen, she switched on an overhead light, then walked to the control box and punched the keys in the right order. Not so hard for her to remember since they were her parents' wedding date—0483.

The beeping stopped, and she walked farther into the kitchen. Pretending she was thirsty, she opened the refrigerator and got out one of the bottles of water that they'd bought the day before.

She could hear Max in the living room pulling down shades and turning on more lights.

After twisting off the cap on the water bottle and taking a sip, she stayed facing away from the door. Opening a kitchen cabinet, she pretended to check some of the supplies they'd bought, desperately trying to avoid thinking of what a newly engaged couple would be doing when they got home. When she heard his footsteps in back of her, the image grew even stronger. Like wouldn't she and Max screwing each other's brains out be a good way to defuse some of the tension blooming between them? They could get the sex part out of their systems and focus on the murder investigation.

And what would Max think about her then? That she'd picked up some bad habits in New York? He probably wouldn't realize that her busy schedule had kept her from having much of a personal life.

Glad that her back was to him, she dismissed the sexual thoughts as completely inappropriate. She wasn't going to do anything of the sort with Max.

He cleared his throat. "We've got a lot of work to do."

"Right."

"Maybe you should start by telling me what you're not saying about your school days."

The words and the tone of his voice made her go rigid, then whirl toward him. "What do you mean?"

"Why are you worried that what happened to Gary, Patrick, and Angela could happen to you?"

Chapter 5

"I'M NOT SURE WHAT YOU MEAN," OLIVIA SAID, although she was pretty certain she knew where Max was going with this.

"What do the four of you have in common?"

"We were all popular."

"What else?"

Olivia was saved by her cell phone ringing. Relieved, she said, "I have to get this."

But after she'd dug the instrument out of her purse and looked at the number, she went rigid all over again.

"What?" Max demanded.

"It's not about the murders," she snapped, then ordered herself to calm down as she clicked the icon to answer. She'd been on edge all day, and this was one more reason to set her nerves jangling.

"Olivia. I left a message for you to call," Jerry Ellison, her agent, said. Of course, she'd told him she was going to be out of town for a few days, and while he hadn't flat out told her she couldn't come down to Maryland, she'd known he was opposed to the idea. Jerry was the kind of guy who liked to wield power—especially over people who worked for him. And she silently admitted that one of the reasons she'd been so anxious to get away was to give herself space to evaluate her career. She'd walked into the Ellison Agency as a wet-behind-the-ears wannabe. She'd felt like fortune had smiled on her when he'd taken her on. Now she knew he'd seen the potential in her. She'd had raw talent, but he'd taught her how to walk and turn, how to hold her head and body. And he'd gotten her jobs that built her career, starting her off with runway gigs, where she had received good reviews as a promising newcomer from the fashion press—which had led to magazine and television work. Those jobs had allowed her to stop starving herself and gain a few pounds. But she'd still kept up her killer schedule. Partly that was because Jerry had pushed her to take on any good job that was offered and partly because she was afraid that if she said no, they wouldn't ask again.

At first all the attention had been exciting, and she had learned from Jerry and stretched her own talent to see what she could do. Plus she'd basked in his praise. But as she got into the higher ranges of her profession, he had become more demanding—and more critical. Now she was thinking about leaving him, but that would mean walking away from several lucrative contracts that he had negotiated. If she did that, everybody would know. Would that mean no other top agent would take her on? And if they did, could she make sure the terms were more in her favor? She'd blindly signed the contract Jerry had offered her. Now she knew she'd take any new contract to a lawyer. And she'd negotiate terms.

"I've been busy," Olivia told him.

"When are you planning to come back?"

"I told you I needed some time off," she said, hedging. She hadn't shared anything with him about Angela's murder or her determination to find out who did it. And for that matter, she hadn't said anything about the fake engagement. He'd go ballistic if he heard about that. But how would he, unless someone at the meeting tonight blabbed?

"I need you back here."

"I can't come right now."

"Yeah, well, Million Dollar Babe moved up the schedule. They want to start shooting the week after next." He was referring to a chain of boutiques that was spreading across the country, establishing itself in suburban malls. They came out with a catalog of new fashions every quarter, and Olivia was one of the women who had been invited to model for the winter season. They weren't using her in the full set of shots. This would be a test to see how she worked out. When she'd gotten the offer, she'd been sure she was going to be added to their go-to list. Now she was jeopardizing that status.

"Jerry…"

"Now you're saying you won't come back for an important job?"

"Yes."

"Are you crazy?" Jerry's voice rose. "This is a crucial career move."

"I've been running on fumes for a long time."

He went on as though she hadn't spoken. "They want to have you try on some of the outfits before the actual shooting. If you can't do it, they'll get somebody else."

"If that's what they feel they have to do," she heard herself say, marveling that the words had come out of her mouth.

There was a short pause while Jerry grappled with the unheard-of thought that his top client wasn't doing exactly what she was told to do. "You're kidding," he said.

"I've come to the conclusion I have to take care of

myself," she answered. And she wasn't saying that just for effect. Angela's death had made her realize that life was short. If you spent all your time chasing the brass ring, you could very well wake up one day and find that things hadn't turned out the way you'd expected. And in Angela's case, that was devastatingly true. She knew her friend had been looking forward to a long and successful career as a prominent Ellicott City businesswoman. Angela had been thriving, but her life had been cut short.

"Maybe you're focused on the wrong priorities," Jerry snapped. "A lot of people depend on you."

The last part hurt, because she knew it was true. Before she could come up with an answer, he clicked off, leaving her listening to dead air.

When she looked up, Max was watching her with chilling intensity. In the midst of the tense conversation, she'd forgotten about him. Now she realized she'd given him an unwitting insight into her private life. When she'd hired Rockfort Security, she'd been thinking in terms of the murder investigation. She hadn't realized that she'd be laying herself bare.

"Trouble?" he asked.

She sighed, wishing she didn't have to explain the call. Actually, she didn't, but it was awkward to ignore the conversation now. "My agent is angry that I'm not rushing back to New York because an important client wants to start earlier than they initially said." As she explained the problem, she watched Max, anxious to see his reaction.

"Does that guy run your life?" he asked.

She pushed back the thick wave of hair that had fallen across one eye. "I sort of let him do that for a while."

"And now?"

"Now I have to think about what comes next. And I'm not ready to discuss it with anyone," Olivia added, wondering why she had put it in those terms. Had she already made a decision she couldn't admit? Had being back home shifted her priorities? Or had her attraction to Max reminded her she should think about her personal life? That was an interesting thought. They'd only been together for a few days, and they'd be saying good-bye when this job was finished for him. At least that had been her original thinking.

"Understood," he clipped out, reminding her that as far as he was concerned, they were sticking to the original deal.

They stood facing each other for a charged moment, and she tried to take the level of tension in the room down a notch

"Did you get enough to eat at the meeting?" she asked. "Or should I fix something?"

"I had the equivalent of dinner—if you consider dinner to be buffalo wings and chips and dip. Not exactly a balanced meal, but filling enough." She saw him making an effort to relax as he said, "I'm going to change into something more comfortable."

"Probably a good idea," she agreed, glad that they were off the subject of the phone call and steering away from anything personal.

They both climbed the stairs to the second floor, then separated in the hallway. Max was sleeping in what had been the spare bedroom. She was back in the room she'd occupied when she'd lived with her parents. She could have taken the master bedroom, but that would have felt too strange, since her mother and father had slept there for so many years.

She quickly took off the pearl gray slacks and dressy knit top she'd worn to the reunion committee meeting and pulled out jeans, a T-shirt, and running shoes.

After dressing, she started down the hall to the bathroom and almost bumped into Max coming from the other direction, also dressed in jeans, a T-shirt, and running shoes. The bathroom situation was one of the least convenient aspects of the house. It had only one full bath on the top floor, although there was a powder room in back of the kitchen.

Max stopped short. "Go ahead. I can wait."

She wanted to say she could also wait. But there was no point in making a trip to the potty into some kind of…pissing contest.

"Thanks," she said, then ducked into the room and closed the door. When she heard his footsteps recede down the hall, she used the facilities and washed her hands, then walked back to the steps. In the living room, she picked up her iPad from the end table and got into her email, most of which was either ads or messages from newsgroups she subscribed to.

There was also a message from Jerry reminding her about the Million Dollar Babe shooting schedule, as though they hadn't spoken about it a few minutes ago. It wasn't like it was next week. She could still do it if they resolved the problem down here in time. But Jerry wanted a definite answer.

"Sorry," she emailed back. "If you have to get someone else, go ahead and do it."

His jaw was probably going to drop to his knees

when he read her response. But she wasn't going to cave. Not just because the murder investigation was important. Wasn't it possible for a top model to pull back and work on an easier schedule? What if she was married or something?

She made a snorting sound. She wasn't married to Max—or even engaged. She was just pretending to be his fiancée. When this was over, he'd go back to his work with Rockfort Security, and she would... Go back to New York? Probably. Where else did she have to go, really?

Attending the reunion meeting had made her realize more than anything else that she had severed her ties with Howard County, Maryland. Leaving had been a deliberate move on her part. You could even say calculating. She had turned away from her old life, determined to build something of her own. And she'd worked hard to do that. She'd had a goal, and mostly she had achieved it. The climb had been difficult—and exciting. Each new milestone had made her feel more like she belonged in that glittering world of success. But now that she had reached a level of success she'd hardly dared to imagine, it didn't feel as awesome as she'd expected.

Was she passing up the chance to get married and have a family?

There it was again. Thoughts of marriage, which she'd firmly put out of her mind while she focused on her career. Was a normal life now impossible for her?

Hearing footsteps, she looked up and saw Max coming down the stairs.

He was carrying his laptop, and he sat down in the easy chair opposite the sofa and raised the screen.

She lived alone in an apartment in New York.

Probably he had his own apartment in Rockville. And now here they were together—yet still separate.

Was this a typical evening for a modern family? Long ago, the people who lived in this house might have been gathered around the piano after dinner, with one person playing and the others singing. Then had come the era of listening to the radio—followed by the new invention, television. And now everybody had his own computer, which separated them again.

Max didn't speak, and she didn't ask him if he was checking his email or doing research on some of the people they'd met at the meeting, probably because she didn't want him to ask *her* any questions. They'd been in the middle of a discussion about what she, Patrick, Gary, and Angela had in common, and she was still trying to come up with an answer that would satisfy him—and not make her cringe when she talked about her past.

Damn, she'd jumped into this arrangement with Rockfort Security without knowing that Max Lyon was a bulldog when it came to digging answers out of suspects. Well, she wasn't exactly a suspect. Maybe witness was a better way to put it. But she was a witness who didn't know if the secrets buried in her past were relevant or not.

You're lying to yourself, she silently admitted. *Maybe you're here because you're tired of hiding from yourself*. But was she really ready for that?

Keeping her head down, she focused on the computer screen, opening messages that she might have skipped if she'd been pressed for time.

—◦◦◦—

Max fought the urge to shift in his seat because he knew Olivia would catch the movement. It was unsettling to be sitting across from her like a married couple relaxing in the evening.

And in this house, of all places. Back in high school, he'd imagined the lives of his classmates. He'd pictured their houses and the conversations they might be having around the dinner table with their parents.

And he certainly hadn't pictured the most stunning girl in school living in this house. He'd just assumed that Olivia Winters went home every night to one of the McMansions that had sprung up around the county or at the very least to one of the upscale developments in Columbia or Ellicott City. He hadn't known she lived in a farmhouse with rusty plumbing and wood floors that needed refinishing. All those years ago he hadn't realized that in some ways she was as much an outsider as he was himself.

Max stole a glance at her. She was looking at her iPad screen like it held the secrets of the universe, her fingers on the inefficient built-in keyboard. He knew she was hiding from him. Hiding in plain sight because getting up and leaving the room would be like admitting she couldn't handle the two of them here together.

Of course, he was doing the same thing, if the truth be told. It was clear there were things she didn't want to talk about. And the same was true for him.

Was he going to come out and ask her if she remembered the time they'd actually bumped up against each other when they were both in high school? It had been at a fast-food restaurant in Columbia, a pizza place on Route 108. She'd been there with one of her girlfriends.

Maybe even Angela, although he couldn't be sure, because his focus had been on Olivia. The girls had been at a table, sharing a large pizza, and two guys had come up and tried to start a conversation. Not local guys, because he didn't recognize any of them. Olivia and her friend had done their best to ignore the unwanted attention. But Max had been across the room, and he'd heard the increasingly personal comments and invitations to go someplace where they could get to know each other better. It was obvious that the nice, polite high school girls hadn't known how to handle the situation.

Finally Max had gotten up and crossed the room, moving in on the boys with cool deliberation. At first they'd looked ready to fight with the guy who dared to interfere with their plans for the two babes. Then they'd taken a second look at Max and caught the recklessness below his calm exterior. Maybe they'd decided that tangling with him might get their teeth knocked down their throats. Pretending it was what they'd intended all along, they'd backed away, and the girls had gratefully thanked Max. He'd been torn, but he hadn't taken the opportunity to sit down with them. Instead, he'd gone back to his own table, without a glance over his shoulder. As if he wasn't burning to get to know Olivia Winters better.

Well, now he had that opportunity. But where would it get him? They were together for the moment. But when this case was over, she'd be going back to New York.

Max knew she hadn't loved the idea of playing house with him. He hadn't loved the idea either, but it was the plan that made the most sense if he wanted to mingle with her former classmates without drawing attention to himself. Actually, the pretend engagement had been

Shane's idea. And Max had wondered if the suggestion
was some kind of perverse payback for Max giving him
a hard time when he and Elena Reyes had been tracking
down a thief and a killer at S&D Systems. The take-
down had involved a scam—which had been Elena's
idea. She'd put herself in a lot of danger by using herself
as bait, but they'd gotten to her in time. And now she
and Shane were a happily married couple. Like his other
partner, Jack, and his lady, Morgan Rains.

Neither of the two married guys had been willing to
play Olivia's fiancé, which was how Max had gotten
the job. And maybe in a secret sort of way, he liked it.
Who wouldn't love being seen as the lover of a top New
York model?

And how did she like being engaged to a washed-up
cop? That shouldn't even enter into the equation, but he
couldn't stop the thought from lodging in his head.

So what did that mean? He wanted her to like him?
More than like him? Did he think she was going to actually wind up climbing into bed with him?

He repressed the urge to laugh out loud, because this
engaged couple's game was some kind of cosmic joke.
Would he have chased the boys in the pizza parlor away if
one of the girls hadn't been Olivia? He had been very aware
of her in high school, of course. Probably everybody had
because she was gorgeous, even back then. And now she was
even more striking because she'd learned how to enhance
her natural beauty with the right haircut and makeup. But
under normal circumstances, he never would have met her
when they were all grown up and out in the world.

Back in his Donley days he'd been on the fast track to
the juvenile detention center. Another lost kid with no one

to rein him in. His dad had battled with his mom constantly, and finally the drunken jerk had just walked away one day when Max was twelve. After that, his mom worked long hours to try and support herself and her son. It hadn't been an entirely successful effort. She'd kept a roof over their heads in one of the subsidized apartment complexes in Ellicott City. But clothing and food were another matter.

By the time he was thirteen, he was tired of wearing the secondhand shirts and jeans that they got from church charity sales. And he was tired of his stomach growling because all there was for dinner was a mayonnaise sandwich or a package of cheese crackers that he'd lifted from a gas station convenience store.

By his sophomore year at Donley, he'd taken matters into his own hands. He and another guy in similar circumstances had started breaking into houses in affluent neighborhoods and stealing anything that they thought they could sell for cash. They'd been pretty good at it. And for over a year they'd gotten away with a string of robberies that made the local papers.

Then they'd gotten caught, and Officer Cliff Maringer had taken Max into an interrogation room and sat him down for a long talk. Did he want to go to juvie, where he'd be living with a bunch of badass guys who would teach him to be the kind of loser who grew up with nowhere to go but federal prison?

Max had pretended to be tough. Inside he'd been a scared kid. Maybe he'd responded to Cliff as a father figure. And responded to what Cliff was offering him—a way to make something of his life and not just drift along from one bad situation to another. Cliff got him a job at a fast-food restaurant in Columbia, where he could earn some money and where he could eat for free when he was on shift. It wasn't the best food in the world, but it was better than what he'd gotten at home. And there was certainly more of it.

The relationship with someone who cared had turned him around. And when he'd gotten a little older, they'd become friends. When Cliff had died of an early heart attack, Max had vowed to honor his memory by going to the police academy.

He'd joined the Baltimore City PD as a patrol officer, then graduated to detective. Since he'd turned his life around, the values he'd absorbed from Cliff had been his guide in his job—and in his life. The memory of his old pain had spurred him to help troubled teenagers make better decisions, partly by sharing his own sordid story with them. And he'd always made it a point to go the extra mile for the little guys who expected the cops to stick it to them—not defend them. He'd been secretly glad of making a difference. And then bad luck had slapped him in the face.

Which was another reason he wasn't so glad to be back here now.

His dark thoughts were interrupted by a beeping sound, and he was instantly transformed from reflection to protective mode.

"Stay down," he ordered Olivia as he hurried toward the keypad for the alarm and looked at the readout.

"What?" she asked.

"Somebody's out there."

"Or it's just an animal," she suggested. But the little quaver in her voice gave away her jittering nerves.

"Yeah, well, we're not going to take a chance on it being a deer chomping down the cornfields."

Chapter 6

As Olivia's pretend fiancé, Max hadn't gone armed to her reunion committee meeting. But his weapon was handy. He walked to the desk in the small room that had been set up as an office and opened the bottom drawer. Taking out two Sigs, he checked the magazine on both of them, then handed one to Olivia. After accepting the assignment, Max had been relieved to find out that she could shoot. Apparently that had been part of her lifestyle out here on a farm where there were acres of open space around the house. She'd said her dad had taken *In Cold Blood* to heart. It was the true story of a couple of killers who went looking for cash in the home of a farm family and ended up murdering all of them, told in vivid detail by Truman Capote. After reading it, Farmer Winters had taken Olivia and her mother out onto the property for regular target practice sessions, although neither woman had ever needed to use a weapon to defend herself.

"I'm going out to investigate. You stay in here. I'll lock the door behind me."

Her face had gone pale, but she nodded.

Max was thinking it was too bad Farmer Winters hadn't taken the next step and built a safe room they could use in an emergency. Of course, those had been simpler times. How many farmers would have thought of a safe room?

He walked around the first floor switching off lights, then turned to Olivia. "You have your cell phone?"

"It's upstairs."

"Go get it. And stay up there. If you hear anything, call the police."

"Anything like what?"

"A gunshot."

She winced, but she was already moving toward the stairs.

"And let's make sure you don't shoot me when I come back in. If it's me, I'll call out 'Jack Brandt,'" he said, naming one of his partners instead of himself.

"Okay."

"And if everything's okay in there, answer with 'Runway,'" he said.

She made a face but didn't voice an objection.

When she was halfway up the stairs, he headed for the back door, turning off more lights as he went and peered out the window into the darkness. He could switch on floodlights, but that would only make him a target for whoever was out there watching. Of course, it might not be a person at all. There were plenty of animals in the area. Raccoons, opossums, foxes. But only a deer would have been big enough to trip the sensors that he, Jack, and Shane had put around the property.

However, he wasn't going to take a chance on the intruder being a four-legged animal.

Although he and his partners had set up sensors as an early-warning system, they extended only about seventy yards from the house. Any farther out and someone would still have freedom of movement.

Max silently cursed the hasty arrangements to protect

the Winters property. But the quick job was out of necessity, he told himself. They'd only had so much time before the meeting tonight. And in any case, they couldn't cover the whole damn farm with motion sensors.

Plus they'd only gone with the sensors—no electric fences or explosive charges like they employed around the safe houses that Rockfort Security sometimes used. Those defenses would have been a dead giveaway that more was going on besides Olivia Winters and her new fiancé coming back to spend some time at the old homestead.

Max stepped outside into the darkness. After locking the door behind him, he listened intently, hearing nothing. His gaze swung to the barn, and he saw that the door was closed. And it looked like it was still secured by the padlock that Olivia's father had installed years ago.

Of course, someone could have cut it and made it look like it was intact, but judging from when the sensor had gone off, he didn't think anyone would have had that much time.

He tested the boards of the back porch, wincing when they squeaked a little. At the bottom of the steps, he walked a few paces from the house, then looked back the way he'd come. When he swung his gaze up, he saw that all the lights on the top floor were off—which was a good move on Olivia's part. But was she standing at the window, staring out? He would have warned her not to, but he was pretty sure she would have done it anyway. He would have. Staying inside without a clue about what was going on outside would have been difficult for anyone except a timid person who hid from danger. And he already knew that didn't describe Olivia. She could have stayed in New York and continued modeling.

Instead she'd cleared her calendar, come down here, and looked for a detective to help her investigate her friend's murder. Of course, she apparently hadn't cleared it with her agent as well. What did that mean exactly?

He switched his focus to his surroundings as he moved silently across the property into the darkness, aware of every sound around him, from the wind rustling the leaves of the trees to the buzz of insects. When he reached a patch of woods about fifty yards from the house, he stopped and listened. The alarm had been silent out here, but it had told him the threat—if there was a threat—was coming from the northwest corner of the property, a wood lot that had grown unkempt in the absence of an on-site resident.

Anyone could be hiding in the deeper shadow under the trees or in the underbrush. And going in there could be dangerous. But it might flush out whoever was stalking the house. There were a lot of possibilities for who it might be—from the fairly innocent to the frankly malevolent. Someone from the meeting they'd left a few hours ago could be curious about the newly married couple and could have come around to check out their story. It could be a neighbor who passed the property often and had noticed that someone was living here after years of the place being vacant. Maybe they thought that whoever was in the house didn't belong here—and they wanted to check *that* out. Or it could be the killer, coming for Olivia.

He'd taken this job for the satisfaction of bringing down a killer. The idea of someone going after Olivia had only been an abstraction. Now that it was suddenly a reality, he felt a surge of protective emotions. Like he was a knight or an ancient warrior charging out to protect his woman. He snorted at the analogy, yet he couldn't shake it. He hadn't known Olivia well back in high school, and they'd only been together for a few days now, but the idea of anything happening to her made him realize that he'd come to care about her with gut-tightening urgency in a very short time. And not just because of her public persona. On the surface, she might come across as a poised, confident model, but he'd learned that she hadn't traveled all that far from her roots.

Those thoughts flickered at the edge of his consciousness, because the bulk of his attention was focused on his surroundings.

If the trespasser was in the woods, he'd have two choices. Either hide from the man who had come out to investigate or make a run for it.

Too bad Max couldn't give away his own location by using a flashlight to flush out the bastard. That might have been efficient from a searcher's point of view, but it would have been a risky strategy when he was out here alone and the intruder could shoot in the direction of the light.

He used the wood lot for cover, moving from tree to tree, listening for the sound of breathing—or anything else that would give the guy away.

He realized he was thinking of the interloper as a man because all his intuition rejected the idea of a woman sneaking up on the house. But it still could be possible—for someone with sufficient motivation. Which was what? Deep resentment at some old slight? Anger that Olivia had come back to stick her nose in where it didn't belong?

When he stopped and listened again, he thought he

heard the sound of raspy breathing coming from his left. At least he'd made the guy reconsider his risky behavior.

Ducking low and correcting his course, Max headed toward a tree with a sizable trunk. Before he reached it, someone broke from cover and ran.

He couldn't see more than a vaguely human shape in the dark. The figure was dressed in dark clothing for concealment.

Straightening, Max pelted after him, but the intruder had spent some time preparing for his attack. As Max followed him, running as fast as he could in the dark, he suddenly smacked into an invisible barrier. Nothing solid. Something that had a bit of give.

Seconds after he hit it, he bounced back, feeling sharp barbs tear into his flesh. Christ, what was that? Gingerly he reached for the thing that had stopped him and got more sharp gouges on his hands.

As he tried to figure out what had hit him, he listened to the thud of footsteps disappearing into the darkness. Then the sound of a car starting told him that the assailant had made a clean getaway.

Now that he knew he was alone, he pulled his phone out of his pocket and activated the flashlight feature, playing it over whatever had blocked his path. He saw that the obstacle was several courses of barbed wire, strung across the route the intruder had been following. The bastard had known to duck low enough to avoid the trap as he ran. With no inkling of the danger, Max had plowed right into the wire. It was at shoulder and head level, and he could see he was damn lucky that he hadn't put out his eye with a barb. Which might have been what the stalker had intended.

"You missed," he muttered as he ducked under the barrier and continued down the trail, still cautious. The intruder might have fled, but now Max knew he could have left other nasty surprises along his escape route.

Caution slowed his progress considerably. He stepped carefully, aware that another booby trap could be lower down. And he moved with his hands in front of him, testing the safety of the path he was walking. Stopping, he called Olivia's cell phone. She picked up on the first ring.

"Max?"

"Yeah."

"Are you all right?"

"More or less."

She sucked in a sharp breath. "What does that mean?"

"I'll tell you when I get back. I just wanted you to know that the emergency's over."

"How do you know?"

He sighed. "Whoever was on the property got away. I'm checking to see where he parked."

"It's a man?"

"I'm just using a convenient pronoun. I'm hanging up now. I'll be back soon."

Finally he came to a clearing in the woods beside a farm road. Whoever had been stalking the house had probably driven this far and walked the rest of the way.

The day before, Max, Jack, and Shane had walked around the area. The barbed wire hadn't been here then. Had the perp brought it with him? Or dragged it from somewhere on the farm? And when had he done it? If it was while Max and Olivia were at the meeting, it would mean that it wasn't anyone who had been there.

Or they could have come here afterward and been lucky enough to stay out of the range of the sensors until they decided to sneak up on the house. That would mean that whoever it was didn't actually know that the property had been wired for motion detection. They'd come too close and set off the alarm. At least that part of the defensive strategy had been successful. Too bad Max hadn't seen the barbed wire before plowing into it.

In the clearing, he played his light over the ground and saw nothing notable—except that the weeds had been beaten down by the vehicle's tires. The marks were wide apart, probably from an SUV or a pickup truck.

It hadn't rained in over a week, which meant the ground was too dry for the car to leave tracks, just impressions in the dust. But Max would come back here tomorrow anyway to have a look around in daylight.

With a shake of his head, he turned and started back toward the house, moving faster now that he wasn't in danger. He was anxious to get back to Olivia.

"Jack Brandt," he called out as he approached the house, using their agreed upon signal. And really, saying the password made sense since he could have gotten bushwhacked between calling her and coming back.

"Okay," she answered. Then, "Uh—runway."

A low light was on in the kitchen, and she opened the door before he reached it. He saw that she still had the gun in her hand, which showed that she hadn't let her guard down.

As he stepped inside, she switched on the overhead light. He watched her take in his appearance, then drag in a sharp breath as the full impact hit her.

"Max, you're hurt. What happened?"

"I got a little cut up, is all. It's not bad."

"With what?" she asked.

"Barbed wire."

"How?"

"The bastard set a trap out there in the woods," he said.

"It looks wicked. Come up to the bathroom where there's more light."

"In a minute. I want to check the surveillance output."

"You think you'll find anything?"

He made a dismissive sound. "Unfortunately, no. I'm betting the sneaky bastard didn't get close enough to the house to get his picture taken. But I can't dismiss the cameras out of hand."

"You think it has to do with the murders?" she asked.

"I thought of some other possibilities while I was outside. But that was before I ran into the booby trap."

Before she could ask more questions, he strode into the office and sat down at the desk, where he called up the surveillance program and scrolled back through the video to the point where the alarm had gone off. Leaning forward, he watched intently, but his gut feeling had been right. The guy hadn't gotten close enough to the house to show up on camera.

Olivia was standing in back of him, watching the computer screen.

"He's not there," she murmured.

"Like I said."

"Then come up and let me take care of those cuts."

He would rather have taken care of the problem himself, yet he wasn't going to make a big deal out of it, either.

Chapter 7

Olivia saw Max hesitate. "You're too macho to let me take a look at those cuts?" she inquired in a voice that she tried to make both quiet and challenging. "I mean, they're on your face. You need to close your eyes to disinfect them."

Turning, she walked down the hall, her breath shallow as she waited to see if he was following her. At first she heard nothing but the snick of the lock and realized he was securing the door. Still, she didn't start breathing normally until she detected the sound of footsteps behind her.

She climbed the steps, reached the bathroom, and turned on the light.

Max followed her inside, and when she got a better look at him, she made a low sound.

"What?" he growled.

Wordlessly, she gestured toward the mirror over the sink, watching him take in his own appearance. There was a cut across his left eyebrow, perilously close to the eye, another one on the right side of his forehead a half inch farther up, and bloodstains on several places across the front of his T-shirt and on his arms, corresponding to tears in the fabric.

"I guess the shirt is going in the trash," he muttered as he began to pull up the hem.

She watched him ease it over his head, being careful of

the injuries, then turned away, opening the medicine cabinet and seeing only items that must have been there for years, like her father's old shaving cream and deodorant.

"There's nothing we can use," she murmured.

"I have a first-aid kit in my bedroom."

She nodded, watching him turn and stride down the hall. When he came back he was carrying his T-shirt and a metal box, which he set on the edge of the sink.

"Do you always travel with first-aid equipment?" she asked.

"It's standard operating procedure for Rockfort Security."

"You get hurt a lot?"

He avoided a direct answer by saying, "It's best to be prepared."

Balling up the shirt, he tossed it toward the trash can.

He was half undressed and standing very close to her, and she had to remind herself why they had come into the bathroom. He'd been injured because someone had been sneaking around outside her house.

Reaching past her, he lowered the shade, brushing his arm against hers. She could smell the male scent of his body and see his well-muscled chest and arms in close detail—a lot closer than she'd like. She hadn't counted on any kind of intimacy with Max, and she felt a little shiver travel over her skin at the sudden contact. Trying to stay on task, she opened the box and examined the contents, finding what she needed—antiseptic and sterile pads.

But being so close to half-naked Max was making her breathing unsteady and her heart flutter inside her chest like a bird trying to get out of a cage. Fighting the unwanted sensations, she desperately searched for a way to cool herself down. When her gaze landed on a puckered indentation to the left of his navel, she focused on it.

"What happened to you?" she asked. "I mean... before," she clarified, pointing toward the old injury.

"I was shot."

Maybe it was none of her business, but she wanted to know. "When?"

"In a drug raid eighteen months ago. That's why I left the Baltimore Police force, if you want to know. They were going to keep me on desk duty for months, which was a stupid move on their part. A waste of manpower."

"Because you thought you were fit for the street."

"I know I was. I worked hard getting myself back in shape."

"So you quit?" she guessed.

"And got partial disability, which meant I had some time to figure out my next move. Then I met the other two Rockfort guys, and we decided we made a good team."

Her curiosity piqued, she asked, "How did you meet the other two Rockfort men?"

He laughed. "In jail."

Her head jerked up. "Did I hear that right?"

"We all happened to be in a Miami nightclub when the place was raided. We ended up keeping order in a holding cell with a lot of tough *hombres*. And in the morning, we went out for breakfast—and decided to stick together."

She tipped her head to the side, studying his open expression, which could be as fake as a three-dollar bill. "You're not making that up?"

"Why do you think so?"

"I got a taste of your storytelling ability at the reunion meeting."

He laughed. "Yeah, well, this story's true. Besides, who would make up a story about getting busted?"

"I guess that's right."

The conversation had helped to take her focus off the sexual awareness, but she'd better remember why Max was standing half naked in front of her. "We should wash the cuts first."

He answered with a little nod, and she wondered if he was reacting to her the way she was reacting to him.

She knew he was attracted to her. That was something a woman could tell. But she also knew he wasn't going to do anything about it unless she invited the attention. And she wasn't going to do that. Fooling around with him would interfere with their investigation, and that was as good a reason as any to douse her overheated imaginings with a bucket full of cold reality.

Struggling to change the direction of her thoughts, she turned temporarily away from Max's masculine temptation. At the sink, she turned on the water, letting it warm up while she stepped around him and into the hall, where she opened the linen closet and retrieved one of the clean washcloths she'd brought to the house.

When she came back, she saw him leaning toward the mirror, inspecting his face, his dark eyes narrowing as they took in the damage.

He straightened as she reached to turn the water lower and wet the washcloth.

"I guess I was lucky."

"You mean because it missed your eye."

"Yes. Whoever was out there wanted to stick it to me." He laughed. "Literally."

"Or me," she countered.

"I hope you wouldn't be sneaking around after dark if you heard someone outside. That would put you in the 'too stupid to live' category."

"Oh, thanks."

"But you didn't do it."

"What category does it put *you* in?"

"Doing my job," he snapped.

"So you're saying the attack really was aimed at you?" she said as she squeezed most of the water out of the cloth.

"That seems likely."

"Because?"

"Like I said, it was my job to investigate. And if I went out there and ended up with my ass in a sling, they could go after you."

She winced as she followed his logic. "Let me clean your face. Close your eyes."

When he'd complied, she lifted her hand, pressing the wet cloth against the wound before gently wiping away the blood.

"It's not deep, right?" he asked.

"No." She cleaned both wounds on his face. "Keep your eyes closed so I can disinfect the cuts."

As he stood before her with his eyes shut and his face badly scratched, he looked more vulnerable than she had ever seen him.

Fighting the urge to gently touch his lips, she grabbed a premedicated packet and tore it open, extracting the pad inside and carefully wiping the wound over his eye and then the one on his forehead.

"Thanks," he said in a husky voice when she had finished.

"There are the ones on your chest and your arms."

"I can do those."

Knowing that was the smart course of action, she took a step back and to the side, giving him access to the sink. Maybe she should leave and give him some privacy, but she couldn't stop thinking about what had happened to him because of her. He might say the attack was directed at him, but that was only because he was guarding her.

"You say it was aimed at you. But we've only been here for a couple of days."

"Did you ever come down here alone?" he asked.

"A few times."

"Okay."

"What's that supposed to mean?"

"I'm just responding. Did anything ever happen when you were here?"

"I came back once because the guy who rents the fields from my father complained that someone had vandalized his tractor."

His head swung toward her, his mind obviously focused on business now. "You never mentioned that."

"I didn't think it was important. I mean come on, what does a vandalized tractor have to do with Angela's murder?"

He made a huffing sound. "Maybe nothing. But in light of the barbed-wire trap, we have to consider that everything's important."

She didn't like the way he said that.

"It was a few months ago. And it didn't seem

relevant," she repeated, hating the way he'd so easily put her on the defensive.

"Uh-huh."

He kept working on the cuts on his chest and arm, first washing them as she had done with his face and then using the disinfectant.

"Do you think you need an antibiotic?" she asked.

"No."

"And you're up to date on your tetanus shots?"

"We all stay up to date on those. I mean me and my partners," he clarified.

He had brought a dark T-shirt with him, and he picked it up.

"Wait a minute."

"Why?"

"One of the cuts on your chest is still bleeding."

Despite her previous decision not to touch him again, she pulled a square compress from the box, pulled away the adhesive backing, and pressed it to the cut, her hand resting against his warm skin for a moment, feeling his heart beating steadily but perhaps a little fast.

"I guess I didn't think about pulling it off again," she said as she noted the way it was stuck to his skin.

"My punishment for walking into the barbed wire in the first place."

"You couldn't see it in the dark."

"Yeah. I guess that was the idea."

"It was a mean trick."

"Right again. Which suggests we're dealing with someone who doesn't mind hurting people."

She dragged in a breath and let it out. "Do you think it has something to do with the murders?"

"I wish I knew for sure. It could be that the people who were murdered were harassed first, but we can't exactly interview them to find out. And I didn't consider that we'd need to interview the man who rents the farm property. What's his name?"

"Bill Yeager."

"And where does he live?"

"On the next property over."

"Okay."

"Why would vandalizing his tractor have anything to do with me?"

"Well, I was thinking that this farm is valuable land. What if someone wanted to encourage you to sell?"

"I hadn't thought about that."

"We can't discount it." He changed back to another line of speculation. "Did Angela mention anything to you about being harassed?"

She thought before she answered. "Not specifically, but I got the feeling she was nervous about something."

"What?"

"She never said. And I didn't press her."

"Why not?"

"I figured she'd tell me if she wanted me to know. Both of us were busy, and we were going to sit down for a long chat when I got here." As she said the last part, her chest tightened.

"Sorry," he said.

"We're never going to have that chat."

"I know. Death makes you think about what you regret not doing."

"You have regrets?"

"Some."

"What?" she asked.

"People I should have made time for. There was a guy who mentored me. He'd called me and suggested that we go to dinner, but I was studying for exams and asked if we could wait until the next week. Then he died of a heart attack, and I wish we'd gotten together one last time before it happened. I mean, maybe he had a premonition that he wasn't going to be here much longer."

Maybe she shouldn't be pushing for information, but she couldn't help herself. She wanted to know about him—to feel closer to him. "You said people."

"Yeah."

"Who else?"

He didn't answer for a long moment. "My mom."

"She passed away too?"

"Yeah. She had a tough life. I tried to make it easier for her when I had the money to do it. I got her a nice apartment and some furniture." She saw his Adam's apple bob. "But I didn't visit real often."

"I didn't visit my dad either."

He raised one shoulder. "You didn't get along?"

"He always had his own ideas about how I should live my life. Since I didn't agree, I didn't give him a lot of chances to carp at me about it." She raised one hand, turning it palm up. "It was easy to block him out. But there was plenty I couldn't."

"What do you mean?"

"Over the past few years, I've spent too much time doing stuff I didn't want to and not enough time doing things I wanted to do."

"Why?" he asked

"To get ahead. You didn't do the same kind of stuff?" she challenged.

"If you mean police work, I guess that's right."

Again, she couldn't stop herself from pushing beyond what would be normal boundaries. "You were in an organization where discipline was important. Did that ever get to you?"

"Yeah."

"And you could have waited out the desk assignment, but you quit."

"Right. I guess I'm with Rockfort Security because I reached the decision that I wanted to do things my way."

"You're lucky."

He laughed. "It took a long time for me to find the right balance."

She wanted more insights into what made Max tick, but he switched the subject to her again.

"Is this going to change the way you live?"

"What do you mean by—this?" she asked in a voice she couldn't quite hold steady.

"The murders."

She took a moment before answering. "I think it will."

"What if your being down here makes you lose that job you were talking on the phone about?"

"I guess I'll have to let it go."

"Did you ever let a job go before?"

"Like I said, I'm reevaluating my priorities." She stepped into the hall, hoping that the tone of her voice made it clear that she didn't want to discuss her business decisions with him. Or anyone else—because there wasn't anyone who could give her the counsel she needed. Certainly not Jerry Ellison.

Apparently he picked up on her determination to close the subject because he said, "What about Angela's mother? Would Angela have said anything to her about her problems?"

Olivia thought about that as they stood in the darkened hallway. "Her mother's in a nursing home. I'm betting Angela wouldn't have bothered her with anything negative."

"But we could talk to her tomorrow."

"You want to do that?"

"I want to follow up whatever leads we have. And I didn't feel like I got much tonight. Most people at the reunion meeting were on their best behavior. They were trying to project how successful and well adjusted they were."

"Well, except for Tommy Larson trying to kick you out."

He laughed. "Yeah. Was he always so aggressive?"

"He was a football player."

"Right."

"And you think that person on the property changed things?" she asked.

"Don't you? I mean, don't you think someone coming here brings the investigation closer to you?"

She wished she could deny it, but she could only nod in agreement.

"I have the name of the nursing home in my notes. We can go over and see her tomorrow."

"What about tonight?" she asked.

"What about it?"

"Do you think whoever strung that barbed wire is going to come back?"

"No."

"Why?"

"Because he turned tail like a scared ferret when he could have confronted me. I think he's playing it safe. And if I'm wrong about that, I'll hear the alarm."

She shifted her weight from one foot to the other. "Then I guess I'll go to bed."

"I'll stay up for a while." He stopped in the doorway and turned back to her. "Think about what might link the killings together."

"I have."

"And what might link you with the victims," he added.

She winced. "Thanks."

"We have to be realistic." He paused. "Do you ever use bedtime to give yourself a problem to solve?"

"What do you mean?"

"It's a useful technique. For example, I might focus on something I'm wondering about and tell myself I'm going to process it while I sleep."

"That works?"

"Sometimes. Maybe you could try it."

"Give me an example."

He looked like she'd put him on the spot, but he finally said, "A few months ago we were trying to help Shane's wife figure out who had kidnapped her brother. Well, she wasn't his wife then."

"I didn't know he was married."

"He and Jack both are," Max said then switched back to the subject at hand. "Anyway, we were working on the situation with the brother, and I'd think about it when I got in bed—running down lists of bad guys in the area."

"Did the technique help?"

He laughed. "Unfortunately, no. I didn't have enough information at the time. But you might have better luck with class members. I mean, you remember them. And being at that meeting brought back more memories, right?"

"Yes." She cleared her suddenly clogged throat. "Maybe I'll try."

"Something you haven't thought about before."

He left the bathroom and headed for the stairs. She started to turn away, then changed her mind, realizing she might as well get ready for bed. She wanted to go to sleep and forget the murders, and the plan he'd suggested made her nerves jangle. She firmed her lips. If she tried it and failed, maybe he'd stop pressing her for high school memories.

Again she turned on the water and couldn't help picturing the scene a few moments ago when she'd washed off Max's wounds.

A lot of guys she'd met were babies about being hurt. Apparently Max was too macho to let her know if he was hurting.

Trying to get him out of her mind, she reached for her toothbrush, but as she brushed her teeth, her mind continued to wander. When she'd come down here with the idea of finding out who had killed Angela, she'd felt unsettled, and she'd even thought of herself as a target. But there had been no proof. From what had happened with the intruder tonight, it seemed she'd been wrong. And now she was reevaluating the whole plan. What if she just gave the investigation up and went back to New York? And then what? Get back into the rat race she'd vowed to escape?

Was she planning to run away so somebody else could get killed instead?

That thought made her grimace. Really, what guarantee did she have that someone who sneaked around her family farm wouldn't come up to New York and stalk her there? Maybe it would depend on how focused they were on her.

She went back to her bedroom, closed the door, and changed from the clothes she'd been wearing into shorts and a T-shirt. Not what she usually slept in, but she didn't want to be wearing a nightgown when there was a strange man in the house.

No, not a strange man. The man she had hired to track down Angela's killer. And her best bet to stay safe was to stay here and stick close to Max Lyon, who had already demonstrated his worth in a couple of tight spots. But staying close to Max presented its own problems. She could admit to herself that she was attracted to him, but she was very sure that it wasn't smart to act on that impulse—for a whole lot of reasons.

Chapter 8

MAX WALKED DOWN THE STEPS, LISTENING TO THE stair treads and then the floorboards creak. The house was old and showing the usual wear, but it was solidly built, not like the cheap apartments where he'd grown up, where you could hear the people above and below you talking and flushing the toilet.

The toilet upstairs flushed, and he shook his head. Well, that wasn't so different. But this had been a one-family home, not an apartment where you were supposed to have some privacy.

He crossed the darkened living room and pulled the shade aside, looking out at the farmyard. Everything was still and quiet. But he hadn't expected to see movement. If someone came close enough for a visual sighting, he'd hear the alarm again first.

Still, it was reassuring to look out and see nothing that caused concern.

He sighed. Important aspects of this job had changed in the past few hours. When he'd accepted the assignment, he hadn't really thought of Olivia as a target of the Reunion Class Killer, as he now dubbed the murderer. But seeing the former classmates at the meeting had made him consider everyone as a target, including Olivia. And the attack tonight had reinforced that conviction.

Before tonight, he'd assumed that he could leave her here alone while he went out and did some poking around. Now he was thinking that he'd better stick with her—or, more likely, keep her with him when he went out, although he was sure she wasn't going to like that. He didn't like it, actually. He was used to having time alone. Even with Jack and Shane, he wanted his own space, but he'd have to put his own needs on hold until he found out who had killed Angela Dawson, Patrick Morris, and Gary Anderson. There were some other deaths he'd like to investigate as well, but right now he was focused on the most recent.

Of course, he could get Shane or Jack to come over here while he went out investigating. But he wasn't going to call in his partners every two seconds. They'd been outside checking the area around the restaurant tonight. That was enough for now.

Was he rationalizing? Maybe he wanted an excuse to tell Olivia she'd better stick with him. He snorted, annoyed that he was second-guessing his motives the way he'd try to second-guess a suspect.

Dropping the shade back into place, he brought his laptop over to one of the easy chairs and sat down. There were a lot of problems with this assignment, including the large number of suspects. The killer could be anyone in the reunion class or anyone from the school who had something against the class members. Like what if they'd been involved in a prank that had pissed off a janitor or a teacher? And, of course, it could turn out to be someone from a rival school, although that would mean they'd been involved enough with Olivia's reunion class to go after a lot of the people. It was a possibility, but he'd bet it was closer to home. Which led him back to the idea of a homicidal janitor or teacher running around. He'd get a line on as many of them as possible and have Jack and Shane check them out. There would surely already be some evidence.

He returned to his laptop and accessed the files that Jack and Shane had already compiled, looking at some of the material they'd entered. One of their jobs was to see which class members were living in the area. He scrolled down, counting the names, and found more than two hundred. Great! A lot of suspects that the other guys were going to have to check out while he was working from this end. He sent an email telling them what had happened tonight, then knew he'd better turn in if he was going to be any good in the morning.

Still, he sat for long moments on the sofa with the computer in his lap. He and Olivia had been sitting here before the attack, and his mind went back to that domestic scene. They were playing an engaged couple—a role he'd never expected to fill. Not that he thought marriage was a bad idea for his two Rockfort partners. But they hadn't lived with the turmoil in his parents' apartment. The yelling. The slamming doors. The late-night beatings. He'd decided long ago that a kid who'd been through that was doomed to repeat his parents' mistakes. And he'd figured that the best way to avoid it was to steer clear of the institution of marriage.

He laughed. And now here he was playing at being engaged and enjoying it on a certain level.

Well, don't start trying to decide whether Shane or Jack should be your best man, he cautioned himself. *A few days with a gorgeous model shouldn't change the convictions you've built up over a lifetime.*

It was good advice. The question was, could he follow

it? Or was he already getting sucked in over his head? He looked toward the ceiling. He and Olivia had been uncomfortable with each other from the start—partly because of the attraction simmering between them. In the bathroom when she'd been tending his wounds, he'd felt like they were two cats, a female in heat and a tom, thrown into a burlap bag where they couldn't escape from each other. He knew she'd felt the same sexual pull. He'd seen it in the brightness of her eyes, smelled it in the scent of her body. They'd both fought the attraction—and managed to cool themselves down.

But they'd also gotten to know each other a little better. Some of it was from observing her behavior at the reunion meeting, and some of it was from their conversation. Which was good for the working relationship, he told himself.

When he realized he was still looking upward toward her bedroom, he lowered his gaze. There were no noises from the second floor. Olivia must be in bed, and he was headed there soon. Not to her bed, he reminded himself.

Upstairs, Olivia plumped up her pillow and tried to relax. At first all she could think about was Max. He'd probably be glad to come up here and relax her. For a few tempting minutes she let herself think about what the two of them could be doing. When she found her body starting to heat up, she pushed Max Lyon out of her mind. Instead she focused on the relaxation exercises she'd learned from a DVD, deliberately tensing various muscle groups, then relaxing them. As her body settled down, she found herself thinking of the assignment that

Max had given her. She'd never tried anything like that before, and she was pretty sure it wouldn't do her any good. But she was going to try it so she could tell him in the morning that it had been a waste of time.

Why was that so important? Because she wanted to needle him? Or distance herself from him? She wasn't sure of her own motivation, but she knew that it was counterproductive to be at odds with him. The better she learned to work with him and be comfortable with him, the faster she could get him out of her life. He was the wrong kind of man for her. He was too aggressive and too sure of how things should be done.

Like her father. And maybe like Jerry, she silently admitted.

The thought brought her up short. Was that the problem with her view of Max? That he reminded her too much of the men who had run her life? And that she'd let strong men have too much power over her?

She made a dismissive sound, but now that the notion had lodged in her head, it was worth examining. Had she left her strong-willed father back in Maryland and wound up in a similar situation in New York? And could she really say that her father had ruined her life? It had felt like it when she was living here because of all his rules and his reactions when you didn't follow them. And she'd vowed to get out from under his thumb as quickly as she could.

Her father had been very sure of his values—and of how the women in his family should comport themselves. He was the one in charge, and his word was law in the Winters' house. He hadn't been harsh—if you fell into line with his plans. It had been easier to comply than to overtly rebel. A few times she'd done stuff she knew would make him angry and lied to him about it to cover up. Maybe her teenage behavior had been *her* failing. But she'd told herself Dad was the reason she'd gone off to New York without even considering furthering her formal education. Dad had argued against her making the break. But she'd been too determined to be swayed. She'd been nineteen at the time and sure that the best thing for her was to get away while she still could.

Then Jerry had taken her under his wing. She'd told herself he was making her career possible. And that was why she'd fallen in line with all his advice. But was she really just repeating her experience with Dad?

And here she was back at the old homestead—with another aggressive man. Like Jerry and Dad, he was telling her what to do. She knew it was for her own good.

And to be fair about Max, he hadn't been trying to force his will on her—at least not unless he thought she was in danger. He had very strict ideas about safety, and she knew she'd be foolish to ignore the advice he was giving. Not simply because she was paying him her hard-earned money to solve her friend's murder—she didn't want to end up as another one of the class whose life was cut short.

She was safe at the moment with Max in the house.

She closed her eyes, getting comfortable on the bed as her mind drifted back to the meeting they'd attended this evening, thinking about the men and women who had been there. They'd been in their teens the last time she'd seen them. Some of them seemed pretty much the way they had been in high school. Others had changed— mostly for the better.

As she thought about the meeting, she felt herself drifting off. Getting to sleep had never been a big problem for her, and soon she crossed the divide. For a little while, she slept peacefully, despite all the stress of the evening. Then everything changed as she fought to figure out where she was and who held her captive.

Chapter 9

OLIVIA WAS SOMEWHERE ELSE. NOT IN HER BED. IN THE middle of chaos. Back in her own past in a crowd of high school kids frantically trying to get away from danger.

Around her people ducked behind furniture or tried to stampede up a flight of stairs. A lot of them were charging toward her, and someone grabbed her, trying to pull her to safety.

They crashed to the floor, and she cried out, "Let me go," even though she knew he wanted to drag her out of danger, away from the terrified crowd and a gunman behind them.

"Take it easy. You're all right." The words were spoken by a hard male voice that sounded too deep to be coming from one of her high school classmates

But she couldn't take it easy. She was frightened, and she lashed out, striking the man who held her. When she landed a blow to his face, he grunted, and pinned her arms down so she couldn't hit him again.

As she struggled against him, she realized that she wasn't lying on a cold tile floor as she'd thought. She was on a bed, and the man who had spoken was lying across her, holding her down, with a terrifying restrained power that sent panic zinging through her.

She redoubled her efforts to get away, and he circled her wrists with his hands, keeping her in place. She knew from the way he held her that this man could hurt her, yet she also knew that he was trying to be gentle.

"Olivia, don't. You're all right. You were having a bad dream."

Finally the familiar voice registered.

Her eyes blinked open and she found herself staring up at Max, illuminated by a shaft of light coming through the bedroom door.

"Max?"

"Yeah."

She felt heat rise in her face and was glad of the darkness. "I hit you. I'm sorry."

"You were having a bad dream," he repeated.

"Yes," she murmured, dragging herself back to present reality. She wasn't in the middle of some wildly panicked scene. She was in her own bed, and Max Lyon was lying there with her. And as she looked up at him, she saw that he was naked. Or maybe he was wearing shorts, she couldn't be sure.

Embarrassed by her out-of-control behavior, she stammered, "You... you told me to work on the case while I was sleeping, and... and I think I did that."

"Okay. Yeah."

She heard his automatic reassurance but knew he couldn't understand what she was talking about. He hadn't been there with her in the dream. He'd only come in when she'd been trying to free herself from the nightmare.

When he started to pull away, she involuntarily gripped his arm, needing the physical connection on some deep, primal level. Like the sky would come down around her if he left her now. She couldn't tell him that. All she could say was, "I don't want to be alone."

"Okay."

Before she could stop herself, she moved over to make room for him, and as he settled down beside her on the bed, she saw that he was wearing a pair of boxer shorts.

He lay on his back, and she lay beside him, her shoulder touching his. As her emotions settled, she decided that she probably shouldn't have invited him to stay in her bed. Somehow doing that in the house where she'd grown up felt very wrong, but she wasn't going to send him away because she hadn't lied to him. The dream was too vivid for her to cope with it alone.

She wasn't sure what he was feeling when she heard him drag in a breath and let it out.

"Can you tell me what was so upsetting?" he said.

Although she was the one who had stopped him from leaving, the idea of talking about the dream brought a breathless wave of cold to her body, as though she'd been pulled into an arctic lake and dragged below the surface by a sea monster. He probably felt her shiver. And when she remained silent, he prompted, "You said you were working on who might have killed Angela?"

Yeah, that was the crux of the problem. "Yes," she answered in a low voice.

"And that's what triggered the dream?"

"I think so."

When she went silent again, he shifted toward her, his hand stroking her arm. "Can you tell me about it?"

She swallowed hard. "Okay. I was back at a party in my senior year of high school. With a lot of the same people who were at the meeting tonight… And some who weren't…" Her voice trailed off. "Well, I guess it was yesterday."

"Some who weren't?" he asked.

"Well, like Angela."

He waited for her to say more.

"I can't be sure if it was exactly the way it really happened back then."

"Why not?"

She swallowed hard. "Because in the dream, you were there."

He laughed. "I guess that means it was a total fantasy trip, since I didn't run in your circles."

"We did meet once," she said.

She felt his hand go still. When he spoke, his voice had thickened. "You remember that?"

"Of course."

"But you never mentioned it."

When she didn't respond, he asked, "What do you remember, exactly?"

"Angela and I were in a pizza parlor. Some guys we didn't know were harassing us, and you came up and stopped them. Then you left, and I never got a chance to thank you."

In the darkness he swallowed hard. "I didn't do it to get thanked. I did it because I didn't like seeing what was happening. But I thought you didn't remember."

"How could I forget something like that?" she asked.

"Because it was me."

Her head shot toward him. "What's that supposed to mean?"

"I was a guy your crowd avoided."

"Maybe they thought you were dangerous. But that night in the pizza parlor you proved you weren't what I'd assumed." It was her turn to swallow hard. "But

I wasn't going to go looking for you after that. I had enough problems."

He could have asked what that meant. Instead he said, "Maybe we'd better talk about that dream, before you forget the details."

It was an interesting transition back to the nightmare, but she knew that he was right. If they were going to talk about it, they'd better do it now before the details evaporated into the mist of her unconscious. Still, it was hard to force her tongue to form the right words.

"Okay. You weren't really there. But a lot of the rest of it was what I remember. At least what I remember now."

"You're saying the dream was about something that really happened to you?"

She had to gulp in air and let it out slowly before saying, "Yes. It was about a party I went to. Until tonight, I'd forgotten all about that night. I guess you could say I repressed it."

"Why?"

She wanted to scream at him to stop pressing her. If she was going to talk about that night, it had to be at her own pace.

"It wasn't one of my better moments."

"But now you think this party was important?"

When she'd come to Rockfort Security, it had been to solve the murder of a friend. Maybe on some level she'd known that she was going to have to talk about her and Angela's high school years. Maybe the dream was her way of forcing the issue.

On a sigh, she said, "If it wasn't, I wouldn't have dreamed about it, would I?" Still, as she said the last part, she began to shiver, fighting the feeling of being dragged under freezing water again.

"Are you all right?" Max murmured.

"I don't know. I mean, all that stuff rushing back at me is a shock."

He gathered her closer, stroking his hands over her back and shoulders and into her hair. It felt good to be held by him—protected. And more. They were in her bed, in the middle of the night. What would happen if she raised her face to his?

It was tempting to do that. Tempting to find out if playing house was affecting him the way it was affecting her. Or maybe in her case, it was because she hadn't been with anyone in a long time, and she was focusing on Max in a way that was better left alone.

Her rational mind knew it was a mistake to get involved with him. Especially now. But her emotions were so tangled up by the evening's events and the dream that she wasn't capable of staying logical. She raised her face, and for a moment their mouths were inches apart. She heard his breath catch just before she closed the gap between them.

When her lips touched his, it was as though an electrical circuit had snapped closed. She felt a jolt of sensation, a frisson of heat that sizzled through her body, and she silently acknowledged what she hadn't told him. In the dream, seeing him had sent a wave of heat coursing through her. Then it had been unwanted. Not now.

She had initiated the kiss, but he didn't remain passive. His lips moved over hers, and his arms gathered her to him, increasing the heated sensation. She closed her eyes, enjoying the kiss and the man, and elated by the knowledge that the sexual pull hadn't been all on her part. There was no doubt he was responding to her, just as she was responding to him. That insight gave her a feeling of power that she hadn't sensed in the relationship before. As she rode the wave of that power, she opened her mouth, darting her tongue out to play with the seam of his lips. He opened for her, and she drank in the taste of him, the sensuality of his tongue gliding against hers. She let the tendrils of fire wrap around the two of them, sealing them together, enjoying the man and her own arousal, and not thinking about where a kiss between two people lying on a bed might lead. But he was apparently more cautious than she.

When he pulled back, she made a small sound of protest.

"Max?"

"I shouldn't have done that."

"I think I started it."

"And I have to put a stop to it, because this is not a good place for us to be kissing."

"Is there a good place?"

"Probably not."

The blunt words cut, and she didn't want to think that he was rejecting her. "Because you're on a job?" she asked.

"Yes."

He shifted her body so that she was facing away from him in the bed, although he kept his arm around her. Closing her eyes, she leaned back against him. But before she could focus any more on what was happening between them, he said, "That dream about the party threw you off balance."

"Yes," she answered, knowing that he intended the comment as a way to save face.

"Tell me more about it."

So there would be no temptation to go back to kissing? She didn't voice the thought, but he was quick to clarify

"While it's fresh in your mind."

"Okay. The party was at Brian Cannon's house, and Angela wasn't the only recently deceased person there. Gary Anderson was there and so was Patrick Morris."

"Gary's the guy who was found dead in the drainage ditch? And Patrick was the one who was overcome by carbon monoxide in his house?" Max said, apparently to make sure he was getting it right.

"Yes."

"So what was the party like?"

"It was getting out of control. The football players had won a game that afternoon, and they were guzzling beer and doing shots at the bar in the rec room. They were getting wasted. Other people were making out or going off to the bedrooms. With all the drinking and making out going on, Angela and I decided we were out of our depth. Angela had her car, and we offered Linda a ride."

"Linda, the one who organized the reunion committee?"

"Yes. Linda Unger."

"But Brian didn't want us to leave. He was blocking us from going up the stairs from the rec room to the first floor. Then Troy Masters came over and told him that if we wanted to leave, he and Tommy Larson could take us home."

"Troy is Mr. Princeton, and Tommy is a local success, too?"

"Right. I was focused on Troy and Brian, and I wasn't

paying attention to the guys at the bar, when suddenly Gary and another guy started fighting."

"Gary, who's now dead?"

"Right."

"Who was he fighting with?"

"I'm not sure."

"Why not?"

She shrugged. "He was turned away from me. But I know it was one of the football players. He knocked Gary down. And when Gary came up, he had a gun in his hand—and he shot it."

"Jesus! What happened?"

"My guess? He didn't really want to kill the guy because he didn't hit him. But everybody went into a panic. Some people were trying to hide, and others were running to the stairs. I was going to get trampled, and I think Patrick pulled me out of the way."

"Patrick who's now dead."

"Yes."

"I guess that was when I also heard you screaming in your sleep. You were in the middle of a riot."

"And I was hitting you. I'm sorry."

"It's okay. I understand." He kept his gaze on her. "I woke you up and cut off the dream. But what happened back then?"

"The football players got the gun away from Gary."

"And then what?"

She laughed. "Well, Gary's shooting the gun broke up the party. Maybe everybody realized that they could have gotten into real trouble."

"And Brian called the cops?"

"Actually, no," Olivia said.

"Why not?"

"I guess you can think of it as a conspiracy of silence. He didn't rat out Gary, and nobody who was there told about how the party had ended."

Max made a dismissive sound. "You're saying a whole bunch of people kept a secret like that?"

"As far as I know. Maybe because it was such a shock. I mean, today there are a lot of guns around. Back then, not so much. And it was only about a month until graduation. Nobody wanted to get in trouble and face the consequences."

"Did you find out whose gun it was?"

"I didn't find out. I'm assuming it belonged to his parents."

"And how did the shoot-out at the party affect everyone's relationship with Gary?"

"Well, after the gun incident, they were more cautious around him. You could say they withdrew from him."

"Yeah, I'll bet. Did that make him more aggressive?"

"I don't know. I really did keep away from him after that. I mean, there was no telling what he might do."

"Right, people knew he had a violent streak. Maybe he went after someone else years later. Which could have been how he ended up dead."

"Yes."

"Which might mean his death's not related to Angela."

"I guess that's true." She shivered again. "What if this is more complicated than I thought? And it's spooky thinking about the implications. I was there with Angela. She's dead now, and so is Gary—and Patrick."

"From what you say, you had direct interaction at the party with Angela and Patrick. But not with Gary."

"Yes. And I had completely forgotten about the party—until tonight." She paused for a moment. "I mean it was pretty…upsetting. I guess it was the first time I saw things get that much out of control—ending with the gun. Until then, smoking in the woods was a big deal. Or somebody getting hold of a six-pack of beer."

"You came from a pretty tame environment."

"Yes. And now you telling me to focus on the murders brought back stuff I didn't want to remember."

He nodded. "Of course, the dream could be important for other reasons."

"Like how?"

"Before Gary shot the gun, what was happening?"

She grimaced. She didn't really want to talk about her own behavior, which she'd avoided discussing. Instead, she made the comment general. "Well, some kids were drinking. Others were dancing or making out, and some had even gone upstairs to the bedrooms. Angela, Linda, and I just wanted to get out of there when we saw how out of hand it was."

"Hmm. It's how I'd expect rich high school kids to act—until the shooting."

"But I wasn't a rich high school kid. We're back in the house where I grew up, and it's not exactly a luxury mansion."

"Okay. But you were hanging out with the rich crowd."

"The in crowd, I'd put it. And I had lied about where I was. If my dad had found out, I would have been in deep doo-doo. And he would have made sure Angela's parents knew about it."

"How did she fit into that crowd?"

"She wasn't one of the rich kids either, if that's what

you're asking. Her parents owned a couple of antique shops. One in Ellicott City and one in New Market. Both of us worked hard to fit in."

"How?"

She was sorry she'd said that last part. "Being friendly. Going along with what the gang wanted."

"Drinking and smoking?"

"Yes."

"Drugs?"

"I managed to avoid drugs."

He looked thoughtful, and she braced for another probing question about herself. To her relief, he asked, "And if we went to the house where they had the party, would we find a bullet hole in the wall?"

"I don't know. Maybe Brian patched it up and painted the wall or something before his parents came home."

"You never went back to his house?"

"No."

"Why not?"

"I wasn't really friends with him. I wouldn't have gone there to hang out. And that night gave me the feeling that it was dangerous to be around him."

"Well, the dream gives us more to work with. Who else was there?"

She thought for a moment. "Claire Lowden and Zeke Pressman. They were making out."

"Uh-huh."

She laid her forehead against Max's shoulder, silently admitting that there was more she should say, but she didn't really want to. Did she have to tell him everything?

He stroked his hand up and down her arm, making her skin tingle.

"Do you remember when the party was? What month?"

She thought about that. "It was May. I even know the date. Brian said they were celebrating Cinco de Mayo. May fifth."

"Good. That may be helpful." He kept stroking her, then finally said, "It's still pretty early in the morning. You think you can go back to sleep?"

She wanted to say she'd feel safer if he stayed there with her, but she knew that asking him to sleep in her bed was a bad idea—as bad as having kissed him. Instead she gave the only answer that she could. "Yes."

—∿∿—

Conscious of Olivia's gaze on his nearly naked body, Max forced himself to climb out of bed and head down the hall to the room where he was sleeping. He wanted to stay. Olivia wanted him to stay, but if he did, he'd end up doing something he knew was unprofessional. Worse than what he'd already done. Deliberately switching his thoughts away from himself, he started thinking about Olivia's dream again. She'd said it was what had happened the night of the party, but she'd hesitated at several points, which made him wonder if she was being completely straight with him.

Was there something she had done? Something that embarrassed her? Or worse?

They were going to have to talk about it again, but he knew from her evasive behavior that he was going to have to give her a little time.

He switched his thoughts back to himself. Or more accurately, the two of them. Her talking about the past had brought up the incident in the pizza parlor, when he'd come over and rescued her from the two creeps.

He'd thought she didn't remember it or that maybe she hadn't wanted to talk about it. But she was the one who had brought it up.

He'd wanted to hear more about it, but that would only be for his personal enlightenment. It had no bearing on the current investigation. Well, he'd established that the other girl had been Angela. But the rest of it wasn't important, he told himself.

Chapter 10

A FEW HOURS LATER, THE SMELL OF COFFEE DRIFTED toward Max as he walked slowly down the steps, through the living room and dining room, and into the kitchen. He and Olivia had been in the house together for a few days, and she'd served him breakfast, in case anyone was watching their morning routine.

As on the previous mornings, he was dressed in jeans, a T-shirt, and a light jacket. He followed the tempting aroma of the coffee and found Olivia standing with her back to him at the stove, scrambling eggs. She was also dressed casually in jeans and a knit shirt, but she looked far from relaxed.

Her movements were as jerky as a marionette's and her shoulders as rigid as a fence rail, and he knew she hated the thought of facing him in the morning. Because of her behavior in bed? Or was she flashing back to the dream and what she hadn't told him about the evening in question?

You could say this was a very weird morning after, considering all they had done was kiss.

"Coffee is in the pot," she said, pointing toward the coffee machine on the sideboard.

He'd used the machine before without comment. Now he made an attempt at conversation. "Was this your dad's?"

Her laugh was brittle. "God forbid that he'd spend

money on a fancy coffee setup. He made do with instant. I brought some luxuries from New York. Good coffee is a necessity I can't live without."

"It wakes you up?"

"It keeps me going all day."

He poured some into the mug sitting beside it.

"And you take it black, right?" she said.

"Right." For the moment, he didn't ask how she'd slept or get into anything personal. For the past couple of hours, he'd been going over lists of things they should do regarding the case. It was a long list, and he figured it should take their minds off the kiss. If anything could take their minds off the kiss.

"We have a lot more to work with," he said as he sipped from the coffee mug.

"Uh-huh."

"I had said we should talk to the guy who's renting the farmland from your family."

"Bill Yeager," she interjected.

"Yes. And I still think that should be first on the list, since somebody was sneaking around here last night."

Maybe the dream had overshadowed the incident out in the woods. Now she rubbed her hands up and down her arms as she nodded.

"I'd also said we should talk to Angela's mother. But I think we might change the focus and talk to some of the people who were at the party."

"Uh-huh."

She turned to face him, and he saw her inspecting the wounds on his face.

"They're healing," he said.

"Yes, you were lucky you didn't damage your

eye. But what are you going to tell people who ask what happened?"

He had decided on a strategy for that. "I'm going to tell them what happened last night."

"Really?"

"Yes. It's actually a good idea. I can get their reactions, and I can say that as your new fiancé, I'm worried about your safety, and I want to know about what happened on Cinco de Mayo—since you dreamed about it after the reunion meeting."

"But they all wanted to forget about that party—the way I did."

He made a dismissive gesture. "That was before someone started killing members of the class—all three of whom were there, as it turns out."

"You don't know the murders are related. You don't even know that Gary or Patrick was murdered. The police labeled each one an accident. That's why I hired you. Well, Angela was the primary reason. But I wanted to know if it was connected."

"It seems to me that you hired me because you thought the deaths were related. Now are you taking the other side of the argument?"

She sighed. "Maybe."

"Because of the dream?"

"What do you mean?"

"Think about it."

She gave him a long look but said nothing.

"One thing I bet we'll find out when we start asking questions is who Gary was fighting with."

"Maybe," she said again.

When she didn't elaborate, he asked, "Why not? You

might not have seen it clearly, but I'm sure somebody did. Like other guys on the team who were right up there with the would-be victim."

She answered with a tight nod, then asked, "Do you want orange juice?"

"That's an abrupt change of subject."

"Subtle, huh?"

He laughed, then asked, "Do you want me to help with anything? I mean, with the breakfast."

"Get forks."

"In the left-hand drawer of the hutch, right?"

"Yes."

As she dished the eggs onto plates, he said, "That's more than I usually eat in the morning."

"Me too."

"Doesn't a model have to stay pencil-thin?"

"That's how you see me?"

He suddenly felt like he'd taken a step into quicksand. "No."

"How do you see me?"

Now he was sinking deeper into the trap he'd created for himself. "Um, as a very attractive woman." He could have added desirable, but she already knew his thinking on that score.

Her gaze held his for a long moment.

"A supermodel has to stay pencil-thin."

"You're saying that's not what you are."

"More like a successful model. That's a whole other level of commitment."

He resisted the temptation to look her up and down. "Still, you're breaking your training, aren't you?" he said.

"Yes. But I like the freedom," she answered as she set

the plates on the table. "And anyway, I read about a new diet in a women's magazine. You eat what you want five days a week and diet on two."

"That works?"

"It has for me."

Deliberately switching the subject away from anything personal, he looked around the kitchen and said, "I guess you all did some remodeling."

She seemed relieved to get off the topic of diets. "Yes, maybe ten years ago. Right before my mom died. Dad did it for her, so he kind of wasted the money."

Although he'd vowed to keep the conversation off of anything personal, he couldn't stop himself from asking, "What happened to her?"

Olivia pulled out the chair opposite him and sat down. "I guess you could say it was bad luck. She was having terrible pains in her chest and abdomen. She was afraid she was having a heart attack, but it turned out to be her gallbladder. She went into the hospital to have it removed and got one of those awful skin-eating bacteria. She died a week later."

He winced. "Your dad took it hard?"

"We both did. She'd always been a buffer between me and him. With her gone, it was like the two of us were cooped up here."

Like us, Max thought, but didn't say it.

"That was in your senior year?"

"Yes."

"Before or after the party?"

"After."

When she reached down to fiddle with her fork, he knew she hadn't wanted to get back to the subject of the party.

"Her dying was a major factor in my getting out of here. It was in the summer, and I was trying to decide what to do. Then I suddenly had some money I could use any way I wanted." She kept her gaze focused on her food. "Dad and I never really got along, and I knew I had to get out of the house—one way or the other."

"Why not?"

"He came from a long line of male chauvinists. Rural men who were the breadwinners and the law in their little world. They were pretty isolated, and they could do what they wanted. Maybe he even wished there wasn't so much modern communication. He had very definite ideas on everything—including the role of women in the family. He wanted things done his way, and Mom and I had to conform."

"Like what?"

"Well, I remember Mom wanting to bring in some extra money. But he made it clear that it would shame him for his wife to have a job outside the home. Besides, he said she'd be happier staying home where a wife belonged."

"He dictated what would make her happy?"

"Remember, he thought he knew best. If she wanted to make a difference in their finances, she could do it by saving money. By freezing and canning her own vegetables and fruits instead of buying them at the grocery store. Or by making her own clothes. She made mine, too, actually. She had a natural talent for it. Maybe that's where I got my early interest in fashion. We'd go to the fabric store together and spend a lot of time looking at the pattern books and the materials. She also made the curtains, and she even made rag rugs."

"Why did she marry him?" Max asked. Because of

his own screwed-up family, he was always interested in how unsuitable couples had gotten together. He'd never asked his mom why she'd married his father. Probably he should have. But he'd avoided the subject because it had been easier to ignore the past. Was that why Olivia avoided talking about that party back in high school?

Olivia answered his question. "Maybe he hid his need to dominate from her when they were dating. Maybe he knew that if he came across as too controlling, he wouldn't get her."

"He loved her?"

"I think he loved both of us—in his own way. But he was an old-fashioned man, and he wanted everything on his own terms. And if he didn't get them, he...lashed out. Verbally. And in my case, spanking me with a coat hanger."

"You couldn't get away with that today," he said, his voice turning rough.

"I know it's frowned upon. Nobody would do it in public. But in the privacy of your own home, I think you still can. Unless the kid ratted out the parent, but most kids keep their mouths shut, I think. I mean, if you get your parents in trouble, what happens to you? Anyway, Mom took his frugality advice to heart, and then some. And not entirely in the way he intended. She had stashed some money in a bank account. I don't know if she had fantasies about leaving him, or if it was just that she wanted me to have more choices than she did." She stopped and took a breath. "She'd written me a letter about it that she said not to read unless something happened to her. After she died, I read the letter and got the money. Actually, the account had my name on it, too. When I'd signed the card, I hadn't realized what it was."

"How did your father like your getting the money?"

"He hated it because it gave me some independence. That's how I could afford to go to New York and start trying to get modeling jobs."

"It paid off."

"Well, I've worked steadily since I got my first job modeling for an underwear catalog."

Olivia in sexy underwear. He was tempted to look it up on the web, but he kept his mouth shut.

"This is the first time since I started working regularly that I've taken more than a couple of days off."

"You should have done it more often," Max said. "That's one good thing about working for Rockfort. We can arrange for time off."

"A good policy," she said as she forked up some of the eggs.

"We liked arranging the agency the way we wanted it."

"It's just the three of you?" Olivia asked.

"For now. But we may take on some more partners."

He took a bite. "These are good. What did you do to them?"

"I just put in a little deli ham and green pepper, plus some seasonings."

After he'd chewed and swallowed, he said, "And your boss is mad about your bailing out."

"My agent."

"You probably pay *his* bills."

"Yes, but he was a major part of my success. He saw that I had raw talent, and he showed me how to capitalize on it. He got me the right haircut and took me to a studio that taught me makeup techniques. He showed me how to walk and how to present myself in the best way. He even coached me in fending off the inevitable pushy men—but in a nice way. In case they were important."

Max snorted.

"I was grateful for all the coaching—and for the steady stream of work. Now I'm thinking that he could have let me work at a little slower pace. Of course, there was always the thought in the back of my mind that a model's career is limited."

"By what?"

"Her age, for one thing. There's always someone younger and fresher coming up." She looked like she wanted to say more but had perhaps thought better of it.

He found he was hungry and finished the meal. She had taken less but she also cleaned her plate. When they were done, he cleared the table and loaded the dishwasher while she washed the skillet in the sink.

"I want to go out and look at the barbed-wire trap," he said. "And see if I can find anything else." He waited for a moment. "Do you mind coming with me?"

"No. I want to see." She gave him a quick look. "You have your gun?"

"Yeah. I think that's going to be standard operating procedure from now on."

"That's why you wore your jacket?"

"Yes."

They exited the house, and he locked the door behind him before taking the route he'd followed the night before in the dark.

They headed past the barn and into the woods, with

Max in the lead and walking cautiously. Even during the day, it wasn't that easy to see the barbed wire in the dim light under the trees. It made for a dangerous stroll around the property.

Olivia winced when she saw it. "That could have done a lot more damage."

Nodding in silent acknowledgment, he walked closer. He had assumed the guy who'd strung the wire had gotten away clean, but as he approached the trap, he saw a small piece of dark-colored cloth caught in one of the barbs.

"Well, well." He picked up a stick from the ground and tried to lift the fabric away, but it stuck to the barb. It was good quality fabric, not unlike the shirt he'd been wearing the night before, only darker.

Olivia came closer.

"It looks like a man's dress shirt. I mean, someone who could have come straight here from the meeting," she said.

He made a sound of agreement. "Or it could be a woman, dressed in a man's shirt. Do you remember what everyone was wearing?"

She gave him a quick look. "Women's clothing is my job. I remember the women's outfits. None of the men were dressed in anything memorable. I'm sorry."

"As it turns out, I took pictures."

"How?"

"With that pen I was using to take some notes during the strategy session."

"Clever."

"I wanted a record of the people there. I wasn't really interested in the clothing."

Now he took a plastic bag and some thin rubber gloves out of his pocket and carefully untangled the fabric from the barbed wire. The material was stiff in one place, and when he held it up to the light, he thought he saw blood.

"I think the bastard cut himself when he was getting the hell out of my way."

She stared at the cloth. "If he cut himself, can you get his DNA from that?"

Chapter 11

OLIVIA WATCHED MAX CONSIDER THE QUESTION. "THE short answer is yes. But there are a lot of factors in play. I'm not officially in law enforcement, which makes a difference in how the analysis would have to be handled. A police department's not going to work with me. Of course there are civilian labs, like the National Forensic Support Lab, but they're expensive, and it might take weeks to get the results. And once we knew the individual, we'd still have to look for a match in the state or the FBI database. With Maryland, we'd only get people in the state system."

She cleared her throat. "Don't you have a friend in the police department that you could ask?"

"That's a possibility. Maybe better than looking for someone with a nasty scratch on his arm."

"Not very scientific."

"It would be a clue."

She followed him out of the woods and into the house, where he pulled out his cell phone and made a call—to his partners, she presumed, because he reported the barbed wire and the piece of shirt fabric.

"We might as well go ahead with an analysis," he said, then listened for a few moments.

"Yeah, it may not pan out, but I'd like to at least see what we've got. I'll mail it off as soon as I can."

When he hung up, she gave him a questioning look. "I thought you said we might as well not bother."

"We might get lucky. And maybe with those photos I took."

He went to his computer and opened a file. She sat down next to him as he brought up one of the pictures he'd taken with his pen the night before. It showed Tommy Larson sitting across the table from Max. He was wearing a yellow polo shirt, nothing like the scrap of fabric Max had found on the barbed wire.

They went on to the next picture, which was of Tommy and his date. Even though Tommy's shirt didn't match the fabric, he *was* looking at Max with an annoyed expression on his face. Pictures of Brian and Troy showed shirts that were nothing like the fabric, but they revealed similar expressions.

She dragged in a little breath.

"What?"

"They don't like you."

"They could be remembering me as the school bad boy."

Olivia put her hand on his arm. "You weren't as bad as they thought."

"Why not?"

"You came to my rescue at the pizza parlor. And if you did that, you probably did other stuff that damaged your bad-boy reputation."

He snorted. "You mean like walking old ladies across the street?"

"Did you?"

"I don't remember."

Pressing him, she asked, "That night, would you have done it for anyone, or was it me specifically?"

He made a low sound. "What's the better answer?"

"What do you mean?"

"Is it better for me to have wanted to help you specifically—or any girl?"

"I don't know."

"Well, I don't know the answer."

"You don't remember what you were thinking that evening?" she probed.

"It was a long time ago."

She was pretty sure he *did* remember but that he didn't want to share the memory with her, because he was deliberately backing away from an opportunity to get closer to her.

He clicked to the next picture, and she took the opportunity to lean closer to him, as she looked at the group shot of several people at the food table. No one was wearing the shirt in question.

Finally they'd gone through all the pictures and found nothing useful—besides the negative attitude toward Max. Not from everyone but from a lot of the men.

She put her hand on his arm. "I'm sorry."

"About what?"

"I was too wound up with myself, and I wasn't seeing all the stuff you had to deal with while we were there."

He shrugged. "Part of the job. A private detective gets that a lot. Too bad it doesn't give a clue to the killer."

She wanted to tell him that she wished she'd been more of a partner at the meeting. But it seemed that he wanted to stay on task. "So either it wasn't one of those guys, or he changed his shirt."

"Yes."

"Do you have a padded envelope and a mailing label I can use to send the sucker?"

"It wasn't something my dad would have needed."

He clicked away from the pictures and found the address of the lab he'd used on previous occasions. Then he filled out an online form to accompany the sample and printed it using the portable printer he'd brought to the farmhouse.

Their next stop was the closest mailbox store, in one of the new shopping centers Olivia had seen when they were driving home the night before. The detour took an hour, and it was close to noon when they drove back to the farm next door.

"We're going to have to use the engaged couple story with the Yeagers," Max reminded her.

She winced, thinking that she might as well take out an ad in the *Howard County Times* announcing her status.

Max caught her reaction. "Sorry. When this is all over, you can send out announcements setting the record straight."

"How will that make you feel?" she suddenly asked.

He hesitated. "Like I completed my assignment."

"You mean because you caught the killer?"

"Yeah."

"You won't care that everyone will know you weren't really engaged to the hot model?" she probed.

"Oh well."

And how would she really feel about it? She'd hired him to do a job, but she was thinking it was more than that to him now. And to her. Was that what she wanted—something romantic with Max Lyon? It hadn't started off as part of her plans. Now it was hard to avoid considering it. Still, she switched her thoughts away from herself and Max as they got out of the car.

Bill Yeager's wife opened the kitchen door when

they knocked. She was a woman in her late forties or early fifties with a weather-roughened face. She'd changed since Olivia saw her last: She wasn't as thin as she had been, and her hair was now a salt-and-pepper mix. Olivia felt a twinge of sadness for the woman, who apparently led a hard life, not unlike her own mother's.

Mrs. Yeager was obviously concerned that the owner of the farmland her husband rented had dropped by. "Ms. Olivia, what can I do for you? Is anything wrong?"

"We just need to ask your husband a few questions about any…unauthorized visits to the farm."

"He don't do that."

Realizing her answer had done nothing to set the woman at ease, Olivia hurried to explain. "What I meant was, if someone he doesn't know has come by."

"Oh, well, he's out in the south field inspecting the corn."

"Yes. It's good we've had rain," Olivia, a farmer's daughter, said. "We'll drive over there."

As they returned to the car, Max commented, "She seemed nervous."

Olivia laughed. "I guess it's from years of dealing with my father. Maybe she expects the same from me."

"Was he hard on them?"

"Not exactly. But he stuck to the letter of their agreement. Like when there was a bad year and half the crops dried up, the Yeagers still had to pay as much as if they'd done well."

He turned his gaze toward her. "You don't do the same thing?"

"No."

"Why not?"

"I don't need the money, and I know the Yeagers do," Olivia said. "Plus, I feel like they're doing me a favor, helping me keep the land."

She directed Max back along the farm road, then told him where to stop. They both got out and walked to the field.

A tall thin man wearing worn jeans, a plaid shirt, and a straw had glanced up inquiringly when he saw them on his property.

"Everything okay?" he asked, looking from Olivia to Max and back again.

"No problem about you," Olivia said.

"But?"

"We were wondering if you'd seen anyone suspicious around the Winters' property?" Max said.

"Well, you, for starters. You're the guy who was nosing around with two other fellows," Yeager said.

Max glanced at Olivia, thinking she probably hadn't expected the farmer to comment on what he and his partners had been doing there. When she said nothing, he explained. "I'm Olivia's new fiancé."

Yeager's gaze bored into Max. Instead of offering congratulations, he said, "What—are you thinking about selling the property?"

"No," Olivia answered quickly.

The farmer looked relieved, then finally said, "Congratulations."

"Yes, thanks," she managed to reply, wishing she could sink into the ground beside the cornfield. Or wishing that Max had just come here alone, although she knew that wouldn't have been practical, for a whole lot of reasons. Starting with she was the one who knew

Yeager and ending with Max had said it was dangerous for her to be alone at the farm.

Yeager looked her up and down. "So you're giving up your career?"

"No," she answered quickly. Or was that really what she was considering?

To her relief, Max jumped back into the conversation. "I guess you saw me and my buddies setting some security devices. I was concerned about her safety after her friend was killed."

"What friend are you talking about?" Yeager asked.

"Angela Dawson was in her class at Donley High. She had a shop in Ellicott City. You didn't hear anything about that?"

Yeager's gaze turned inward. "Yeah, I do remember reading something about it in the *Times*. It's a damn shame what this world is coming to."

"Yes," Olivia agreed.

Max continued. "So a couple of my buddies and I were just making sure nobody could sneak up on the house." He paused a beat, then added, "In fact, somebody tried to do that last night."

"Oh yeah?" Yeager asked, looking genuinely surprised, and Olivia was sure he hadn't had anything to do with it.

"Uh-huh," Max answered but didn't elaborate.

The farmer took off his wide-brimmed hat and swiped his arm across his forehead.

"We were wondering if you'd seen anybody hanging around the property," Max said.

Yeager thought for a moment. "As a matter of fact, I did see a car parked up the road." He gestured toward Olivia's house.

"The farm road or the highway?"

"Highway."

"When?" Max asked, and Olivia caught the sharp edge in his voice.

"A couple of days ago."

"After we got here," Olivia murmured.

"And nobody before that?" Max clarified.

Yeager creased the brim of his hat. "Not that I saw. Course, I wasn't looking out for anyone. And I don't spend all my time scanning the road. I got work to do."

"Understood," Max answered. "Can you tell us anything about who you saw?"

"It was just a car parked. A cheap model. Probably Jap."

"Okay. Did you see who was in it?" Max asked.

"A fellow did get out and stare toward your house."

"Young? Old?"

"Hard to tell. He was pretty far away, and he was wearing a baseball cap pulled down kind of low. But maybe he did move like a younger man."

"Anything else you remember?"

Yeager gave Max a sharp look. "You're askin' a lot of questions. You sure you're not a cop or something?"

"No," Max said evenly. "I'm just concerned about my sweetie."

Olivia shot him a look but said nothing.

"Well, I can't give you any more details. I was too far away."

"If you remember anything, could you call?" Max asked.

"Sure. But I don't think there's much else to say."

"You have my cell number," Olivia said.

Yeager nodded.

"Thanks for your time," Max said.

He and Olivia both turned and walked back to his SUV. They waited until they were inside the vehicle with the doors closed before speaking.

"So someone *was* hanging around," Olivia said.

Max nodded. "It doesn't prove anything. It could be someone just getting out to stretch his legs."

"Is that what you think?" she asked.

"Actually, no. Too bad we don't know much about him besides that it was a guy driving a cheap car. Which doesn't mean that's what he usually drives. He could have used it for the occasion."

"So we have no idea who it is. And we don't even know for sure if it was the guy who strung the barbed wire."

"Unfortunately." He turned toward her. "How do you evaluate Yeager's reaction to our asking questions?"

She thought for a moment, then said, "He was a little on edge. But like his wife, he could be worried that I'm going to try and get him off the property."

"Can you?"

"Well, he's got a lease. But I suppose I could break it if I was looking to sell. Or buy him off."

"Would that put him out of business?"

"No. He's got his own fields. He's just taking advantage of my acreage to grow more corn."

"And your dad got along with Yeager?"

"What's that supposed to mean?"

"Well, it could have been Yeager sneaking around last night."

"Why would he?"

"It depends on how secure he feels with his rental arrangement. He saw me and Jack and Shane poking around the property. Then he saw lights on in the house. He could have been investigating."

"But he wouldn't string barbed wire."

"When Jack and Shane came out here with me, we didn't go into the woods where the barbed wire was strung. We only had time for a quick and dirty security setup. That means the barbed wire could have been there when we were on the property, but we didn't see it."

"Okay." She dragged in a breath. "So what's next?"

He reached to start the car, then dropped his hand. "I was going to suggest we talk to Brian Cannon, but now I'm wondering if there might be something more productive to try."

"Like what?"

"You dreamed about the party at Brian's. Is there somewhere else you and your friends used to hang out after school or on weekends? Somewhere away from adult supervision?"

Chapter 12

MAX HAD THOUGHT OF THE QUESTION AFTER HIS EARLY morning session in Olivia's bed, and he'd been waiting for the right time to spring it on her. Now he watched her face go pale. She looked like she wished he hadn't brought up the subject, then made an effort to relax.

"Like where?" she asked in a voice that had gone thin. *Interesting reaction.*

"Somewhere more private than somebody's house. Maybe you all thought of it after the party, when you realized you could have gotten into trouble."

She swallowed hard. "You said 'you.' Do you mean, me—specifically?"

"No. Any one of your gang."

He was pretty sure she knew about some other place but didn't want to talk about it. In fact, he had heard kids talking about a hangout they thought was very private. He hadn't been there himself because he hadn't wanted to horn in on a party where he wasn't invited.

Now he kept his voice even, though he wanted to push her. "I'm not talking about The Mall in Columbia. I'm talking about a teenage hangout where you wouldn't be tripping over adults."

She was silent for several moments.

"This could be important," he pressed, hoping she would be honest with him. He'd felt like they were getting closer. Now he knew she was pulling back.

"Why?" she asked.

"I'm trying to understand the dynamics of what happened."

She swallowed hard, then said, "There was a place we went sometimes."

He kept his gaze on her, waiting for further clarification.

"Some kind of county maintenance facility that they weren't using anymore, I guess. Or maybe it belonged to the water company."

"Want to show it to me?"

"Not particularly."

"But you will," Max said.

"If I have to."

"What's wrong with the place?"

"A girl was raped there," she said in a low voice, like she didn't want to say it at all. "After that we stayed away."

"She reported the rape?" Max asked.

"Actually, no."

"Because?"

"It was like what happened with Gary at the party. She knew she would get into trouble if her parents found out she was hanging out there, so she just kept it to herself."

"That would be enough to keep a rape to herself?" Max asked.

"I guess so."

"So adults were the enemy?"

"Weren't they for you?" she asked.

He raised one shoulder. "I guess that's right. But we're not talking about me. I was skating on the wrong side of the law. You were supposed to be good kids."

"Yeah, well good kids rebel against parental authority, too."

In his case, it hadn't been "parental authority." It had been any authority, but he didn't feel the need to correct her.

"And you did it at a place that only you and your friends knew about?"

"Right." She knitted her fingers together in her lap. "That party isn't the only thing I haven't thought about in years. This whole deal is bringing back a bunch of memories I must have just edited out of my mind."

"Who was raped?" he asked.

Olivia dragged in a breath and let it out.

For a moment he thought she wasn't going to answer. Then she said in a low voice, "Angela."

Max's head snapped toward her. "And you didn't think this was relevant information?"

"It may be relevant."

"Who raped her?"

"She didn't know."

"Why not?"

"People drank out there, and someone must have put something in her drink. You know, like that date-rape drug."

"But a bunch of people must have been around. Didn't anyone notice who she was with?"

Olivia sighed. "She never said. Maybe she knew and didn't want to go through what it would take to press charges."

He thought about the explanation. And he could see it from the point of view of a teenage girl.

"And she told you about it later?"

"Yes. And later there was a rumor circulating that a girl was raped, but most people didn't know who it was."

"So she could have been lying about it."

Olivia's jaw tightened. "Why would she lie about something like that?"

"To get herself out of some other kind of other trouble?"

"How does rape get you out of trouble?" she snapped, unable to keep herself from reacting.

"Well, if she'd gotten pregnant and didn't want to admit she'd been fooling around."

"She wasn't pregnant."

"You're sure."

She took her lower lip between her teeth. "Well, I don't know for sure, but if she was, she hid it pretty well."

"Claiming you were raped would be a way to call attention to yourself."

Olivia's expression turned angry. "Listen, Max, give it a rest. The stuff you're suggesting doesn't make any sense to me. Angela was upset. She needed to talk to someone. I thought it was true. Can we stop talking about it now?"

He knew the conversation was upsetting her, which might mean that pressing her would draw out information she was deliberately holding back. On the other hand, he had to work with her until they solved the murders. And he needed her to trust him. More than that, he needed her to feel that it was safe to confide in him. He pulled back a little, taking the focus off Angela. "But somehow word got around?"

"Someone left a note at the hangout saying a girl had been raped."

"Interesting. Who would that have been besides her? Or you? If nobody else knew about it."

"The guy who did it."

"What would be *his* motivation?"

"Maybe he wanted to have private parties out there, and he wanted to keep other people away."

"That's what you really think?"

"You asked me a bunch of questions, I was trying to come up with answers."

Max felt the tension crackling in the car. He was sure there was more to the story—facts he'd have to drag out of Olivia.

He started with, "Let's go see the place."

"I haven't been there in years."

"But you know how to find it."

"Yes."

He started the engine. "Give me directions."

"I'll bet you know where it is," she whispered.

"What's that?"

"You might not have gone there, but you probably knew about it."

He sighed. "Okay, yeah. But I never tried to find it."

"Why not?"

"What would I have done there—hung out with the rich kids?"

"I guess not." She swallowed hard, then said, "You know where Wilkins Dam Road is?"

"Yes."

"Head that way."

He pulled onto the blacktop and drove back to the Winters' farm, where he turned around and headed toward the area where the Suburban Sanitary Commission had built a reservoir and a dam and then planted the woods along the reservoir with thousands of azalea bushes. In the springtime, people flocked there. It was a showplace bursting with the color of the blossoms that rivaled the National Arboretum in D.C. During the rest of the year it was a pleasant place for nature walks.

From the corner of his eye, Max saw Olivia sitting rigidly next to him. He pretended that he wasn't watching her as he turned onto the two-lane highway that led to the dam, which had been built in the early '40s. The road ran through a hilly area that had once been completely rural. But as more people had moved to Howard County, builders had taken advantage of the forested lots.

All the development made him wonder if the hideout had been abandoned in the wake of approaching civilization. Then they entered a wooded area with no houses that was probably part of the reservoir property.

He saw Olivia tense and wondered if she was going to let him drive on past. Instead she murmured, "Slow down."

He slowed and she pointed toward a gravel track that led off into the trees.

He turned right and stopped when he encountered a chain stretched across the one-lane road. Hanging from the middle of it was a rusty sign that said "No Trespassing."

"I guess we can't go up there," she whispered, sounding like the sign was going to stop them cold.

"You kids ignored the sign."

"Yes," she murmured.

"We'll be quick," he answered. "How far is it?"

She raised one shoulder. "I never measured it. I guess it's less than a quarter of a mile."

"Walking won't be a big deal."

For a long moment, he thought she was debating whether to refuse or send him up there himself. Finally, an expression of resignation bloomed on her face as he turned the SUV around and pulled down the road about twenty-five yards to a small clearing beside the shoulder.

They both climbed out, then walked back to the chain. Max scanned the highway, waiting until a car had passed before stepping around the barrier, looking back at Olivia.

She followed, and they silently started up the rutted gravel track, as the loose stones crunched under their running shoes. The road was narrow, with weeds and small saplings encroaching on either side. Max could see that the surface hadn't been maintained recently, and he had the feeling that the site had long ago been abandoned—at least as far as its intended use was concerned.

"Did you all walk up here or drive?" he asked.

"We walked. But usually we parked farther down the road and came through the woods," Olivia volunteered.

Max thought she could have told him about that strategy earlier but didn't bother to voice the complaint. Her body language and lack of conversation told him she obviously didn't want to be here.

But he couldn't stop himself from making a comment about the location. "So you all drank up here?"

"And did pot," she admitted.

"Did they do pot at that party, too?"

"Yes," she snapped.

"Why didn't you mention it before?"

"I wasn't thinking about it. Do you think it's a big deal?"

"Not really."

"Good."

Did that mean she'd been into it? *He* had when he was in high school, but he didn't volunteer that information as they walked uphill, farther into the shade of the trees, the highway noises receding behind them.

As they walked farther into the woods, he was thinking, *So this was where the rich kids hung out when they wanted to be alone.* And now one of the rich kids was leading him up here. Only she wasn't really rich the way he'd assumed—from her being with the in crowd and from her clothes. Now it turned out that her mom had made her clothes. He'd assumed she was out of his league back then. And it had been true—if for no other reason than that hanging out with him would have been out of the question for anyone in the in crowd. Now she was truly a lot farther above him than when they'd been teenagers. He had a respectable job. But he couldn't really see a model with a big-time career hanging out with a PI.

He snorted.

"What?"

"I was thinking about assumptions I'd made."

"You mean when we were kids?"

"Yeah."

She raised one shoulder. "We all do."

"And what about now?" he asked.

"What do you mean?"

Instead of focusing on a personal relationship, he asked, "What if you decide to trust me? Don't you think we have a better chance of solving Angela's murder if you do?"

"Yes."

"But you're still uncomfortable with that?"

"This place makes me uncomfortable," she answered. "Ask me when we get safely out of here."

"Safely?"

"A figure of speech."

―᠁―

As the road made a sharp turn into the woods, Olivia felt the temperature drop and foliage close in around them. She could hear birds chirping, but the highway noises had become only a vague rumble in the background. She felt totally cut off from the real world. Up ahead she saw a structure through the leaves and tree trunks.

On the drive here, she'd been hoping that a bulldozer had come and mowed it down, but there it was, about the way she remembered it. She struggled for objectivity as they got closer, trying to see the place from Max's point of view. The place was like a small house or cabin with weathered siding. It could have been something from a hundred years ago, except for the attached carport sticking out from the right side.

The exterior siding was made of boards, running vertically along the walls and held down by narrower strips of wood—a construction style that she knew was called board and batten.

There were two windows and a door in front, all of them with boards nailed across to keep them closed. Probably the building had once been painted dark brown, which she could see in a couple of protected places, like under the window frames, but most of the paint had faded and flaked off, giving the exterior a desolate look.

"This is it?" Max asked, his voice startling her.

"Yes," she answered, hearing the tightness in her own voice.

Was that why he gave her a studied look? Did he realize that coming here was the worst thing she could imagine? Or was he just sorry he had to put her through something unpleasant?

She struggled to pretend that coming here was no big deal, but of course it was. Things had happened at this isolated cabin in the woods, things she had pushed out of her mind like a soldier slamming the door of a bomb shelter. Only now she felt like she was trapped inside.

Drawing in a deep breath, she let it out slowly.

"What?" Max asked.

"This place is disgusting," she managed to say.

"Yeah." He looked around at the trash scattered on the ground. There were beer bottles and soda cans, wrappers from candy and junk food, and...

Olivia followed his gaze, spotted a presumably used condom lying in the weeds at the edge of the carport and felt nausea rising in her throat

"I guess people are still coming up here to party," Max said. He glanced around at the woods. "This is about how the area looked when you used to come here?"

Struggling for a response, she whispered, "Well, maybe the underbrush is a little thicker."

He gestured toward the building. "Did you go inside?"

He had pitched his voice low, and she wondered if the place was getting to him, too. Did some evil magic cling to the atmosphere?

She wanted to wrap her arms around her shoulders, but she forced herself to keep her hands at her sides. She glanced at Max. His face was grim. Maybe he was reacting to the way the place looked now. She was reacting to memories she wasn't going to share. Or was he picturing wild parties up here? Drunk kids doing God knows what because there were no adults around to stop them.

"We went in," she said in a thin voice, thinking about turning and fleeing down the path. But if she did that, he'd question her, and she didn't want to talk about what had happened here.

"You've seen it. Can we leave?" she whispered.

"Soon. You haven't been back in ten years?"

"No. And I wouldn't be here now if you hadn't dragged me," she said.

"Sorry."

"Are you?" she couldn't stop herself from saying.

"I'm trying to figure out who murdered Angela. And if something bad happened to her up here, then I want to understand as best I can."

When she didn't answer, he turned back to the building, looking at the closed-up windows and doors. "How did you get in? The guys took the boards off the door or a window to get inside?"

She sighed. "No. Around back, there was a place where the siding was loose. There's no insulation, and we could just climb through."

"Show me."

She gave him a pleading look. "I want to leave."

"I know. But I want to understand what happened here."

"You can't understand!" she almost shouted, before resignation settled in. "I suppose the sooner I show you, the sooner we can split."

She stomped away toward the back of the house. Max caught up and was right behind her as she stepped to the rear of the cabin, glad to have an excuse to turn away from Max so that he couldn't see her face. She wasn't sure if she looked scared. Or would it be angry? But she didn't want him to ask her what she was feeling. She wanted him to think that she was just reacting to someone else's trauma, because her own trauma was something she had never really faced.

Once again as she knelt by the back corner of the cabin, she was hoping that everything had changed. What if someone had come along and repaired the break in the siding, and they wouldn't be able to get in? But when she pulled on the section of the exterior wood, it lifted up from the side of the little building, and she could see darkness beyond.

Crouching, Max joined her at the opening. "What's inside?"

She sighed, resigned to his plans. "It used to be a big open room, then somebody had the bright idea of tunneling into the ground at the back."

"You mean making extra room inside?"

"Yes."

"Did you go down there?"

"No."

"Then how do you know about it?"

She had kept her responses to a minimum. Now she was forced to explain. "I saw the entrance. And Angela told me about it. There's a room at the end of the tunnel—maybe like a bomb shelter. It was damp and dirty."

"I'd like to see."

She grabbed his arm. "No. Stay out of there."

"Why?"

She gulped. "That's where Angela woke up—after, you know."

"Okay."

"Please, can't we leave? You're not going to find anything after ten years."

———

Max could see the tension in Olivia's features and knew she wanted to get out of this place, but now that they were here, he needed to spend a few more minutes checking it out. "Maybe not."

Or should he just give it up? He was torn. He wanted to see the scene of the crime for himself, but he could tell that Olivia loathed the idea of going inside, particularly into an underground space. And he couldn't leave her out here, not in this isolated location where he wouldn't be able to get to her quickly if something happened.

He decided on a compromise.

"We'll go inside, and you can wait for me in the main room."

"Max, please."

"I need to understand this place to understand the dynamics of what happened back then."

"Coming here scares me."

"Why?"

"Okay, maybe it's just a reaction to the past."

"Then let's get this over with and get out of here."

He held the piece of siding up, and she got down on her knees and crawled inside. He switched on the small but powerful flashlight he carried with him and followed her in. She had moved to one wall, pressing her back against the rough siding as he shone his light around the room, which was about fourteen by fourteen. The floor was made of rough planks, and as he shone the light over it, he saw where a section of the wood had been cut. Striding over, he lifted it up and saw a ladder leading down and a passageway leading away from the house.

"Satisfied?" she asked.

"Not until I go down."

She put a hand on his arm. "Don't."

"Why not?"

"It's an old tunnel. It could collapse."

"If I think so, I'll get out. And I'll be quick."

He climbed down the ladder and found himself in a passage with a dirt floor and walls—probably not safe. But at least he could stand up if he bent over slightly. He felt like the walls were closing in around him, but now that he was down here, he wasn't going back without seeing what there was to see.

He shined his light down the passageway and saw an open space. Following the light, he stepped into a small room, no bigger than six by eight, he estimated. Someone had floored it with strips of plywood and also laid the same material over the presumably dirt walls. The ceiling was just dirt, and the room exuded a moldy smell, since it was underground and lacked ventilation. In one corner was a bare mattress with a blanket. There were no other furnishings and no sign that anyone had been here recently.

He picked up the mattress and looked under, seeing nothing but the plywood floor. But when he moved it away from the wall, he found a wrapper from a package of peanut butter and cheese crackers. Was it ten years old, or had someone been down here more recently? The place gave him the creeps. You could use it for a cell, if you put something heavy over the trapdoor. Or maybe there was a way to block off this end of the tunnel. And then what? You'd have to give your captive a portable potty and some food. He was thinking about that when the sound of his name reached him from above.

"Max! Are you okay?"

"Yes," he answered.

"Come up."

Olivia was calling him in a voice that bordered on panic, which gave him an excuse to get out of a confined space he didn't much like. He turned and made his way back down the tunnel, then up the ladder.

Olivia was standing as she had outside, her body rigid and her arms folded across her chest, her hands gripping her shoulders—a statue carved in misery.

Hoping to jar her out of it, he said, "Let's go get a pizza."

"What?"

"After taking me up here, you deserve a treat."

She snorted, then asked, "What did you find?"

"Not much. I'll tell you when we get outside."

He stepped through the opening into the sunshine, then turned to help Olivia out. When he straightened and turned again, he went stock-still.

A man had apparently been waiting for them to come out of the cabin. As he stepped from behind a tree, Max saw that he was holding a gun pointed at them.

Chapter 13

"HANDS IN THE AIR," THE MAN ORDERED IN A "GOT ya" voice.

As Max raised his hands, it registered with him that the guy was wearing a dark green uniform.

He wasn't some low-life who had sneaked up on them. He must be a security guard who patrolled the grounds around the dam, and they'd shown up at the wrong time.

"What are you doing here?" he asked, his gaze swinging between them and settling on Olivia.

Instead of answering, she straightened, and her persona seemed to change. She had been upset about coming here, but now her posture subtly shifted into the public image that he'd studied when he'd first considered this assignment.

The guard's focus was entirely on her now. "You're... someone... Where have I seen you before?" he asked.

"On television. Or maybe in a magazine. I'm Olivia Winters."

He continued to study her. "Yeah, the model. That's right. What are you doing here?" he asked with considerably less hostility than he'd exhibited at first.

She kept her head up and her shoulders squared, as though she were wearing a designer gown and getting ready to step on the runway. And somehow she was exuding a charm she hadn't bothered to use on Max or her former classmates. But apparently when she needed to, she could call on some learned behavior that she found useful.

"Did you read about the murder of Angela Dawson a couple of weeks ago?"

"Yeah. What about it?" the guard asked.

"She was my best friend in high school. Because the police weren't making any progress on finding out who did it, I hired a private detective to help me figure out what happened to her."

The guard said nothing, forcing Olivia to keep speaking. "The kids in my class used to hang out up here." She stopped and swallowed. "Actually, Angela was raped up here when we were in high school." She stopped and inclined her shoulder toward Max. "Detective Lyon wanted to see where it happened because it could be relevant."

"She was raped here? Seriously?"

"Yes," Olivia answered. "Otherwise we wouldn't be here."

Max joined the conversation. "I'm digging into the motivation of the killer. I think it has something to do with the relationships between the class members ten or eleven years ago."

Olivia added, "So I brought him up here. I'm sorry. I know I should have gotten permission, but we thought we'd be in and out of here before anybody noticed."

"What did you think you were going to find after so long?" the guard asked Max.

He thought about the underground room but said only, "There probably isn't any physical evidence, but I wanted to get a handle on this hangout. It looks like the kids had free rein up here back in the day. It's good that you're patrolling the area now."

"Yeah," the guy said, and Max wondered what that meant, exactly. But he didn't ask for clarification. Beside him, Olivia was also silent.

After long moments, the guy finally said, "Go on, before I change my mind about pressing charges."

"Thanks," Max said. Actually he wanted to ask a bunch of questions—starting with, how often did he patrol this area? How many guards worked here? What was the patrol route, and whom did the guy work for, exactly? But he decided not to press his luck by making the guy think twice about letting them go.

"And I hope you find out who killed your friend," the guard said to Olivia.

"Thanks so much," she answered.

"Yes, thanks," Max added, thinking that being discovered could have gotten them into a hell of a mess.

They both turned and started back the way they'd come.

"Don't run," Max murmured.

"I'm not."

Until they made the turn in the gravel road, Max could feel the man's gaze on the back of his neck.

When they were out of sight, he whispered, "It was like pulling teeth to get you to say anything about this place. But then when a complete stranger confronts you, you blurt out the rape."

She turned to him, a plea for understanding on her face. "I knew he wasn't going to just let us go unless he knew we were on a serious mission."

"Murder is serious."

"I could tell from his face that it wasn't serious enough."

"You read people that well?"

"Sometimes."

He couldn't stop himself from saying, "And can you always get guys to respond like that when you turn on the charm?"

She turned to him, a challenging look in her eyes. "What's that supposed to mean?"

"That if you weren't Olivia Winters, top New York model, we'd be on our way to the police station."

"Do you see that as an advantage—or is it a criticism?" she asked in an even voice.

"In that case, it was definitely an advantage."

"Thanks." She kept her gaze fixed on the trail ahead, and he was sure she wanted to cut the conversation short, but he wasn't able to drop it.

"You didn't use that technique at the reunion meeting," he observed.

"I already felt like enough of an outsider. I wasn't going to emphasize the fact." She waited a beat before adding, "And I like having the chance to be a normal person."

"But in a case like this, celebrity can be useful."

"Let's not focus on that."

They were both silent as they kept heading down the gravel road toward the car. When they got to the *No Trespassing* sign, Olivia cut Max a glance.

"You still think it was a good idea going up there?"

"Yes," he answered, then shook his head. "Sorry. I didn't like that encounter any better than you did. Maybe less, because I didn't like getting you into trouble."

"It worked out."

"Actually, judging from the amount of trash lying around on the ground up there, it looks like we ran into bad luck getting caught." He paused and couldn't stop himself from adding, "And the guy might not have known we were up there if you'd shared the information about parking farther away and coming through the woods."

She gave him a narrow-eyed look. "Oh, now it's my fault?"

"No." He didn't like the tenor of the conversation and made an effort to get his emotions under control. Obviously this place was affecting both of them. "It was my idea. And I don't think it was a bad judgment call. We did learn something valuable."

"What?" she shot back.

"That there was ample privacy up there for a girl to be raped."

Her expression turned guarded. "Now what are you saying? That you thought I was making it up?"

"No."

"Then what?"

"I wanted to see for myself." He thought for a moment. "A security guard could have interrupted a rape, but not if she and the guy were inside. Especially if they were underground."

She shuddered. "What did you find down there?"

"Not much. A small room. A mattress. A good place to get a girl by herself."

"Yes," she whispered.

"And you were never down there?"

"No," she answered in a barely audible voice. "You asked me that before. Are you trying to see if I'll change my story?"

He considered his answer and settled on, "No." He

was thinking again that she was holding something back. But he wasn't going to interrogate her. This little jaunt hadn't helped their working relationship, and he was thinking that if he was too rough on her, she might shut him out—or fire him. That last thought sent a chill through him. He hadn't wanted this job, but now he wanted to see it through. Because he'd gotten invested in solving the murders? Or because he couldn't stand the idea of someone coming after Olivia?

They reached the car, and both climbed in. He had intended to stop for pizza, then head for the next stop on their list, but when he turned to Olivia, he saw that she was sitting with her shoulders hunched, shaking, which made him wonder if her reaction had as much to do with her past as the present.

He could have said, "Are you all right?" But he knew she wasn't. He wasn't so great himself. Instead of speaking, he leaned across the console and reached for her, pulling her close.

At first she stayed stiffly in his embrace, then he felt her give in to the feel of his arms around her shoulders. She hadn't put on her seat belt yet, and he slid his seat back, lifted her up, and settled her in his lap.

She kept her head down and her face against his shoulder. He stroked his hands over her back, then into her lush hair.

"Thanks for getting us out of there," he murmured.

"It was worth a try," she answered in a barely audible voice, raising her head to look him in the eye.

"It was quick thinking on your part."

"Then you don't assume I'm just an airhead model?"

"I never thought that."

"Then why…" Instead of finishing the question, she let her voice trail off.

"Why what?" he pressed.

"Have you been keeping me at arm's length?"

The question shocked him. "Because I knew it was what you wanted and because we have to maintain a professional relationship."

"Do we?"

Before he could answer, she brought her mouth to his. They'd both been through an experience he wouldn't want to repeat. That was no excuse, he told himself as the feel of her lips on his radiated to every cell of his body. He'd picked her up to comfort her. Suddenly his reasoning wasn't so clear. He'd wanted her in his arms. Now he was shaking with the need for her. As he kissed her with a passion gone out of control, she returned the fervor, her hands moving over his back and into his hair, holding his mouth to hers. The world had vanished around them. The only thing in his universe was the woman in his lap, her hip pressing against the erection suddenly straining the front of his jeans. He slid his hands under the back of her knit shirt, pressing them against her warm skin, reveling in the feel of her. But it wasn't enough. Acknowledging his own surrender, he angled her away from his chest so that he could move his hands around to the front of her, cupping her breasts through her bra. They were small, but sensitive, and she moaned as he stroked his fingers back and forth across the hardened nipples where they poked through the clinging fabric.

Neither of them spoke, but words were unnecessary. She lowered her head, her teeth digging into his shoulder and her long hair hiding her face. For long moments, she stayed where she was as he continued to caress her. Then she moved, shifting her body so that she was straddling his lap, only a few layers of fabric separating his cock from her sex. It was a clear indication of what she wanted—a perfect echo of his own desire.

Chapter 14

MAX DIDN'T KNOW WHAT WOULD HAVE HAPPENED IF A loud horn hadn't blasted through the bubble around them. Her head jerked up, her expression startled, and he followed her gaze, seeing that a huge truck had come around the curve in the road and slowed so that it was opposite them. The driver, who was much higher than the SUV, leered down at them.

"Get a room," he called out.

Olivia slipped off Max's lap and turned her head away, using her long hair as a curtain and waiting until the driver had started up again and disappeared down the road.

"Sorry," both of them said at the same time.

"Not your fault," Max said, his voice thick with frustration and passion. "I picked you up and put you in my lap."

"It's just as much on me," she answered. "I shouldn't have started anything out here."

He didn't ask what that last part meant. Would it have been all right to start something if they were in the privacy of the farmhouse?

She pulled down the visor, inspected her face and ran her fingers through her hair.

After taking a breath and letting it out, she asked, "We were going to see Brian Cannon?" she asked.

"You don't want pizza?"

"After we finish with Brian."

He reached for the starter button, and she reached for her seat belt. When he started the vehicle with a jerky motion, she grabbed the door handle.

"Sorry," he said again.

She made a dismissive sound. "We're going to his office? And you know where it is?"

Again he answered in the affirmative.

"Are we going to call him first?"

"Better if we just drop in."

"What if he's not there?"

He shrugged as he drove back the way they'd come. "There are a lot of other suspects we can try. Like maybe Tommy Larson."

"Is he a suspect?"

"He was on edge at the meeting."

"Right."

"But everybody in the class is a suspect. Maybe everybody who was at Donley when you were."

"You mean teachers or custodial staff?"

"It's possible. Did you worry about any of the janitors?"

"No."

He turned off when they reached the outskirts of Columbia, the town that had been built from scratch on Howard County farmland by James Rouse, who had wanted to make the new city a model for America. Back then, the local residents had resented the intrusion into their way of life, Olivia's father probably among them. Had he vowed never to let his family shop at the Columbia Mall, but the decision had finally become too inconvenient?

The New Town, as it was still called forty years later, was divided by Route 29, with most of the more recent development on the east side of the major highway, and much of it built since the last time Max had been in Howard County.

Cannon Limited was in an upscale office park off Broken Land Parkway, and Max pulled into a parking space several rows from the glass and brick building. When they climbed out, Olivia looked down at her front, grimaced, and tugged at her bra before pulling at the hem of her knit shirt. Max inspected his own clothing, but didn't see any sign of their previous behavior. Still, he ran a hand through his hair before they started for the building.

"Let me do the talking," he said.

She gave him a quick glance. "Glad to. I'd like to hear what you're going to say."

"I told you what I was thinking, but I always play situations like this by ear."

He'd looked up the address but not the suite number. Pausing at the directory in the lobby, he scanned the entry and found Cannon Limited on the second floor.

They were both silent in the elevator and didn't speak as they walked down the carpeted hall and into an office reception area that was decorated in tasteful shades of beige. On the wall were expensive-looking modern oil paintings of the slash and dribble variety.

An attractive, dark-haired young woman sitting at a desk to one side looked up questioningly as they approached her workstation. The metal tent sign on her desk said *Allison Holiday*.

"May I help you?" she asked.

"We were hoping to speak to Mr. Cannon."

"And you are?"

"Max Lyon and Olivia Winters."

She consulted a computer screen. "I'm sorry, I don't have you on his appointment list."

"We're from the Donley reunion committee. We were talking to Brian at the committee meeting the other night, and we were hoping he had a few minutes to see us now."

"Just a moment," she said, got up from her desk and walked down the hall.

Olivia glanced at Max. "Smooth."

"I practice."

A few moments later, Ms. Holiday returned. "He can give you a few minutes. His office is at the end of the hall."

"Thank you," Max said.

As they walked down the hall where the same kind of paintings lined the walls, Olivia said in a low voice, "He must be doing pretty well in the commercial real estate business."

"You mean you think he spent a lot on this artwork."

"Yes."

"Maybe he got his dog to do it with its tail."

She snorted.

"Or get me some paint cans, and I'll make you some."

The door at the end of the hall was opened, and Max stepped through the door ahead of Olivia.

"This is about the reunion?" Brian asked. "Did they put you in charge of fund-raising or something?"

"No. But I hope you can give us a few minutes of your time," Max said.

Max took one of the guest chairs in front of the desk, and Olivia took the other.

"I've been talking to Olivia," Max said when they were seated. "About the murders of your classmates."

"You started that conversation last night. I wish you'd drop it," Cannon said, sounding annoyed that Olivia's new fiancé was rocking the boat. Whatever boat that was.

"I'm afraid I can't. I didn't know about any of this when I got engaged to Olivia, but as soon as I found out, I realized it was my duty to protect her."

"Isn't that the job of the police?" Cannon asked.

"They don't seem to be doing a very good job," Max countered.

Cannon was silent, and Max recognized the technique. If you said nothing, the other person would eventually fill the silence. In this case, Max was prepared with his story. Which was true as far as it went.

"After the meeting last night, Olivia had a nightmare. I woke her up, and she was quite upset."

"Maybe she shouldn't have gone to the meeting," Cannon suggested.

"It's too late for that." This time Max was the one who paused. After their encounter in the SUV, he'd vowed to keep his paws off Olivia, but he couldn't stop himself from reaching over, taking her hand and knitting his fingers with hers. The sign of a concerned fiancé, he told himself, noting that Cannon followed the gesture.

"What was it about?" Cannon asked, sounding wary.

Max kept his gaze on the man. "About a party at your house."

"I had a lot of parties at my house."

"This was the one on Cinco de Mayo, your senior year. The one where Gary Anderson shot off a gun."

Cannon blanched, and his gaze shot to Olivia.

She shrugged.

"Oh, that party," the man across the desk muttered.

"We were talking about the members of the class who died under strange circumstances—or were killed. Both Angela and Gary were at that party. And also Patrick Morris."

"Jesus! You're including him."

"He's dead," Max countered.

"From a faulty furnace giving off carbon monoxide."

"It might not have been an accident."

Cannon's accusing gaze shot to Olivia. "Three dead people who died from unrelated causes don't prove anything." He kept his gaze fixed on her. "And we agreed not to talk about what happened that night."

"That agreement was ten years ago when we were teenagers. I did my best to wipe that party out of my mind," she answered in a low voice. "But last night Max woke me out of a nightmare and asked me what was wrong. I didn't actually want to tell him about it, but he could see I was upset, and he wanted to know why. I decided it would be better to tell him."

Cannon looked exasperated.

"Olivia says she was near the door, and she wanted to leave. When she heard the gun go off, she couldn't see who Gary shot at."

Cannon focused on her. "Is that what you told him?"

"It's the truth."

"The truth? Did you tell him you were so out of it that you didn't know what was going on?"

"I don't remember that part."

"Of course not," Cannon shot back. "You were too drunk. Lucky you didn't throw up all over the rec room."

"Let's not get sidetracked. I don't think that's relevant," Max said.

Cannon's gaze swung back to him. "You weren't there. You don't know what's relevant." As soon as he'd spoken, the other man looked like he wished he hadn't made the assertion.

"We'd like to know which football player was involved in the incident," Max said.

Cannon hesitated for a moment. "Craig Pendergast."

Beside Max, Olivia caught her breath. "Didn't he die when his car went off the road?"

"Yeah," Cannon confirmed. "So if you think he was the one who killed Gary, that can't be true."

"I wasn't implying that he killed anybody," Max said in a controlled voice. "Now we know for sure that four people who were at the party are dead. Why don't you tell me what else was going on that night."

"The usual kid stuff."

"Which is?"

"Don't tell me you didn't drink and smoke pot back then," Cannon said. "And weren't you arrested for breaking into houses and stealing stuff?"

"Yeah. What of it?"

"So what right do you have to come here and question me?"

"What I did back then isn't relevant to this investigation."

"But what I did is?"

"Yeah."

"Why?"

"Because it's your class with the dead members. And it looks like four of them were at your house that night."

Brian's voice grew hard. "And you're calling it an investigation?"

"I guess I am."

"I don't have to answer any more questions."

"Don't you want to catch the killer?"

"I'm not convinced there *is* a killer. I mean, we're talking about a bunch of people who died in different ways. Don't serial murderers usually have a pattern?"

"It depends on why they're doing it. If it's for sexual gratification, then they probably have a similar MO. But if it's to punish people or to keep them from talking, not having a pattern would be a good technique for disguising what was going on."

"What are you, a cop in disguise?" Brian suddenly asked.

"I'm not a cop."

"Then why are you digging into this like a squirrel digging up nuts?"

"To make sure nothing happens to Olivia," Max responded. "Suppose something happened at that party? Something the killer didn't want anyone to know about."

"Then he waited a long time to start his killing spree."

Max kept his gaze on the man. "An interesting way to put it. But it goes back at least five years—when Gary died."

Brian dragged in a breath.

"You're the one who came here talking about a serial killer—or whatever you want to call it. And maybe it's time for you to leave, because I can't give you any more information."

"I think you can."

"Like what?"

"Olivia told me the people she remembers at the party. I'd like you to give me your list."

"I'm supposed to remember everybody who came to a party ten years ago?"

"It was at your house, and it was a pretty memorable event."

Cannon sighed. "Okay, I'll do my best." He began rattling off a list of names, many of them the same names Olivia had given him, although there were more.

"Can you write it down?"

"Now?"

"I'd appreciate it."

"How about I email it to you. That will give me time to dredge up people I might have forgotten."

Max would have liked to stay in the office, putting the guy on the spot, but he thought there was no more to be gained by pressing him. "Okay," he agreed and gave the guy his email address.

Cannon visibly relaxed when he knew they were going to stop questioning him.

Max gave him another jolt by saying, "You're in danger, too."

Brian's eyes widened, but he only said, "Oh sure."

"Don't be so cavalier about it." Max leaned forward. "This is more urgent than you might think. Last night someone was sneaking around Olivia's property. They ran away when I came outside with a gun."

The other man blinked. "You're kidding, right?"

"I wouldn't kid about something like that. So any help you can give us would be appreciated."

"Okay. Sure."

"Thanks."

Max and Olivia stood, and the businessman gave them a long look and shook his head.

"What?" Olivia asked.

"I never would have figured you'd end up with the school thug," Cannon said, probably delivering a line that he'd been hoping to work into the conversation like a skunk cabbage in a wedding bouquet.

"He's not a thug."

"He was back then."

"Some people are able to overcome their beginnings."

"What's that supposed to mean?" Cannon asked.

"I'm just saying that Max turned himself around."

Cannon shrugged.

"You had every advantage," Olivia continued.

"And what's *that* supposed to mean?"

"Your parents had money. You had anything you wanted. You could afford to go to one of the top colleges."

"And I had the grades to do it."

They were apparently talking loudly, because Ms. Holiday stuck her head in the door.

"Do you need anything?" she asked her boss.

"No," he snapped. "Mr. Lyon and Ms. Winters were just leaving."

Max took Olivia's arm and they headed for the door. The receptionist stepped aside to let them pass, followed them down the hall, and watched them exit the office suite.

"That went well," Olivia murmured as they headed for the elevator.

"Depends on the objective. We pissed him off, but we got some valuable information. We know about Pendergast. And we know Cannon's hiding something," Max said.

"How?"

"By his behavior. I'd love to have a bug in the office and find out if he got on the horn to someone as soon as he saw us in the parking lot."

"Who would he call?"

"Someone else who was at the party who has an interest in hiding what really happened that night." He slid Olivia a glance but didn't ask the question that was in his mind. Cannon had said Olivia hadn't seen what happened at the rec room bar because she was wasted. Was that a smoke screen, or was he telling the truth? Max would like to know. But perhaps now was not the time to ask.

They reached the car and got in.

"Now where?" Olivia asked.

"Back home."

She looked relieved, like she'd had enough excitement to last for a couple of days. He drove to the farmhouse and paused at the mouth of the access road.

"What are you doing?" Olivia asked.

"Just looking around."

"To see what?"

"Someone was here last night. I'm looking for evidence that they came back."

"You think they're going to leave a sign?"

"Not intentionally."

He walked twenty yards up the driveway, scanning the fields for anything out of place, then came back to the SUV and steered the vehicle up the rutted lane to the gravel area beside the house.

They both climbed out and went inside, both of them obviously on edge, with no way to avoid being alone together. He hadn't planned the frantic grappling in the car, but it had happened and it had crossed a line that Max wasn't sure he could step back over. Olivia knew he wanted her. He knew she wanted him, although perhaps he could still rationalize that their emotions had been supercharged by the encounter with the security guard—and by her reaction to going back to the cabin in the woods. Before he could decide his next move, his phone buzzed.

Chapter 15

IT WAS A TEXT MESSAGE FROM SHANE.

> New confidential development in the case.
> Need to talk.

Okay, Max texted back.

> Need to talk to you alone. Meet me at restaurant where you had meeting last night. South end of parking lot.

Max glanced at Olivia.

"What?" she asked.

"I've got to take care of something."

"Just you?" she asked.

"Yeah."

"I thought you didn't want to leave me alone..." Her voice trailed off before starting again. "Will you be gone long?"

"I don't think so. Lock the door behind me, and don't let anyone in. I'll set the alarm before I leave."

He strode to the desk and pressed some buttons on the computer there.

"It will chirp if anyone comes near the house."

"And what am I supposed to do?"

"Call my cell phone. I won't be far."

He stepped outside onto the front porch, hearing the lock click behind him. As soon as he was by himself, he called Shane to ask for more details. The call went right to voice mail. But Shane had just texted him. What was that about? Maybe leaving wasn't such a good idea.

He tried another text. Why aren't you answering phone?

A moment later, another text came through. Want to keep conversation off the air.

Because?

Sorry. It's something you need to know about Olivia.

He'd almost decided not to go. But he didn't like the implications of his partner's message. Obviously Shane had some confidential information about Olivia. What was it? Something about her background that had come to light? Or was it worse than that? Had Shane found evidence that she was involved in the killings?

Max fought the clogged feeling in his throat, hating that he was going to have to wait to meet with his partner to find out the answer. Why the shit couldn't Shane simply call him?

Teeth clenched to avoid snarling in frustration, he climbed back into the car and backed out of the parking area, then reversed direction and bounced down the drive.

———

Fighting the goose bumps peppering her arms, Olivia rubbed her shoulders as she watched the scene out the window. It looked like Max had decided not to leave, then changed his mind. Now he was speeding back down the access road. What kind of message had he received? And where was he going? He hadn't even told her who he was meeting.

She couldn't help feeling confused—and disappointed. She'd thought that maybe the two of them were starting to work together pretty well, on the murder investigation and maybe on a personal level, too. Or was that simply what she wanted to be true?

She watched the cloud of dust raised by the SUV's wheels, then stayed at the window, staring out. It was only a few minutes later when she saw a car turn into the driveway.

Her heart leaped. It was Max coming back after all.

But as she stared through the dust, she saw that it was another vehicle. At the same time, the alarm in the other room began to chirp, alerting her that someone was approaching.

Oh Lord, Max was gone, and she was alone. She fumbled in her purse for her cell phone and pulled it out, thinking she would call him back. Then she blinked when she saw who got out of the car. Putting the phone back, she watched Claire Lowden heading for the front door. Claire was one of the women from her class. She'd been pretty involved with the in crowd at school, and she'd been at the party Olivia had dreamed about. But Claire hadn't been at the meeting the other night. Olivia hadn't known her well, but they had traveled in the same circles.

In school, she'd always been well dressed. Today she was wearing rumpled jeans and a sweatshirt. Her dark hair looked like she hadn't combed it after getting out of bed, and she looked like she hadn't bothered with any makeup.

She glanced up at the house, then hurried toward the front steps, her face pale and drawn.

Olivia moved from the window to the door. On the other side of the barrier, Claire knocked as though a hoard of evil aliens was after her, and the only safety was in the house.

"Olivia? Are you there? Olivia, I see your car out here. You must be home. You have to let me in," she demanded, her voice rising in desperation.

Max's instructions were to keep the door locked, but the woman's obvious terror tore at her.

"Claire, what are you doing here?"

"Please, you have to let me in," the visitor begged.

"What's wrong?"

"Someone's after me."

Not evil aliens—but "someone."

The dread in Claire's tone was simply too much. Surely Max couldn't have been talking about a defenseless, terrified woman when he'd laid down the law about no visitors.

"Olivia, please."

Unable to ignore her classmate's plight, Olivia unlocked the door, and Claire flew into the front hall.

"Thank God," she breathed, coming to a quick stop and looking around as though she was now wondering what she was doing here at all. Up close, she looked like she hadn't washed her hair or changed her clothes in weeks. Or taken a shower, Olivia thought as she breathed in the odor coming off the woman.

"What is it?" Olivia asked.

Claire clenched and unclenched her hands at her sides but said nothing.

Olivia gestured toward the living room. "Come in and sit down. Can I get you a glass of water?"

Claire was still staring at her as though she'd suddenly lost her sense of direction. "I don't know," she answered in a vague, airy voice.

"Come into the living room," Olivia said again, turning and hoping Claire would follow.

When she heard footsteps behind her, she let out the breath she hadn't realized she was holding.

"What's that noise?" Claire demanded to know, apparently just becoming aware of the alarm her arrival had triggered.

"Just something in the other room," Olivia answered. "I'll turn it off."

She went into the office and disabled the beeper. When she returned, Claire was still standing, her hands clasped tightly in front of her.

"Let's get comfortable."

When Claire didn't move, Olivia took one of the easy chairs and made a show of settling into the cushions.

Claire hesitated for a moment then dropped onto the sofa, leaning forward, every muscle in her body radiating tension

"What is it? What's happening?" Olivia asked.

"Someone's stalking me," she said in a rush.

"How do you know?"

"You think I'm lying?"

"No. No. Of course not. Just tell me what's happened."

The other woman answered with a high-pitched laugh before she began to speak. "I started getting phone calls a couple of weeks ago. First hang-up calls when I said hello. Then it changed, and I could hear someone breathing on the other end of the line."

"That is pretty scary. Did you call the police?"

"No."

"Why not?"

"When I went out to go to work one morning, there was a note under my windshield wiper. It said that if I contacted the police, I would be killed."

Olivia sucked in a sharp breath. "That would have certainly made me call the cops," she said.

"Maybe not if it was happening to you," her visitor said in a strained voice. "How do you know how you would act?"

Not wanting to antagonize Claire, Olivia nodded. But she was pretty sure she wouldn't have sat back and simply let someone systematically terrorize her. And although she hadn't called the cops when Angela had been murdered, she'd taken action by looking up private detective agencies and settling on Rockfort Security.

After they had accepted the assignment, Max had been with her most of the time since she'd hired them. Too bad he'd chosen this afternoon to leave her alone. Should she call him? He'd seemed uptight when he'd left. Maybe she'd better try to handle this by herself right now and hope that he'd be home soon.

She had kept her gaze on Claire, noting the woman's pale skin. As Olivia watched, her visitor lifted a hand to her mouth and began to chew on a hangnail. She seemed ready to fall apart, and Olivia knew that she was going to have to handle her gently.

"Was the note handwritten?"

"Typed. Or I guess from a printer."

"Did you save it?"

"Yes." She fumbled in her purse, pawing through the contents, then looked up. "I thought it was here."

"That's okay. What else happened?" she asked in a soft voice.

"I heard noises outside the house. In the morning there would be things on the doorstep."

"Things?"

"Like little dead birds and animals."

Olivia sucked in a sharp breath. "You can't be serious."

"I'm not lying," Claire insisted, her voice rising in desperation or outrage.

Olivia held up a hand. "Okay. I'm sorry. It just seems so…" She didn't finish the sentence. What did it seem like, exactly? She'd been about to say crazy, but stopped herself in time. Now she was thinking that someone was trying to intimidate and scare the wits out of Claire Lowden, and it looked like they had done a very good job. Maybe they'd somehow even intensified the effects with drugs—if that was possible.

"Why did you come to me?" Olivia asked, trying not to sound like she was making an accusation and praying that she could get the situation under control.

"He said you were the only person who could help."

"He? Who are you talking about?"

"The guy who's been after me. This afternoon, he finally said something over the phone. He told me to come to you—or I'd be sorry."

As she took in the distraught woman's words, Olivia felt as though she'd suddenly stepped off a high cliff into empty air, and now she was plunging downward

at a terrifying speed. "Wait a minute. Let me get this
straight. You're saying the guy who was stalking you
sent you to me?"

"Yes."

"When?"

"Like I said, this afternoon. Just a little while ago. I
was so scared. I came straight over."

"Okay, that's good," she said automatically. But as
soon as the words were out of her mouth, she remembered
the way Max had taken off on some mysterious errand.
Did that mean the man had found a way to get Max out
of the house before sending Claire here? It sounded like a
complicated maneuver, but unfortunately it fit the situation. Which meant that they were both in danger.

Olivia shifted in her seat. "We have to call the police."

"No!"

Olivia pushed out the chair, strode to where she'd left
her purse on the sideboard and picked up the cell phone
she'd laid beside it.

Claire's eyes widened. Leaping up, she followed on
Olivia's heels.

"No!" she shouted again. "You can't call. You'll get
us both killed."

"We can't handle this by ourselves."

When she started to press 911, the other woman
made a grab for the phone. Olivia wrenched her hand
away and took a step back. Still on the attack, Claire
lunged forward and smacked Olivia across the face
with surprising force. Stunned, she reared back as
Claire reached out again. But this time Olivia was too
disoriented to hang on to the phone. Claire snatched
it from Olivia's hand and threw it on the floor, where

she crushed it under the heel of her shoe with a crackling sound.

Olivia stared at the phone in horror.

—⁓—

Max pounded his hands against the steering wheel.

"Come on," he muttered, speaking to Shane, who obviously couldn't hear him. He had been waiting in the parking lot for ten minutes and Shane hadn't showed. In frustration, he kept scanning the entrances, waiting for his partner, but so far he was sitting here in his car all by himself.

Unable to stay still any longer, he got out his phone again and texted. Where are you?

There was no answer for several moments, then another text message flashed onto the screen. Almost there.

OK.

To get a better view of his surroundings, he got out of the car and craned his neck scanning the highway outside the parking area. A vehicle came down the road, and he breathed out a sigh when he assumed it was Shane. But it drove on by, leaving him tenser than ever. Once again, the minutes ticked by again and still no Shane.

Max cursed under his breath. It wasn't like either of his partners to pull this kind of stunt. He'd joined up with them partly because he knew they were both reliable. So what the hell was going on? Had Shane flipped out?

He squeezed the cell phone in his hand, then relaxed

his grip. He was still holding the instrument when it rang. When he scanned the number, he didn't recognize who it was, and he didn't have the patience for anything extraneous now. But ignoring the call didn't appear to be an option, because the phone kept ringing.

"All right. All right," he shouted as he stabbed the answer button, almost putting his finger through the damn screen.

To his surprise, Shane's voice came over the line like there was nothing out of the ordinary about the call. "Just want to give you a heads up."

"What the hell are you talking about? I've been waiting in this parking lot for you for half an hour."

"Huh?"

"You texted me. You said you had some information about Olivia."

The man on the other end of the line swore. "That wasn't me. I've been running around for the past few hours trying to find out what happened to my phone— and get a new one. It was acting wonky, and I took it to the repair shop—where it disappeared."

Max's heart had begun to thud. "Jesus, what are you talking about?"

"Someone went to a lot of trouble to steal my phone. They must have jammed the signal. I dropped it off at the repair shop, and when I went to pick it up, they told me it had disappeared, and they'd give me a replacement."

"And you didn't think that was strange?" Max asked in a hard voice.

"Yeah, I thought it was strange. I've been trying to figure out what was going on, but I sure as hell didn't think it had anything to do with you."

Max was already starting the engine as he struggled to speak coherently. "Well, whoever took your phone did it so he could send me a bunch of text messages that I'd think were from you."

"What messages?"

"That you had confidential information about Olivia that you didn't want to tell me over the phone—or in front of her." Gunning the engine, he headed for the parking lot exit. "Got to go. Someone used your phone to lure me away from the house, and Olivia is there alone."

"Oh Christ," Shane answered. "I'm sorry."

"Yeah," Max agreed as he sped back the way he'd come, praying that he wasn't going to find a disaster when he arrived at the house.

"Do you want us over there?" Shane was asking.

"I don't know." He hung up because he knew he was driving too fast to focus on the call and stay on the road.

Fear pounded through him like massive blows from a boxer's fist as he raced toward the farmhouse, cursing himself for leaving. Christ, he'd wanted to protect Olivia, and he'd let some bastard sucker him into charging off to a bogus meeting without confirming who was texting him. But the messages had come from Shane's phone, for Christ's sake. And Max had been all too willing to believe there was something shady in Olivia's background that would be a major factor in the case.

Clenching the wheel in a death grip, he sped back the way he'd come. Interspersed with the curses were prayers that he wouldn't be too late.

———

Olivia stared in frozen horror at the woman who had just cut off their only means of communication, because she and Max had come to the house on short notice and hadn't bothered to contact the phone company about reinstating the hardwired service. They hadn't seen the need for it, and it probably would have taken days to get it hooked up, anyway.

"We have to get away," she said to Claire, glancing out the window toward the car she'd left in the parking area out front.

Claire shook her head. "No. It's too dangerous. He said to stay here."

Bad news, Olivia thought. The guy who'd sent her former classmate rushing over here wanted the two of them in the house together.

She grabbed the other woman's hand. "Come on."

"No. Don't you understand? You're going to get us both killed."

Claire jerked away and lashed out again, landing a blow on Olivia's cheek that stunned her. She tried to speak, but the only sound that came out of her mouth was a muffled gasp.

Oh Lord, she had to get away from Claire. But then what? What if the guy who had been stalking her was outside right now?

Olivia contemplated her chances of getting away from the house. It would all depend on if he was already here or if he was still on the road. But maybe her best chance was to leave. And abandon Claire?

She didn't want to do it, but the other woman had

proved she wasn't capable of rational thought. In fact, from the way she was behaving, she was almost as much a threat as whoever was stalking her.

Olivia backed away, but before she could get out of the room, Claire grabbed her arm.

"You have to stay here. With me. It's the only thing that's important."

"Okay, but we can't stay in the house."

"We have to stay together."

"Then come on."

"No. He wants to talk to both of us."

"That's what he said?"

"Yes."

"You believe him—after all the nasty things he's done?"

"He said he'd stop."

She wanted to scream, "Are you crazy?" But she already knew the answer. This woman had passed beyond sanity.

Claire gave her a pleading look. "Just listen to what he has to say."

Olivia hadn't heard a car pull up outside or any indication that trouble had arrived. But just as Claire finished speaking, one of the windows shattered as a missile came sailing into the house. It hit the floor and began spewing smoke into the room.

Chapter 16

As the smoke filled the living room, both women began to cough. Wide-eyed, Olivia backed away from the thing.

"Come on," she tried to shout to Claire, but her voice came out as a hoarse croak, and the other woman didn't move, only stared at the billowing smoke in confusion.

Olivia crawled to her and grabbed her arm. "We have to get out of the house."

Claire only shook her off and started coughing as she crawled away.

"Claire, no. Stay with me. He told you to stay with me, remember?"

At least that halted the other woman's progress. "That's right," she agreed.

"We should go in the other room," Olivia choked out, thinking that if they got through the dining room into the kitchen, she could pull Claire out the back door. But then what? They'd be out in the open. Maybe that was what the man out there wanted, after all.

Another missile crashed through a second window, landing on the carpet and spewing more smoke. Tears ran down Olivia's cheeks from the acrid smell, and she could barely see the other woman.

Claire had been crawling toward Olivia. Now she stopped in her tracks.

"Claire, you came to…me for help," Olivia tried, her

eyes stinging and her lungs burning. "Let me help you. We're under…attack," she managed to say between coughing fits. "We have to get out of here."

Claire made a muffled sound as the door crashed open.

Olivia prayed that it was Max coming back. But when he didn't call her name, she decided it wasn't him. It must be the guy who had thrown the smoke bombs, coming in to put the finishing touches on his plan. But she wasn't going to let him kill her without fighting back.

Max had made sure she was armed and knew how to use a gun. There was one upstairs in her bedroom and another down here in the drawer of an end table. Knowing she had to get to it before the guy found her, she abandoned Claire and began crawling along the floor until she reached the front of the sofa. Trying not to cough and give away her location, she kept moving. It seemed to take forever to travel a few feet, but finally she reached the end table and eased the drawer open, rising up enough to fumble inside and wrap her fingers around the butt of the automatic Max had left there. She hadn't thought she was going to need it, but now she was damn glad that it was in her hand. Whoever had come in was probably thinking that she was going to roll over the way Claire had, but he had another thing coming.

She pulled out the weapon, made sure the safety was off, then backed up to the wall where she had a view of the room through the smoke.

A figure loomed in the doorway, and she squinted through the hazy atmosphere, stifling a gasp as she tried to interpret what she was seeing. It might have been a monster with a darkened, elongated face that made him look part man and part animal. Then she realized it was a man wearing a gas mask. Gun in hand, she eased back around the corner of the sofa so that she was partially hidden by the arm. It took all her willpower to stay where she was, but she knew that if she moved, he would spot her. She saw him turn his head from side to side, then start toward the spot where she'd left Claire on the floor.

Claire gasped as she took in the terrible-looking figure looming over her, but before Olivia could do anything, she heard a concussion reverberate in the room and realized the man had fired a shot—probably point-blank at Claire.

Knowing she would be next, Olivia raised the gun in her hand and fired. But just as she did, the assailant ducked toward the woman lying on the floor and the bullet went over his head.

He whirled toward Olivia and fired in the direction from which the shot had come, but he hadn't actually spotted her, and at this distance in the thick haze, it seemed he couldn't be sure exactly where she was. She let out the breath she'd been holding as the bullet whizzed past her. But she had to grab another breath, and dragging a lungful of the smoke unleashed a coughing fit. She waited for him to come toward her, but now that he knew she was armed, he apparently didn't want to take the chance. Still with the gun trained on him, she picked up an ashtray from the end table and heaved it across the room, where it crashed against the wall.

The assailant whirled and fired. While his back was turned, she pushed herself out of the living room and into the dining room where the air was clearer, keeping her face to him and putting the table and chairs between them.

When he realized that she'd fooled him with the ashtray, he turned back in her direction, and she heard an angry snarl from under the gas mask.

He waited a moment, trying to locate her, she assumed. After long moments, he headed straight for her hiding place. She shrank back, wondering if she could get off a shot at him before he killed her.

It was then that she heard someone call her name.

"Olivia!"

It was Max. Thank the Lord.

At the sound of his voice, the man in the gas mask stopped dead in his tracks, turning away from her and toward the new threat.

Olivia gasped. "Watch out, he's got a gun," she shouted.

The man cursed and fired several rounds in her direction, but he was blocked from getting a clear shot by the table and chairs.

Max pounded into the living room, starting to cough when he hit the smoke.

"I'm under the table," she shouted. "Aim high."

The assailant dashed past her and into the kitchen. She heard the back door slam open, then footsteps rushing away from the house.

Max came streaking past, heading for the back door. She heard several more shots and assumed he was shooting at the fleeing guy. She wanted to get out of the smoke, but at the moment she knew she was safer where she was. She crouched there with her heart pounding, praying that Max was all right.

"Olivia, it's me. Don't shoot," he called out as

he came back into the house. Then, when she didn't answer, "Olivia, are you all right? Olivia?" he shouted, his voice urgent.

She tried to talk, which triggered a coughing fit. "Sorry," she wheezed and managed to say, "It's okay, Max. I'm here. I'm all right."

"Thank God." He followed the sound of her voice into the dining room. Reaching down, he helped her up, then saw the gun in her hand.

"Good girl."

"Thanks."

He started to cough. "We need to get the hell out of here. I don't think there's a fire. Just the smoke."

They reached the back door, and she took a grateful breath of fresh air. But when Max tried to tug her outside, she dug in her heels. "Wait. We have to see if he killed Claire."

"Claire? You're not here alone?"

"No. Claire Lowden showed up. That's how it all started." She stopped and coughed several times, then started again. "She came to me. She said someone was stalking her. I was trying to talk her into calling the police when the guy threw that smoke bomb through the window. She's on the floor in the living room. Over by the far chair."

"Claire Lowden? You mean one of the other people who was at that party?"

"Yes."

"Jesus," Max clenched his fists, then relaxed them. "You stay by the kitchen door. I don't think he's coming back, but I don't want you exposed in the house."

She did as he asked, watching him disappear into the smoke. When he didn't come back immediately, her heart blocked her windpipe. Finally he emerged, alone.

"She's dead," he said in a gritty voice.

"I was afraid she was. I heard a shot. Then he went after me."

"Only you defended yourself. But why didn't you call the cops—or me?"

"Because she came here in a panic, and it only got worse. I tried to call 911, but she was in such a state that she grabbed my phone, threw it on the floor, and crushed it under her shoe."

"Jesus." He looked from her to the interior of the house where smoke still billowed. "Wait here a minute."

Stepping onto the porch, he glanced around, then motioned for her to follow him. They both stood on the back stoop, taking in big gasps of air. When he turned to her, she saw the look of relief on his face.

He reached out, and she came into his arms, clinging to him. He stroked his hands up and down her back and into her hair, touching her with a possessiveness that shocked her.

"Olivia, I'm so sorry," he whispered, his mouth against her cheek.

"For what?"

"I never should have left."

"But you came back in time to save me."

"You were doing a pretty good job of that yourself."

"At least I held him off." She dragged in a breath and let it out. "Why did you leave?"

"Because I was an idiot."

Before he could say more, they were interrupted by the sound of tires crunching on the driveway.

"Stay here."

In a flash he was at the end of the house, gun in hand, and his posture told her that he was ready for another attack. Then she saw him relax.

"It's Shane and Jack."

"Over here," he called out to them.

The two other Rockfort agents came around the corner, and they all stood where they had a view of the fields and driveway.

"What happened?" Shane asked as he looked at the smoke billowing from the broken window.

"After he lured me away, he came after Olivia and another woman from her high school class—Claire Lowden."

Shane turned to Olivia, an apologetic look on his face. "I'm sorry," he said in a low voice. "My phone was stolen. I didn't know it had anything to do with this case. Apparently he was texting Max."

Olivia's gaze swung to Max. "About what?"

She watched his face contort. "He said he had confidential information about you."

"What?"

"I don't know." She could see Max's face redden. "And believing it was Shane texting me could have gotten you killed. It did get your friend killed," he added.

"She wasn't my friend. She was just one of the girls I knew in high school."

"And now she's dead," Max reiterated.

"Don't blame yourself. You didn't know it wasn't Shane," Olivia murmured. "Whoever called you had the whole thing planned out pretty carefully."

"Don't make excuses for me," he snapped.

She saw he was still cursing himself, and she wasn't sure how she felt about his leaving her alone. But she understood why he had believed the messages had come from his partner.

Max was speaking again. "I'd like to say we should just clear out of here, but another member of your class is dead, and we have to call the police."

"Did you see who did it?" Shane asked.

"I saw someone I think was a man. But I couldn't see his face because he had on a gas mask."

Max made a snorting sound. "It hid his face and kept the smoke from getting to him."

In the distance, they heard the wail of a siren.

"That sounds like the cops," Shane said. "Or the fire department."

"How did they know to come here?" she asked.

"Maybe your neighbor, Mr. Yeager, heard the shooting," Max said.

She nodded, thinking that was probably right. That and the smoke.

Two police cars with flashing lights came roaring up the driveway.

"Put your guns down," Max muttered.

"Why?" Olivia asked. "We didn't do anything besides try to defend ourselves."

Max gave her an urgent look. "They don't know that. Haven't you read stories about innocents getting shot by cops?"

"Yes," she answered. To his relief, she put her gun on the ground. Max and the other two Rockfort men did the same—just in time.

"Raise your hands," Max ordered Olivia. "They don't know what happened here. Surrendering is the only way to make sure we don't get shot." He hoped. He'd known some trigger-happy cops in his day, and he was praying these weren't some of them.

She gave him a quick look, but apparently understood his logic and complied as four uniformed officers got out of the two squad cars and made it official. "Keep your hands in the air," one of them shouted.

The cops eyed them with suspicion. "What's going on here?" a guy who seemed to be in charge called out. Unfortunately, he wasn't anyone Max had met when he'd been with the Baltimore PD.

"We were attacked by a man who came here with a gun," Max answered. "He's gone, but he shot a woman. She's in the house."

"Ambulance?" the officer asked.

Max shook his head. "It's too late for that."

"Don't move," the officer in charge ordered.

They all stayed where they were with their hands in the air.

"We're unarmed," Max said as two of the cops went into the house. They were back pretty quickly, coughing.

"She's dead all right," one of them confirmed. He looked at Max. "Smoke bomb?"

"Yeah."

"Turn around. Hands against the wall. Legs spread," the man in charge said.

Max heard Olivia gasp.

"It's okay. They have to be sure we're the good guys."

They all complied, and Max endured a very thorough pat down. He knew his partners understood why the police had to do it, but he was sure Olivia was hating the process and being a suspect when she'd just almost been killed. Turning toward her, he saw that she wanted to speak, but he shook his head. "Not yet," he mouthed.

When it was clear they were unarmed, the lead officer said, "Okay. Let's get this sorted out."

Max glanced at Olivia.

"I was here alone, and a woman I knew in high school came over in a panic, saying someone was stalking her," she said. "While I was trying to calm her down, he showed up and threw a smoke bomb through the window."

One of the officers walked several yards away and turned his back, and Max assumed he was using his body mike to call in a detective.

The officer who had been asking the questions looked at the three Rockfort agents. "And how are you involved?"

"I was here earlier, but the assailant lured me away from the house with text messages," Max answered. "When I realized what was going on, I came rushing back, but it was already too late for the other woman."

"Claire Lowden," Olivia supplied.

"She thought she was being stalked, but she didn't report it?" the officer asked, sounding like he didn't believe the story.

Olivia answered. "From what she told me, I think he'd convinced her that if she asked for help, she'd be killed. He told her to come here. He said it was the only way for her to stay safe, but I think he was planning to kill us both."

"This is the fifth member of the Donley High ten-year-reunion class who's been murdered," Max said.

The officer swung toward him. "Oh yeah? Then why don't we know about it?"

"You know about Angela Dawson," Olivia said. "But the other murders didn't look connected—or even like murders. And they happened over several months—and years."

"And the Howard County PD didn't figure it out?" the officer asked in a hard voice.

When Olivia started to answer, Max put a hand on her shoulder.

"Let me handle this."

The cop swung back to him with an inquisitive look on his face and asked, "And what is it that you want to say?"

"This is the first time the guy has come in shooting. Three of the previous murders looked like accidents. But one was that Ellicott City businesswoman, Angela Dawson, who was strangled." As the officer stared at him, he kept talking. "I'm a private detective from Rockfort Security. Olivia hired me to protect her after the Dawson murder."

It wasn't exactly what had happened. She'd really hired him to find out who had killed Angela, but he knew that the cops weren't going to like hearing that someone had been called in to do their jobs.

To his relief, Olivia didn't correct his false statement, and he thought everything was going to work out okay, until another car came speeding up the driveway. It was an unmarked cop car, and the man who got out looked them over, then zeroed in on Max.

Chapter 17

MAX CURSED UNDER HIS BREATH.

"What?" Olivia murmured.

"Trouble."

The chunky man came stamping toward them. He was wearing a rumpled tweed sports coat and dark slacks, a white shirt that had seen better days, and no tie. His name was Archie Hamilton, and Max had tangled with him on a couple of cases a few years ago. That was one of the factors that had convinced Max it wasn't worth going back into police work after he'd been shot. Hamilton had a tendency to act like a bad cop in a film-noir drama. But Max didn't have time to explain any of the background to Olivia. He had to deal with the guy right now.

He came straight toward Max. "Lyon, what are you doing here?" he demanded. "I thought you got canned."

"I wasn't canned. I took disability retirement over a desk," Max clipped out, then silently cursed himself for feeling like he had to explain his decision to this guy, and at the same time hating that they were having this conversation in front of Olivia and his partners.

"And you're here now because?"

"I'm with Rockfort Security," he answered. "I was hired as a bodyguard by Olivia Winters."

"And she's in danger from what?"

Olivia jumped into the conversation. "My best friend

from high school was murdered. I wanted to make sure it didn't happen to me."

He tipped his head to the side, studying her, and Max was pretty sure she wanted to pat her hair back into place. "You're that supermodel? The big Howard County success story that I read about in the *Baltimore Sun*?"

She raised one shoulder. "More like a successful model."

"What's the difference?"

"Money. Celebrity."

"But you're in New York."

"Yes, I've worked in New York for the past ten years, but I grew up here." She gestured toward the house. "Right here. I was just attacked. And another friend from high school is dead."

Hamilton looked from her to Shane and Jack. "And what are you two doing here?"

"We came when Max told us there might be trouble here."

"Yeah, trouble," the detective agreed. "That's why we're going down to police headquarters to sort that out."

"All of us?" Shane asked.

"Until we know what the hell went on here."

"Would a surveillance video help?" Max asked.

The detective gave him a long look. "You're saying you got one?"

"Yes. When I took the bodyguard job, I had cameras installed at the front and back doors. You can get the digital output. It's on the laptop computer in the little office off the living room."

The detective sent a uniformed officer into the house to get the computer.

"Can we go in to get some clothing?" Max asked.

"You know I can't do that," Hamilton answered.

"My things are in a suitcase upstairs in my bedroom," Olivia said. "If you could just have an officer bring the suitcase, I'd be very grateful."

"And maybe he could pick up my bag too," Max said.

"In the same room?" Hamilton asked with a grin in his voice.

"No. Down the hall," Max answered, making an effort to rein in his annoyance. If he got into a pissing match with this detective, he was going to end up soaked. From his years on the force and then as a PI, he knew that the cops always won.

Hamilton turned to one of the officers. "Go up and get the stuff."

At least the detective was being magnanimous.

"Yes, sir," the uniform answered.

The man went into the house, and Max waited tensely until he reappeared with Olivia's suitcases and his duffel bag and set them down on the ground. The first man had already come out with Max's laptop.

"And now we're going down to police headquarters."

Max knew they were in for several hours of interrogation; it was standard procedure. And he also knew it was going to be worse because he was involved. In the eyes of many cops, Hamilton included, there was nothing worse than a PI who thought he could do a better job than the police and who fucked up a case with his own investigation. Well, he took that back. Maybe the worst thing was a former cop who had gone over to the PI dark side. But Max knew his only alternative was to cooperate. And now he was regretting his decision to lie about what he was actually doing here because Olivia might tell a different story at headquarters.

He knew they wouldn't drive him and Olivia up to headquarters together, and he caught her arm as they waited for more cars to arrive so that they could all be separated.

"Bodyguard," he said, hoping she caught the import in his voice.

She nodded, and he prayed that the story they told was going to match.

More cars roared up the driveway, and she was led off to one. He was escorted to another, and Jack and Shane were each put into separate vehicles. As Max was driven to headquarters, he considered what his friends were going to say. Shane would tell them about the phone being stolen. He knew that Max had been lured away by the false text messages. But that was all he knew about what had happened before he'd arrived. Jack knew only what Shane did. But there was one factor that he was sure they weren't going to share with the cops. In addition to the readout from the surveillance cameras on the laptop, the video had been transmitted to Rockfort Security headquarters. They wouldn't have to wait until the cops released the computer. They could watch the video and see if there was anything they could figure out from the pictures.

Fifteen minutes later, they pulled up at the modern redbrick police headquarters building on one of the hills above the river valley where Ellicott City had first been established. By the time Max arrived, he saw Olivia disappearing into the building under escort and knew there would be no chance to confer at headquarters.

They were all being taken to separate rooms, where they would each tell their separate stories.

Max cooled his heels in an interrogation room. After glancing at the one-way mirror on the opposite wall, he sat down at the scarred table and stretched out his legs. Pretty sure Archie Hamilton was making him wait until everybody else was done, he folded his arms on the table, leaned over, and used them for a pillow. A few minutes later, he was sleeping.

—∿—

"Wake up!" Hamilton barked.

Max lifted his head and looked at his watch. He'd been here an hour and a half.

As he took in the detective's annoyance, he stifled a smile. Probably Hamilton had thought Max would be bored to tears—or sitting with his stomach churning, wondering if he could make his story match Olivia's.

"You know the drill."

"Yeah."

Hamilton pulled out a chair opposite him. Instead of speaking immediately, he opened a folder he'd brought with him and consulted his notes.

Max kept himself from starting the conversation.

Finally the detective looked up. "What are you really doing in Howard County?" he asked.

"I told you. Acting as bodyguard for Olivia Winters."

"That's not what she says."

"Well, it's the truth, so I don't know why she would have said otherwise," Max answered, hoping Hamilton was using the standard law-enforcement technique of lying in the hopes that he'd change his story.

Again the detective was silent, and Max thought
that he looked more like Archie Bunker than someone
named Archie Hamilton. Finally, he sighed.

"Okay, I guess that's close enough."

Max nodded.

"And what about the engagement story?"

"That was to make it look logical for me to be spending all my time with her."

"Why didn't you just say you were her bodyguard?"

"She didn't want any publicity," he answered, hoping
she'd remembered he'd said that at the reunion meeting.

After listening to the explanation, Hamilton said,
"You mind giving me your account of what happened
this evening?"

"Like I said before, I got a series of text messages
that I thought came from one of my associates—
Shane Gallagher. He said he wanted to meet with me
away from the house. After I left, a woman in Ms.
Winters' high school class came rushing over. She
said she was being stalked and that only Ms. Winters
could save her."

He stopped, took a breath, and then continued.
"Apparently the guy had told her to come to the house so
he could kill both her and Ms. Winters at the same time."

"And you weren't doing your bodyguard bit."

Max kept his voice even as he said, "I was lured
away, by the perp. He went to the trouble of stealing my
partner's cell phone so he could make it look like the
messages were legit.

"You looked at the tape?" Max asked.

"Yeah."

"And it confirms what we've said?" It wasn't really a

question. He wanted Hamilton to acknowledge that he'd seen the action.

"As far as it goes."

Max wanted to ask what that meant, but he kept the question to himself as Hamilton started asking the same questions over again, probably hoping he could shake Max's story, but he answered the same way he had earlier, and he hoped the way Olivia had answered.

Finally, the detective got tired of going over and over the same ground and getting the same results.

"You can go," he said.

Max stayed where he was.

"What?" Hamilton demanded.

"We don't have to be working against each other," Max said.

"What do you mean?"

"Neither one of us wants another murder out here."

"Yeah, so you guard the model, and I'll investigate the case."

Max struggled not to sigh. He'd hoped he could make peace with the guy. Apparently Hamilton wasn't having any.

"You had an interesting reputation when you were with the Baltimore PD," Hamilton said.

"What's that supposed to mean?"

"It means you poked your nose into cases that weren't yours."

Max figured any rejoinder would be the wrong answer. Without saying anything else, he exited the room and strode down the hall to the lobby, where he found Olivia, Shane, and Jack waiting for him.

"Are you okay?" Olivia asked.

"Yeah. Let's get out of here."

"While you were still waiting, a uniformed officer gave us a ride back to the farm," Jack said. "We've got our vehicle, and yours."

"Great."

They all walked out of the building to the parking lot, and Max was surprised to find that it was full dark. He'd been at the damn police headquarters for hours, when he should have been doing something constructive, like finding evidence that linked Claire and Angela's murders so they could get the guy who had tricked him into leaving the farm. He understood the feeling of urgency. He wanted to make up for his failure earlier in the day. Not just his leaving Olivia alone, but his reason for rushing away. He hadn't trusted Olivia because he was putting his own spin on her behavior.

Shane broke into his dark thoughts with a welcome piece of information. "And we've got the video."

"Did you look at it?" Max asked.

"We were waiting for you."

"We can't go home," Olivia said.

"And we need to keep you safe," Max said to her, "now that we know that you're a target."

"Then where are we going?" Olivia asked.

"We've booked you a suite under an assumed name, at one of the local hotels. The Marriott Courtyard," Shane said

Max nodded.

"You can follow us over," Shane said.

He and Olivia climbed into his SUV. She leaned across the console toward him, and he leaned toward her, putting his arms around her and holding her tight, his hands stroking over her back. There wasn't time to say much now, but he needed to hold her, and she seemed to feel the same.

"Thank God you're okay," he repeated what he'd said at the farm.

"You, too."

"Nothing happened to me."

"I'm sure Hamilton—um—how would you say it, tried to crack you."

Max laughed. "He tried."

There was a lot more he wanted to say. But it would have to wait until later.

Easing away, he started the engine.

"Thank you for sticking to the bodyguard story," he said.

"I could see it was important to you. But why?"

He sighed as he pulled out after Shane's SUV. "Some cops hate having anyone poking into their investigation. Hamilton's one of them, and in this case, he and I have a history."

"Like what?"

Max hated dredging up old business, but since he was working for Olivia, he didn't see that he had a choice.

"I was with the Baltimore PD, and he was here in Howard County. The two departments were working on a case involving major thefts from businesses in the area. I thought it was a relative of a delivery man, and Hamilton didn't agree. One night the relative broke into a Columbia warehouse that was supposed to be empty at night—except for the security guards who patrolled the industrial park. But the warehouse manager was there, and the thief shot him. Not fatally."

"And?"

"And Hamilton got reprimanded for not following up on my lead."

She laughed. "I guess that *would* make him hostile."

"After that, I tried to stay out of his way, but I couldn't avoid having some other dealings."

"He said he'd arrest you if you interfered in this case."

Max's head whipped toward her. "He told you that?"

"Yes."

Max cursed.

"Doesn't he want to solve the murders?" Olivia asked.

"Of course he does, but he doesn't want any help from me."

"And he's not going to make your job easier." She shook her head. "Of course, he thinks you're just a bodyguard."

"He may not believe that."

"But you're not going to let that stop your investigation."

"Right."

Shane had pulled into the parking lot of the Marriott Courtyard, a beige stucco building, and Max parked a few cars over.

Shane strode to the driver's side of his SUV, and he rolled down the window. "Wait here," he said. "Jack and I will go in the front and open the side door for you. It's locked at night," he added.

When Shane came to the door, they got out of the car and hurried inside, then to a nearby elevator.

After unlocking the door to the suite, Shane handed the key card to Max and gave another one to Olivia.

"But I hope you're not going far by yourself," Max said.

"No," Olivia answered.

They all went into the suite, which had a living room and an adjoining bedroom with a king-sized bed.

"I can take the sofa," Max said.

Olivia didn't object, and they all sat down in the living room area.

"We're just to your right," Shane said, gesturing. "We're all registered under assumed names."

"Because?" Olivia asked.

"Because the guy who attacked you knows that Max works for Rockfort Security. He knew who I was. He knew that stealing my phone would be a good way to con Max."

"Unfortunately," Olivia agreed.

"We're all staying in Columbia until we solve this damn thing," Shane said.

"Even if Hamilton is checking up on us?" Max asked.

"No question," Jack answered.

He had brought in a laptop, and Max looked at the machine. "The tape from the surveillance camera is on there?"

"Yeah. It was networked to the laptop at Olivia's house."

"Does Hamilton have access to all your notes?" she asked.

Max laughed. "If he wants to spend hours trying to figure out the password."

Jack set the machine on the coffee table, and they all squeezed onto the sofa.

Shane queued up the tape, found the current date, and began to play, scrolling the morning and early afternoon.

When he got to the afternoon, he slowed. First they all saw Max come out of the house and head for his car.

Nobody said anything, but he kept his gaze fixed on

the screen, unwilling to look at anyone else in the room and feeling like a grub under a rock. If he had stayed at Olivia's where he was supposed to be, none of this would have happened. Well, Claire would have showed up, but the perp wouldn't have attacked with Max in the house, since he would have gone to a lot of trouble to get rid of him.

Again Shane sped up the tape, but not as fast as before. He slowed it down again when a car came bouncing up the rutted gravel road.

"That's Claire," Olivia murmured.

The car lurched to a stop in front of the house, and a woman got out. Her skin was pale, her hair was a mess, and her eyes were wide.

Jack paused the picture for a moment, and they all gazed at the distraught woman. "She looks like she's been holed up in her house. And finally got forced out."

"We don't know exactly what happened," Max interjected. "I'd like to go over there, but Hamilton is going to make sure we don't get inside."

"Or arrest us if we do," Jack added.

Jack started the tape again, and Claire hurried up to the front porch and disappeared under the overhang.

"She banged on the door, and I let her in," Olivia said.

"Let's see what else happens outside," Shane said.

They kept their eyes on the screen as the view of the outside stayed static for several seconds.

"Okay," Max finally said. "I see something flickering at the left-hand edge of the picture."

"Too bad we can't change the view," Jack muttered.

The flickering continued, and finally a man walked into the frame. He was wearing a dark shirt and pants, and his head was covered with a knit cap. He was also wearing leather gloves. The clothing covered almost anything that could have identified him, and he had already put on the gas mask and was adjusting it as he walked.

Max made an angry sound as the guy stood for several moments watching the house, then started walking again. He had a knapsack slung over one shoulder, and as they watched, he reached inside and pulled out a canister.

"I guess that's the smoke bomb," Olivia whispered, her voice high and reedy.

He hefted it in his hand, then heaved it toward a window, where it crashed through. Seconds later, he rushed forward and looked inside.

On the tape, smoke began to billow out the shattered glass. And it seemed that less than a minute went by before he threw another missile after the first.

"What were you doing after he threw it?" Jack asked.

"Claire and I both started coughing, and our eyes were burning. I was trying to get her out of there. First she wouldn't move. Then it seemed like she'd come with me. But she changed her mind again."

They were still watching the screen. The man was still on the outside looking in, but he probably couldn't see anything through the smoke. Then he withdrew a gun from the knapsack and walked confidently around to the front of the house.

"What a brave guy," Jack muttered. "Going after two defenseless women inside with their eyes stinging and their lungs burning."

"He thought they were defenseless," Max answered. "But Olivia wasn't going to just let him shoot her."

With the gun in his hand, the man disappeared from view.

"I guess that's it," Jack said. "Too bad we couldn't hear anything or see anything more."

Max turned toward Olivia. "From what we just watched, do you know who he is?"

Chapter 18

MAX WAITED FOR OLIVIA'S ANSWER.

Her response was what he expected, given the precautions the guy had taken.

"No."

"Anything at all you can think of?" Jack pressed.

"I was in a panic. In the smoke. He was shooting at me. All I wanted to do was get away. Well, get away with Claire."

"Yeah, but we can go back and look at him on the tape."

He rewound until they had a clear picture of the time after the assailant walked into the frame.

Max went through the tape very slowly.

"He didn't park in the driveway," he said. "It looks like he came through the woods."

"Like when he was here before," she murmured.

"I told you about the man who strung the barbed wire in the woods," Max clarified to his partners. "We don't know for sure that was him, but it would make sense. Which means it would be helpful if we got those DNA results."

"Yeah," Shane agreed. "But once we get the profile, we've got to find out if he's in the system."

"Work on that," Max ordered.

Shane nodded. "He must have been coming to check out the place. "But why announce his presence by setting that trap in the woods? That doesn't exactly make sense."

Max made a sound of agreement, then went back to slowly forwarding the surveillance tape, keeping his focus on the man who had come to kill Claire and Olivia.

"He moves easily. I'd say he works out," Jack observed.

"One of the former football players?" Olivia wondered.

"Not necessarily," Max answered. "Too bad he had on that cap. I'd like to at least know his hair color—or if he's bald."

"See if you can get it," Shane said.

Max stopped the picture and zoomed in on the man's mask-covered face. When the guy turned his head, they saw a bit of hair at the bottom of the cap.

Max enlarged the picture again. "It's dark," he said.

"He could still be mostly bald," Shane pointed out.

"Or he could have dyed his hair," Olivia said.

"It's the only physical evidence we have to go on so far," Max said.

"I'd like to look for shoeprints, but the cops have probably trampled the ground," Jack said.

Max zoomed out again, and they kept going through the tape, frame by frame.

"He could have gotten that shirt anywhere," Max said.

"No," Olivia said.

"You know where he bought the shirt?" Jack asked, and they all turned to her.

"Well, not specifically where he bought it, but I'm pretty good at remembering clothing. It's part of my job."

"You said you remembered women's clothing better than men's when I asked you about the reunion meeting," Max said.

"Right. But last year I was doing some commercials for Ralph Lauren. That shirt was in the male collection."

"You're sure."

"It's a dark, solid color broadcloth shirt with a slight pattern in the weave." She pointed toward the screen. "But look at that checked pattern inside the collar."

"What about the logo?" Max asked.

"He had a handkerchief covering it," she said.

"Good work," Max said to Olivia.

"Does it help?" she asked.

"It's a clue," Max answered. "It tells us he's a guy who can afford to wear expensive clothing to a murder. And that he doesn't mind getting them messed up," he added.

Shane snorted.

Max kept going. "Anything else sartorial that would help?"

Olivia watched for a few more minutes, then pointed to his shoes. "I think those are Gucci loafers. I can't be sure because there are a lot of knockoffs. But it's the style. See the curve of the tongue."

Shane laughed. "I'll take your word for it."

"More evidence that he's well off," Jack said.

"Like Brian Cannon," Max said.

"But he has blond hair," Olivia pointed out.

They kept watching, and Olivia couldn't come up with anything else that would help identify the guy.

When the tape finished, Max turned to Olivia and saw her biting her lower lip. "What are you thinking?"

"If I had saved Claire, we could ask her about him," Olivia whispered.

"You couldn't save her because she wouldn't let you," Max said. "She was too out of it, I think. Maybe she was even drugged so she couldn't think straight."

"I was wondering about that," Olivia conceded. "She wasn't acting the way I remembered her—or acting normal, come to that. But how would he drug her?"

"He could have done something similar," Shane said. "Introduce some kind of gas into her house. Something more subtle than breaking the window. But we can't find out if we can't go over there and investigate."

"That jerk Hamilton is irrational," Max muttered.

Jack shook his head. "We probably wouldn't have access anyway."

"We'd have a better chance of getting some evidence," Max shot back, then glanced toward Olivia. She had thrown her head back and looked exhausted. He'd wanted to talk about the assailant's motivation, but he decided that was going to have to wait.

"I think we've worked you hard enough tonight," he said. "Why don't you take a shower? You probably feel grimy after that smoke attack."

Olivia sat up and looked at him. "Yes."

When she'd gone into the bedroom and closed the door, Max looked at his partner. "I was thinking about something," he said.

"And we're not going to like it," Jack said.

"Yeah. It's about the two of you staying in the hotel with us. I understand why you got yourselves a room, but under the circumstances, it's not the best plan."

"Why not?" Jack asked.

"Because the killer has obviously researched us. Not just me—the whole Rockfort organization. He knows who we all are, and he's got a line on how we operate. He knew enough to get your cell phone."

Shane made an angry sound.

"And use it to trick me," Max added. "Unfortunately, I think if the two of you are in the hotel, that increases the chance of his finding us here."

His partners thought about that for a few moments.

"I hate to admit it, but that makes sense," Shane said.

"So go back to your wives tonight. And tomorrow, try to get those DNA results. Also, we need to do some more intensive research on Olivia's class. We can narrow it down to rich guys."

"Unless he bought the shoes and shirt on sale," Shane said.

"Well, that would mean he wants to look prosperous. We can also focus on guys who think image is important."

"That will take a bit of digging," Shane said. He cleared his throat. "I'm really sorry about the phone."

"Not your fault," Max answered immediately.

"I should have put you in the loop as soon as the damn thing disappeared."

"And I shouldn't have fallen for that damn ruse like a wet-behind-the-ears patrol officer," Max snapped.

"Don't either of you beat yourselves up on that," Jack said. "It was a clever ploy executed with finesse."

"It could have gotten Olivia killed," Max shot back.

"But she's okay," Jack said. "She held him off long enough for you to get back there."

"And we know the guy is smart. Don't underestimate him," Shane said.

"He was clever enough to make his previous murders look like accidents until Angela," Max said.

"And now maybe he's coming unraveled," Jack said.

"Which makes him more dangerous," Max added.

They discussed the case for a few more minutes but

drew no other useful conclusions. When the two other Rockfort agents left, Max was alone with his thoughts — and with Olivia.

He hated the way he'd bought into the idea that Olivia was involved in the case as more than a victim, even when he understood his twisted logic. Partly it was because he was certain that she was hiding something from him. And he'd been using that as an excuse to distance himself from her.

And now that they were alone, he had to talk to her about what had happened, even though the thought of the conversation made him feel like he'd stepped out of a helicopter and was hurtling toward a crash landing onto a concrete slab.

Unable to sit still, he stepped to the bedroom door, listening. The shower went off, and then he heard rustling noises in the bathroom. He was standing by the window when the door opened and she stepped into the living room, facing him.

She looked a lot better than she had twenty minutes ago. She was wearing one of those white hotel robes, and he wondered what she had on under it. Forcing his mind away from intimate thoughts, he folded his arms across his chest and said, "I have to ask you something."

His tense posture and the tone of his voice had apparently made her wary.

"What is it?"

"Do you still want me on the case?"

Chapter 19

Fighting a feeling of disorientation, Olivia stared at the man standing beside the sofa.

"Why are you even asking?"

"Because I screwed up," Max said.

"No."

"Of course I did. I knew it wasn't safe to leave you alone. Then I let myself get lured away—so the killer could come to your house. He obviously had it all set up."

"And he obviously had it carefully planned," Olivia reminded him. "He wanted you to leave so he could come after me and Claire."

"How does that change anything?" he asked in a gritty voice.

"Well, you realize that he could have lured you away to kill *you*," she said.

His eyes widened. "Jesus, I didn't think about that."

"I did. I had a lot of time to think while I was hanging around police headquarters, waiting for you to finish with that nasty detective. Where were you supposed to meet Shane?"

"In the parking lot of the restaurant where we had the reunion meeting."

"So he knew about that. In fact, he could have been there."

"Or not."

She could see from his face that nothing she said was

going to have much effect on the way he felt about what had happened. He was still kicking himself for leaving her unprotected. Probably Hamilton had pounded that into him as well.

Maybe she wasn't totally sure how she felt about his going. But she knew there was only one way to reassure him that she wanted him here with her.

She reached for him, pulling him to her, feeling his resistance and knowing when he finally gave up fighting what he wanted. What they both wanted.

She cupped the back of his head and brought his mouth to hers in a kiss she didn't even pretend was part reassurance. It was all heat and fury and relief that both of them had come through the incident all right.

He made a sound deep in his throat. *A sound of surrender*, she decided, as the kiss changed its focus. She had been the aggressor to start with. Now he took that role, and if she had been surer of him, she would have thought that he was staking his claim on her.

He gathered her close, his hands moving over her back and shoulder and into her freshly washed hair. She felt his erection standing up between them, hard and insistent, and knew that this time things were going to end differently.

He fumbled for the belt of the robe, opening the tie and letting the belt ends drop to the side before he swept the edges of the garment out of the way.

She was wearing nothing underneath, and the feel of his large hands on her naked body sent a shock wave through her. The kiss had aroused her. It was nothing to what she felt now.

She was pretty sure the public made assessments

about her life. Probably they thought she had slept with a lot of men. But it wasn't true. Of course she'd had a lot of offers, but she'd learned to be cautious about relationships. And this was the first man she had let past her defenses in years. Maybe because he hadn't been trying. He'd been keeping his distance, the way she had been until she'd understood what kind of man he was.

His hands moved over her stomach, her ribs, then reached to cup her breasts. He made a needy sound as he took them in his hands, and she echoed that sound when he stroked his thumbs across nipples that had hardened to tight points of sensation.

When she felt him go still, she raised her head, giving him a questioning look.

"Are you sure you want to do this?" he asked in a gritty voice.

"Very sure."

To make that point, she reached for his belt buckle and pulled the end of the belt free before finding the button at the top of his jeans.

He kept his gaze on her face as she lowered the zipper and reached inside, cupping her hand around his erection through the soft fabric of his boxers.

He sucked in a sharp breath. "That's good. Probably too good."

"Yes," she answered, smiling at his reaction.

Next she tackled his shirt, opening the buttons and pushing the garment off his shoulders. While she did that, he was slicking down his jeans, scuffing off his shoes, and kicking his pants away.

She reached around to his butt, stroking her hands over his curves, and he did the same, then he reached lower into the folds of her sex, caressing her there with knowing fingers.

He let go of her long enough to shrug out of his shirt and push the robe off her shoulders so that they were both naked, with a convenient bed only steps away. She'd already turned down the covers, and he took her down to the surface of the mattress with him, gathering her close and starting to kiss her all over again, beginning with her mouth, then her ears, her neck, her collarbone, and finally her breasts.

"Don't make me wait," she pleaded.

He lifted his head away from one breast so that he could speak. "I want you as hot as I am."

One of his hands traveled down her body while his mouth returned to the nipple he'd been circling with his tongue. When he drew her into his mouth and began to suck, she knew she couldn't take much more.

Sliding her hand down his body, she clamped her fingers around his erection, feeling the heat and power of him.

He gasped. "Olivia."

"Do it now," she answered, rolling to her back.

He followed her, covering her body with his, and she guided him into her.

He went very still, looking down at her, passion and perhaps shock suffusing his face. Olivia knew then that he'd never thought this could happen. But here the two of them were, joined together. And it felt like the most natural thing she had done in a long time.

When he began to move, she matched his rhythm, knowing he was holding back, waiting for her to catch up with him. And all at once she was there, on a high plateau where she knew she might get burned by the heat of the sun. She didn't worry about that. She could only drive for her satisfaction, then come apart in a burst of feeling that carried her into space.

She knew he was with her as she felt his body go rigid and heard his shout of satisfaction.

And then his weight was on her as he gathered her to him, breathing hard.

"That was okay for you?" he whispered.

"Wonderful." She smiled and snuggled against him, feeling happier than she had in a long time. Someone had tried to kill her a few hours ago. But she had kept him at bay long enough for the man who held her in his arms to come back and drive the invader away.

"We make a good team," she murmured.

"Making love?"

"I was thinking of a few hours ago."

He winced.

"Sorry if I reminded you that you left."

"I don't need reminding."

She raised her head and looked down at him. "You saved my life. Don't forget that part." When he said nothing, she added, "I mean that."

He held her close, stroking her, and she might have drifted off to sleep in his arms—until she felt the tenor of the stroking change.

"What?" she murmured.

"There are things I never told you about myself."

"Do they matter?"

Ignoring the question, he went on. "I had nothing growing up, and I had a chip on my shoulder. I envied the well-off kids at Donley."

"There's nothing wrong with wanting more than you had. I wanted more, too. Not just material things. I could see that the other kids didn't have a father like mine—who was always on my case."

"Yeah, well my mom wasn't home enough to be on my case. And the only way I could see to get the things I wanted was to steal them. Another guy and I did some shoplifting—taking clothing, mostly," Max said. "Stuff I wanted to wear to school. And when I needed cash, I broke into a lot of houses in Columbia and Ellicott City."

"But you never got caught?" she guessed.

"Wrong. And the cops who caught me did their best to scare the shit out of me. That was the wrong approach. It only made me more defiant. But then there was this detective who understood how to handle me. And I guess he saw something in me that I didn't see in myself. He turned me around. He was the reason I went into law enforcement."

"And the reason you clashed with guys like Hamilton," she guessed.

"Yeah. Cliff Maringer went the extra mile for me. He looked below the surface. Hamilton just does the minimum, so he can claim he's doing his job, and he resents what he considers interference. I tried to help criminals, if I thought they were worth saving."

When she nodded, he went on.

"After my dad left home, I took out my anger on my mom by paying no attention to anything she told me. Well, really, there wasn't a lot of time for attention. She had a bunch of minimum-wage jobs that kept a roof over our heads, in a housing project in Ellicott City." He turned his head toward her. "Did you even know there was a housing project in Ellicott City?"

"No."

"I guess everyone who lived there was trying hard to fit into the Howard County image." He snorted. "The wealthiest county in the U.S., you know."

"I never thought about that. I mean, it might be the wealthiest county, but I lived in a farmhouse with one bathroom upstairs."

"I lived in a housing project where you could buy drugs in the hallways. It made it hard to keep up."

"But you found your footing," Olivia said. "And you found Jack and Shane. They're important to you."

"You figured that out, too?"

"Uh-huh. I like watching the three of you together. I think you could finish each other's sentences."

"Yeah." He dragged in a breath and let it out. "There's more I have to say. Stuff you might not like as much."

She tensed, knowing he wouldn't say something like that unless he meant it.

"I told you that I thought Shane was sending me text messages. That he had something to tell me about you—and he wanted me off alone when he told me."

Her breath grew shallow as she waited for whatever was coming next.

"I believed him because I know there's something you're not telling me. Something that might be important to this case. I just told you the worst thing there was to tell about myself. I wish you would trust me enough to do the same right now."

She turned away from him. They'd made love, and it was as good as she'd known it would be. Now he was asking for more than she was prepared to give him.

Silently she climbed out of bed and reached for the

robe she'd been wearing. She put it on, closed the front, and tied the belt tightly around her waist.

She couldn't leave the hotel suite, but at least it *was* a suite. She could go into the other room to get away from him.

Without glancing back, she walked to the living room area and closed the door behind her. After crossing the room, she pulled the curtains aside and stood looking down into the building's courtyard. Then she realized that was probably a bad idea. If she could look out, someone could look in. Someone like the man who had tried to kill her.

She wondered if Max would come after her. When he didn't, she sat down on the couch and pulled her knees to her chin, hugging herself.

Did he think their making love gave him the right to demand honesty? It was a reasonable question, and she considered it.

She'd walked away from him when he'd asked for information that he needed to do the job that she'd hired him to do. Really, she wanted to run out of the suite. But that would be a foolish tack, and she wasn't dressed for it. And come to think of it, running away was the same thing she'd done as soon as she'd graduated from high school. That was an interesting comparison. She'd wanted to distance herself from her memories of Donley. And she'd been doing that frantically and successfully for the past ten years. Did that make her a coward? Or had she been trying to live her life the best she could?

It had worked for a long time. Then it had started to fall apart. She'd come back to try and find who had killed Angela. But it had almost been a relief to get out of New York.

Her life there was no longer as satisfying as it had been. Now she was back here. Because she actually wanted to face the past? Or because she was fleeing again?

That was an interesting thought. And the man in the other room had offered her a way to deal with that past. To put it to rest once and for all.

She'd made love with him because she was reaching out to him in a way she had avoided for years. But one night of passion wasn't all she imagined for them. She could see a future for the two of them. It felt tantalizingly real, if she dared to ask for what she wanted. But she couldn't do it while avoiding a subject she had to discuss. She had to come clean with him.

She clenched her hands at her sides. What was he going to think of her?

She dragged in a breath and let it out, struggling for calm. Maybe it was better to get this over with before he distanced himself even farther from her.

She wrapped her arms around her shoulders, holding onto her own body, willing herself to steadiness. As she did it, she realized it was a familiar gesture for her. As if the only person she trusted to protect her was herself. But now she had Max. Or she hoped so. After several deep breaths, she turned and walked back into the bedroom.

In her absence, Max had turned down the lights and straightened the bed. He was lying under the covers. His chest was bare and his hands were stacked behind his head. But from his posture, she knew that he wasn't sleeping. She wasn't sure whether to get back in bed or stay where she was. In the end, she remained standing.

He turned his head and looked at her, and she wished he had kept staring across the room.

Hearing her voice crack, she managed to say, "Angela wasn't the only one raped up at that cabin at the reservoir."

Chapter 20

FROM THE TONE OF HER VOICE, HE MUST HAVE KNOWN what she was trying to say and couldn't quite get out.

"Jesus."

She heard him curse, blinked as she saw him vault out of bed and reach her side in a couple of long strides.

"Oh, baby. I'm so sorry."

The words and the way he spoke them warmed her. When he folded her into his arms, she sagged against him. And then, to her horror, she started to cry.

"It's okay. You're going to be okay."

He lifted her in his arms and carried her back to the bed. Lying down, he cradled her against himself, stroking her back and her hair, murmuring soft reassuring words.

For a few minutes, she let the tears flow. It had been so long since she'd allowed herself to cry, she was astonished that she could still do it. She was surprised that it really did seem to wash away the misery. But finally she struggled to bring herself under control.

"I'm going to get you some tissues. I'll be right back," he said.

He climbed off the bed and returned quickly with several tissues, which he handed to her. She blew her nose and swiped at her eyes.

Reaching for her again, he cradled her close. "I'm so sorry," he said again, his voice rough.

"It was a long time ago."

"And it's still affecting you."

She nodded against his shoulder, then rolled to her back, staring up at the ceiling.

"You were brave to tell me."

"You noticed I couldn't quite say it."

"You said enough."

She turned her head toward him. "I've kept it to myself for so long, but I couldn't keep letting you think that my deep dark secret had something to do with the murders. Or maybe it did."

"We'll find out," Max promised.

She added, "I mean, I wanted everything out in the open—finally." She made a muffled sound. "You know, for years I kept it locked up inside me. Now I know that was a mistake—because you made me face it."

"I knew…something was badly wrong. But I didn't know what."

"And that gave you all kinds of stuff to speculate about."

"Yeah."

"Finally, I knew we couldn't really get close unless I told you. The way you told me about the shoplifting and the breaking into houses. I know that's something you don't talk about, either."

"Uh-huh."

"Sometimes it seems like it happened to someone else. I mean, like I told you about Angela."

He reached for her hand and squeezed it. "And my pushing you made it worse." He made a low sound. "Going back to that cabin in the woods must have been horrible for you. And I was the one who dragged you there. No wonder you were acting so uptight."

"You couldn't know. But that wasn't the worst part. It was being with you."

When she felt him tense, she hurried on. "I was attracted to you, but I was afraid to let you get close. Then I started to realize what kind of man you are, but I still wondered what you would think about me if I told you the truth."

"Jesus, you think I was going to think less of you because some bastard raped you?" He turned his head toward her. "Who was it?"

She swallowed hard. "That's the worst part. I'm not sure. Just like I wasn't sure who Gary shot at."

He said nothing, and she forced herself to go on. "I told you about the party. I told you I didn't see who Gary shot at, but it wasn't because I was looking the other way. Brian was telling you the truth. I was too out of it to follow what was happening."

When he started to speak, she squeezed his hand. "Let me finish and get this over with. You told me what you were like in high school. That you wanted the stuff the other kids had. Well, I wanted that too. Most of the other kids lived in big houses in nice developments. Their dads had jobs in offices. Mine worked a farm and came in sweaty and dirty every night. I wasn't in the Donley school district, but my Dad was determined that his daughter wasn't going to be a second-class citizen. So I went to the best school." She turned to him. "How did you get there?"

He laughed. "There was some kind of county program where they took smart kids from the projects and put them in a better school district. For all the good that did me."

"You probably got a better education."

"When I bothered to study. But maybe I was lucky I didn't run with the in crowd, like you did. Because all kinds of nasty things were going on after school."

"Yes," she whispered. "But back then, I was just trying to feel comfortable with the other kids."

"But you were a knockout."

She laughed. "Thanks."

"You know it's true."

"Okay. And it helped. I won't pretend that it wasn't true. The popular kids invited me to parties, and I would have just stayed in the corner, with no idea how to interact with them. Then I found out that liquor and pot made me…more sociable. So I did a lot of that, and I was likely to be bombed at those parties."

"Were you raped at a party?"

"Up at that cabin near the reservoir, like I told you about Angela." She shivered. "But not in that underground room, I don't think. There were a lot of boys there." She turned her head away before saying, "I can't be sure if more than one of them raped me."

He reached for her, pulling her close and rocking her in his arms until she stopped shivering.

"For the first time, I don't feel like I have to deal with this alone. I mean, Angela and I didn't even talk about it after we graduated," she said, then swallowed hard. "But if I'd told you sooner, maybe you wouldn't have left, and Claire would still be alive."

"You didn't know what was going on with her."

"But…"

"Don't speculate on what would have happened."

"And what about me and Angela getting raped? What if we had said something—back then or later?"

"Again, you can't go there. We have to deal with the situation as it exists now. Focus on that."

"Something else I keep thinking. About that night when you rescued us at the pizza parlor. We were both outsiders. What if we'd actually started talking to each other? What if we'd gotten to know each other?"

"It wouldn't have worked out," he said immediately.

"Why not?"

"Because I was still in my bad-boy phase. I would just have gotten you into trouble."

"More trouble than I was already in?"

"Maybe."

She laughed. "Different trouble, anyway."

He stroked his fingers up and down her arm. "Your dad would have ordered you to stay away from me. Either way, it couldn't have worked out."

"I guess you're right."

"I know you'd rather not, but can we go back to the scene at the cabin? I mean when the rape happened."

"You're right, I don't want to. But I will."

"How did you get there?"

"In someone's car."

"Whose?"

She closed her eyes, thinking. "I'm pretty sure it was Brian Cannon."

"So he was there."

"Yes."

"Who else?"

"A lot of the football players."

"They were a rowdy bunch?"

She made a low noise. "Yes. They thought they were God's gift to the student population—especially the girls. You know how it was. They brought honor to Donley." She snorted. "Honor."

"So it could have been one of them."

She dragged in a frustrated breath. "But I don't know who. And I'm not going to accuse someone without being sure."

"I understand."

She shook her head. "But if I did remember, we might know who the murderer was."

"Yeah. But were you and Angela the only ones?"

"I don't think so."

"So the other girls who were raped could turn out to be victims of the killer," Max mused.

"But why now?"

"The guys and I talked about that while you were taking a shower. It looks like he's out of control. Maybe his life went along okay for a while. Then that changed. Or the reunion coming up made him think people were going to talk about what he did in the past. Maybe they were all afraid of him back then, and now they're all grown up."

"So the men he's killed could have been in on the rape?"

"Or they knew something else he's afraid to have come out."

"And how are we going to find out any of that?"

"We're going to lean on Brian Cannon. And we're going to hope that Shane can come through for us on that DNA sample."

"Okay."

"But there's nothing more we can do tonight, so we're going to put it away."

"I don't know if I can—now that it's all out in the open."

"Oh, I think there's a way to take your mind off what happened back in high school."

He pulled her back into his arms and brought his mouth to hers, and she knew he wanted to give her what she needed. Reassurance—and pleasure.

Like a prisoner finally released from captivity, she lowered every barrier she'd erected around herself, welcoming the gift that Max was offering. And giving back to him in full measure.

———

Olivia woke and felt a moment of panic. Someone was lying beside her in bed. She had slept alone for so long. Now…

"It's just me," Max murmured.

"I wouldn't put it that way," she answered, nibbling her lips against his shoulder.

As she remembered the night before, a satisfied smile played over her mouth.

He noticed and ran his fingers through the hair he'd tousled. "I'd like to stay in bed, but the most important thing is keeping you safe. Which means we have to get up and get dressed."

She nodded, knowing it was true.

"You want the bathroom first?" he asked.

"Yes. Thanks."

She took a quick shower. When she came back, he slipped into the bathroom while she got dressed. In the farmhouse, she'd felt like they were in each other's way. Now sharing the bathroom simply felt like a new intimacy.

"There's a breakfast buffet here," he said. "But it's better if you stay out of sight."

"He knows what you look like, too," she countered.

"Yeah, but I'm just an ordinary guy."

"Hardly."

As she spoke, he pulled a baseball cap down over his face and pulled on a plaid long-sleeved shirt over his T-shirt.

At least he wasn't going to watch her put on her makeup. She always hated to have an audience when she made herself into Olivia Winters—public figure. It meant she could never be herself. Or maybe she had lost sight of who she really was until last night with Max. She'd been afraid that anyone who knew her big secret would think of her differently. That was true of Max. But not in a bad way. It had helped him understand her. Accept her. And that acceptance had been a gift.

She thought about leaving off the makeup. But she couldn't quite go that far. And putting on her face gave her something to focus on while Max was gone.

When she was finished, all she could do was pace nervously through the suite. When someone knocked at the door she whirled and hurried across the sitting room.

"Max?" she asked, seeing him through the peephole.

"Yeah. My hands are full."

After she turned the lock, he stepped inside carrying a tray of food and kicked the door shut.

He set the scrambled eggs, coffee, and sticky buns on the table in the corner and gave her a long look.

"What?"

"You are so beautiful with your makeup on."

She flushed. "I was thinking about leaving it off."

"Good. Because I like you better without it."

"You do?"

"Yeah."

So was that going to be a step into a more normal life? She reserved the thought as she sat down to eat. The free breakfast wasn't bad, and she had finished about half her meal when she saw Max glance at his watch. She gave him a questioning look.

He picked up the remote, clicked on the television, and got one of the local stations.

She kept eating through a couple of commercials, but her appetite vanished when the local news came on. The first thing she saw was a picture of the farmhouse, taken from the road with a telephoto lens.

She stared at the screen in disbelief. "How did they get that? How did they even know about it?"

He swore, his expression grim. "I was afraid of something like this. Probably the local news stations have a police scanner."

They both stopped talking and listened to the reporter who was saying that the home of the late Ernest Winters had been attacked the night before.

"His daughter, the model, Olivia Winters, was staying in the house, and a visitor was killed. Her identity is being withheld, pending notification of next of kin. Ms. Winters is apparently in town in connection with the ten-year reunion of her Donley High School class."

Olivia sucked in a breath. "How do they know that?"

"I guess they contacted people who might know you, and somebody at the reunion meeting talked."

"So they might know you're my bodyguard, not my fiancé."

"Only if Hamilton gives out the information."

"Will he?"

"He shouldn't." Max clicked off the TV and got up from the table. "Come on."

Olivia gave him a questioning look. "Where are we going?"

"To talk to Brian Cannon. The good news is that the press doesn't know where we're hiding out—I hope."

"But it's not just going to be on television. Do you think it made the *Baltimore Sun*?"

"If it hasn't, it will."

When he looked grim, she asked, "What are you thinking?"

"That because you're nationally known, this is going to go farther than the local media."

She struggled to keep down the food she'd just eaten.

To confirm what Max had said, Olivia's cell phone rang. When she looked at the name on the caller ID, she felt her stomach muscles contract.

"Who?" Max asked.

Olivia clicked to answer. "Jerry."

"It looks like you got into some trouble down there," her agent said.

"How do you know?"

"It's on CNN."

"Oh Lord."

"Come back, and I'll keep the media away from you."

"I can't come back. We have to find out what is going on down here."

"You're not a cop."

"Jerry…"

Max took the phone away from her. "This is Max Lyon," he said.

"Who?"

"Olivia's fiancé."

She heard the squeak of surprise on the other end of the line.

"What the hell do you mean, Olivia's fiancé?" Jerry asked, his outraged voice easily carrying through the phone lines.

Olivia started to shake. She hadn't bargained for a confrontation with Jerry. She'd thought she could avoid talking to him until this was over.

"She came down here because her best friend from high school was murdered," Max said.

"You're saying she deliberately put herself in danger?" Jerry asked, his voice clearly audible.

"No," Max answered, then put his hand over the instrument. "Do you want me to tell him to fuck off?"

The blunt question shocked her. Part of her reason for coming home was to put some distance between herself and Jerry. But she wasn't ready to go that far with him.

"I guess I'd better talk to him," she said to Max.

"You're sure?"

"Yes."

He handed her the phone, and she clamped her hand around it in a death grip. "I have to see this through," she said.

"Why?"

"Because it will haunt me for the rest of my life if I don't."

Jerry snorted. Apparently the concept of loyalty to a dead friend was beyond his pay grade.

"This changes everything," he said.

"How?"

"Jesus. You could get pregnant. You could ruin your

figure." He stopped short, then said, "Are you pregnant now? Is that why you're hiding out?"

Olivia glanced at Max, suddenly thinking that she could be. "No," she said.

"You're not doing that Million Dollar Babe shoot are you?" Jerry asked.

"No," she answered, realizing she had made up her mind.

"I think I can get them to take Yvonne Mitchell."

"Sure. Go ahead," Olivia answered. She'd come down here not knowing what she wanted. Apparently she'd made a decision, but she hadn't known it until now.

"We'll talk later," he said.

"Yes," she answered, wondering if they would ever talk again—except through a lawyer. After all, she did have a contract with the man, a contract she'd been eager to sign ten years ago because it had felt like he was offering her the moon and Christmas all rolled together. She remembered that feeling like Superman had taken her hand and was flying her over the skies of New York. Now she was thinking she'd been a fool to trust that he had her best interests at heart. He'd seen a good thing when she walked into his office—a girl with raw talent who could be groomed and controlled.

She clicked off and looked up to see Max watching her.

"I'm sorry," he said.

"Not your fault."

"Well, I shouldn't have said I was your fiancé—not to him. It just slipped out."

Yeah, she thought, like a Freudian slip.

She could mumble something about the heat of the

moment. Instead, she kept her gaze on Max. "Do you want to be my fiancé?"

He went very still, then looked away. "I'd make a lousy spouse."

"How do you know?"

"My background. I don't even know what a good husband is. My dad certainly wasn't a great role model."

"I could say the same for mine. But that's not the point. What if I am pregnant?" she whispered.

"I'd never run out on you and the baby."

She closed her eyes for a moment. She'd asked the question without thinking through the implications. So he'd stay if it was to protect an innocent child, not because he wanted *her*. Or had he told Jerry he was engaged to her because that was what he really wanted?

She couldn't work her way through any of that now. She couldn't even be sure of her own feelings. And maybe she wouldn't be until they solved the murder. As that last thought surfaced, she squared her shoulders.

"Let's go lean on Brian Cannon."

He looked relieved at the change of subject.

"Be right back." She ran into the bedroom to get her purse. When she returned to the living room, he was holding the two sticky buns nestled in two napkins. "We can eat this on the way."

"The nourishing part?"

"The fun part."

"Right. On the way to interview a murder suspect." She stopped and said, "Is he?"

"It's unlikely," Max answered. "But the sooner we find out…" He let his voice trail off, and she didn't ask what he'd been thinking.

Maybe it was, *the sooner we can sort out our relationship*. She hoped so, and she hoped the conclusion would be what she wanted to hear. Which was what? Did she even know? Did he? Were they two screwed-up people who had been thrown together and were now clinging to each other? She didn't like to put it that way. She knew she cared about Max. And he was acting like he cared about her. Plus he'd told her things about his past that he hadn't liked sharing. But what if he'd done it to get her to open up with him? She was still confused, but she couldn't focus on the two of them now.

He was back in bodyguard mode as he said, "Let me go first."

Stepping into the hall, he looked around, then motioned for her to follow. He walked in front of her as they headed for the back elevator, then the side door.

She kept her head down, and nobody paid them any attention as they slipped outside and got into his SUV.

As he drove to the office building where Brian Cannon's office was located, they polished off the buns. After she was finished eating, she pulled down the visor mirror and began to wipe off her mouth.

When he gave her a questioning look, she said, "If I'm not my best, people criticize."

"I'd hate that."

"Not my fave." She shook her head. "And maybe the media are camped out at Brian's."

"Let's hope not."

They found a space near the office building door, and again she was relieved that no reporters were staking out the place.

"I guess they haven't gotten to him yet," she said.

On the second floor, Max hurried down the hall to the office they'd visited the day before, and Olivia lengthened her strides to keep up.

As they stepped into the reception room, Ms. Holiday gave them a wide-eyed look.

"What are *you* doing here?" Ms. Holiday asked.

"We have some unfinished business with Mr. Cannon," Max answered.

"He's not in," she said too quickly.

"Is that what he told you to say if you saw us?" Max asked. "Or the press?"

She didn't answer, but Olivia caught the apologetic expression. Stepping closer to the desk, she said, "You may know that we had a pretty bad experience last night. A woman was murdered at my house, and the man tried to kill me too."

The receptionist gasped. "It was on the news, but I didn't know the part about his coming after you."

"She was in our high school class. I mean mine and Brian's, and I think nobody in the class is safe until we figure out who the killer is."

"What does that have to do with Mr. Cannon?"

"In the first place, he's just as much at risk as anyone else. And in the second place, he may have some information that can help us."

As Olivia kept the woman's attention, Max slipped past them and headed down the hall.

But Ms. Holiday saw him striding toward Brian's office. "Wait a minute. You can't go back there," she shouted after him.

Olivia put a hand on her arm. "It's okay. He's going to feel better after helping us."

"But he told me to keep you away from him. He was
very clear about that."

Just then the sounds of a scuffle interrupted the
conversation.

Chapter 21

Ms. HOLIDAY LEAPED UP FROM BEHIND HER DESK AND charged down the corridor. Olivia was right behind her.

She heard cursing and the sound of knuckles landing on flesh and bone.

They arrived in time to see Max holding a wide-eyed Brian against the wall.

The real estate agent's gaze swung to Olivia, and he looked like he was expecting salvation. "Tell your goon to leave me alone. He's not really your fiancé, is he?"

"He's a PI, and he's investigating the murders. I'm sorry it's come to this, Brian, but we need your help," she said in a soft voice. "Just give us a few minutes, then we'll leave you alone."

He swallowed hard, and she knew he could still order them to get out of his office. Or tell Ms. Holiday to call the cops. It probably depended on whether or not he was the killer.

She chose not to assume the worst. "You could save a life—and it might be yours."

"What the hell does that mean?"

"I think you can guess. If Max lets you go, will you talk to us?"

When he answered with a tight nod, Max relaxed his grip, then turned to Ms. Holiday. "Don't go down the hall and do something stupid—like calling the police."

She looked from him to Brian.

Her boss said, "It's all right. Don't call anyone. Give us a few minutes."

The three of them went into his office and closed the door.

Brian rounded his desk and sat down, looking relieved to have the barrier between them as he rubbed his jaw.

"Sorry," Max apologized as they sat across from him.

"What the hell do you think I can do for you?" he asked.

"Did the cops question you?" Max asked.

"Yes," Brian bit out.

"Did they tell you who was murdered at Olivia's house last night?"

"No."

"It was Claire Lowden."

Brian's face paled. "Oh my God."

"Have you seen her recently?" Max asked.

Brian's gaze shot to him. "Why are you asking? I mean, do you think I killed her?"

"Actually, no."

"Why not?"

Olivia cleared her throat. "Because the murderer had dark hair, and you don't."

Brian stared at her. "Are you saying you saw him? Then why don't you know who it was?"

Olivia could see Max was struggling not to leap across the desk and strangle the guy. She watched him drag in a calming breath and put a hand on his knee.

Last time he had done most of the talking. This time she thought it would be better if she took the lead.

"We're here because we need your help. And we're going to tell you stuff that the cops want kept confidential. You've got to promise you won't tell anyone else."

Brian thought about it, then nodded. "Yeah, okay."

Max looked at Olivia. "Tell him how you saw the killer but didn't see his face."

"He had on a gas mask," she said. "So I couldn't see his features at all. But I saw part of his hair."

"A gas mask? Why?"

"Partly to hide his identity, I'm sure. But he also threw a smoke bomb through the window of my house before he came in and started shooting."

Brian winced. "Holy crap."

"So let's cut to the chase," Max said.

"But I wasn't there last night. I can't tell you anything. Why did you come here?"

"Because Claire's murder confirms what we told you yesterday. So far, everyone who has been killed was at that party at your house. The same party where Gary Anderson shot at Craig Pendergast."

"Christ, I never should have invited anyone over when my parents were out of town. I only asked a few friends, and then the news of the party spread around the school."

"We all do stupid stuff when we're teenagers. You know I did," Max said, probably trying to reassure Brian that they weren't blaming him for anything that had happened. "And you didn't know anyone was going to end up dead."

"You were going to get us a list of the people who were at the party. Did you start working on it, or did you forget about it?" Olivia asked, wondering if she and Max were playing good cop, bad cop, or alternating the roles.

Brian reddened. "I didn't actually get to it. I mean, I didn't think anyone was going to get killed last night."

"Let's try to do it together," Olivia suggested.

Brian gave her a grateful look. "Good idea."

She came around to his side of the desk, where she could see his computer screen, and he opened a notepad and started listing people. She added names, and it gave her the shivers to see how many of those people were dead.

"Is there anything else you can tell us about what happened that night?" Max pressed.

"Like what?"

"Something illegal. Something to do with sex or drugs? I don't know, but I think there was something else going on"

Brian was silent.

"Do you know about kids going up to the cabin up by Wilkins Dam?"

Brian's gaze swung toward Olivia, then away.

"So you know something about it?" Max asked in a hard voice.

"There was some talk." Olivia waited, her breath shallow. Was Max going to ask, "Are you the guy who drove her there the day she was raped?" But he didn't put the question to Brian, and neither man said anything specific about her.

"So maybe something happened the night of the party—something that maybe kept going up at the cabin where there was more privacy. Olivia said most people cleared out after the shooting at the party. Did anyone stick around?"

Brian swiped his hand through his hair. "Okay, there is something. After most people left, Troy and Tommy were still there talking about how Gary fucked up their plans."

"Troy Masters and Tommy Larson," Max said.

"Yes."

"After the party broke up, they said they weren't ready to call it a night. Because it was Cinco de Mayo. A night to celebrate. I think both of them had been hoping for some action." He looked at Olivia again, then away.

"Troy wanted to give me and Angela a ride," Olivia whispered. "I wonder where we would have ended up if we'd gotten into his car. Not at home, I'll bet."

"So what happened next?" Max prompted.

"Troy said he knew where they could get some women—down on Baltimore Street."

"The Baltimore red light district," Olivia said.

Brian nodded. "And they left."

"And that was the end of it?" Max asked.

"Well, the next time I saw Troy, I asked him how it went, and he was evasive. I got the feeling something happened down there that he didn't want to talk about."

When Brian didn't answer the question about the boys' trip into Baltimore, Max pressed, "And Tommy didn't tell you either?"

"No."

Max nodded. "Okay, knowing they went down there is helpful."

Brian shook his head. "It isn't much."

"It's a lead." He cleared his throat. "Claire's death changes things."

"Why?"

"Well, actually that started with Angela. Until then, the killer was stealthy. He made sure nobody knew the previous deaths were murders. Then he came out and strangled Angela. And last night he lured Claire to

Olivia's house so he could kill them both. With a gun. He's not trying to conceal his moves."

"But what's his motive for killing class members?" Brian pressed. "I mean, we graduated ten years ago. Why now?"

"That's the tricky part. It's not like we can draw an arrow to any one motive—unless it's directly related to Gary. Until we come up with more information, we can only speculate. And that makes him more dangerous. If you want some advice, I'd get out of town for a few days."

"I was already thinking about that."

"The guy who killed Claire is out of control. It's like he's trying to wipe the slate clean, and he's getting reckless."

"Yeah."

"So get out of his way for a few days."

"And you'll have it cleared up by then?" Brian asked sarcastically. "When the cops are still standing around holding their..." He stopped and glanced at Olivia. "Sorry, I'm on edge."

"We all are."

"I think things are moving fast," Max said. He looked at Olivia. "Come on, we've got something we can work with."

They left the office, glancing at Ms. Holiday as they passed her desk. She gave them a questioning look.

"Bring your boss a glass of water," Max said. "Or if he keeps liquor in the office, he might want something stronger."

Before she could comment, they exited the office, neither one of them speaking again until they'd climbed into Max's SUV and closed the doors.

"How does what he said about their going down to Baltimore help us?" she asked. "I mean, if they visited a prostitute, it could be anyone."

"Yeah, but I used to work vice down there, and I have some contacts among the working girls. Some of them worked as informants for me."

"Oh."

"Let's start by looking for some of my old contacts."

"But like Brian said, whatever happened with Troy and Tommy was ten years ago."

"Right. But it may be memorable enough to find out what happened." He drummed his fingers on the wheel. "I told Brian he was in danger. Now I'm thinking I should leave you with Shane and Jack."

"No," she answered instantly.

"Why not?"

"Because I want to see this thing through. And I'm not going to be any safer with them than I am with you."

"You'd be out of the action."

"I was the one who called you in the first place. And I'm not going to hide in a closet while you're out investigating."

He sighed. "Okay, I get that. But we're going into a rough neighborhood. Stay close to me and keep your head down."

She expected him to pull out of the parking space. Instead he pulled out his phone and dialed. When someone answered, she could tell he was talking to his partners.

"Olivia and I have some new information. We're going down to Baltimore to follow a lead."

In answer to a question, he conveyed what Brian had said.

After listening to the reaction on the other end of the

line, he said, "Olivia wants to go along, but I figured I'd better clue you in to our location."

Again he listened, and she saw his expression change. "Good. Keep me posted."

"What?" she asked when he'd hung up.

"The results came back on the DNA."

She leaned toward him. "They know who it was who strung that barbed wire in the woods? Then we don't have to go down to Baltimore after all."

He sighed. "I wish it were that simple. The DNA from the blood on the shirt was good enough to type. But that doesn't mean we know who the guy is."

When she looked confused, he explained it to her. "It can be identified as one particular individual. Now Shane is hoping a friend of his in the Montgomery PD will do a search of the Maryland criminal database. But even if his friend will do it, the perp might not have a record. So we'll stick to our original plan unless he calls back with a name we can take to the bank."

"Okay. I get it."

He drove out of the parking lot and headed for I-95, then turned north and into the city.

Olivia cleared her throat. "Thanks for not saying any more about what happened at the cabin."

"I understand why you don't want anyone to know about it—besides whoever already knows. And it looks like there are fewer of them than there used to be."

She winced.

"I don't think Brian was at the cabin," he said, and she knew he was trying to reassure her. "But I get the feeling that if he heard stuff about what happened in Baltimore after the party, he might also have heard about the cabin."

"And that really could put him in danger, which means we did him a favor."

"If he takes our advice."

"You said the killer is deteriorating," she said.

"Until recently he's been very cagey. He never killed in the same way. He made sure it would be hard to connect the dots on the murders."

"I connected them."

"You're smart. And you were on the edge of the action. You probably had a feeling there was something going on, but you couldn't quite put it together—partly because it involved incidents you wanted to forget about."

"Yes," she murmured.

"Back to the killer. For ten years, he was very clever. Now he's doing stuff that's going to get him caught."

"Maybe he doesn't see it that way."

"If not, I'd say his judgment is going. Did he really need to kill Claire?"

"I don't know what she knew about him—if anything. But she was at the party. And maybe she was up at the cabin, too," she added in a low voice.

Max reached across the console and laid his hand over hers. They both knew "up at the cabin" was shorthand for what had happened to Olivia up there. Had Claire also been raped?

Olivia turned her palm up, knitting her fingers with Max's, and he drove with one hand on the wheel for a few moments.

"Or it could be she had nothing to do with any of it," Olivia said. "He could have looked around for someone who he could drive crazy—then used her to get to me. Either way, she's dead."

"And it's not your fault," Max added.

"I know, but I can't help feeling like I could have saved her."

"How? Knocked her out cold and dragged her out of the house? And then what? The guy still had his gun."

They rode in silence into the city. Olivia hadn't been in downtown Baltimore in a long time, and she looked around at some of the new office buildings and condos. Then after a while, she began to notice that they were in a rundown neighborhood. The streets were pocked with potholes. The sidewalks were cracked and littered with trash.

And the housing was all narrow Baltimore row houses, some with redbrick fronts, some with vinyl siding, and some with the ugly formstone that had become popular in the fifties. Most of them also had the famous marble steps that were a hallmark of the city. And a few sported the window screens painted with outdoor scenes, the likes of which Olivia had never seen anywhere else.

There were people on the streets. She saw a few children playing and a few moms watching them. But there were more residents that didn't fit the family mold. Young men in baggy jeans and T-shirts were huddled on some of the corners, and women strolled around wearing revealing costumes like low-cut tops and skirts up to their crotches.

Olivia turned to Max. "Am I seeing drug deals go down—and prostitutes strutting their stuff?"

"Yeah."

She clasped her hands together as she watched the depressing scenery roll past. She'd lived in the Baltimore area until she graduated from high school, and she'd never seen this part of the city. Probably farmer Winters and his wife had never seen it, either. It was as removed from rural Howard County as the Middle East was from Switzerland. "And you spent a lot of time down here?" she asked Max.

"Yeah."

"Is that how you got shot?"

"Uh-huh. But it's more dangerous at night. We should be okay now."

He had slowed, and she saw him look toward a townhouse where the first floor had been converted into a bar called Down and Dirty.

"Some of my contacts used to hang out there." He turned toward her. "And now I'm wishing I'd insisted that you stay home."

"I'll be fine."

He looked like he wanted to say more, but he must have decided there was no point in arguing about something that they couldn't change. Instead he turned the corner and drove slowly down the block. When he found a parking space between a pickup truck and a motorcycle, he pulled in and turned to her.

"I know how these people think. Let me do the talking."

"Of course. I wouldn't know what to say."

He reached across her, unlocked the glove compartment and took out an automatic pistol, checked the safety, and tucked the weapon into the waistband under the light jacket he was wearing.

"I thought you said we'd be okay in daylight," she said.

"Down here, it's best to be prepared."

He stayed close to her as they walked back along the cracked sidewalk to Down and Dirty.

Max pushed the door open, and they both paused as the atmosphere hit them with an almost physical force. Inside, the room was dimly lit, the air was heavy with cigarette smoke and the smell of beer, and loud music played on an old-fashioned jukebox. Immediately, Olivia's eyes began to water.

"I thought it was illegal to smoke in a bar in Maryland," she whispered.

"It is."

"But…"

"It's not worth the trouble to send cops to enforce that kind of law. And nobody in here is complaining."

Olivia was. She hadn't breathed so much smoke since— well probably since some of those high school parties.

She peered through the thick air, seeing that the bar was lined with both men and women, and many of the wooden tables and chairs were also occupied. Apparently it was a popular place for people who had nothing else to do in the middle of the day.

Max had adopted a casual stance as he also looked around the room.

A woman with ratty blond hair at one of the tables saw him, did a double take, and got up. She headed toward them, her hips swaying. From her skimpy outfit, she looked to be in her late thirties or early forties, until Olivia got a look at her face, which was so lined that it was impossible for her to put her makeup on smoothly.

She spared Olivia a quick glance, then dismissed her and focused on Max.

"As I live and breathe, Max Lyon. I heard you were dead."

"I'm hard to kill, Tonya."

"Haven't seen you in ages, lover boy."

Chapter 22

THE SUGGESTIVE TONE OF THE GREETING MADE Max's stomach clench, but he figured Tonya was doing it for Olivia's benefit. He and the prostitute had never been intimate, but she'd been one of his best informants. And he'd tried to take care of her, giving her some protection and also paying her well for the information she supplied. He hadn't seen her since he'd gone off the job, and she looked like she'd aged ten years in the meantime. Unfortunately, that was often the way with working girls. The profession took an enormous toll, particularly for the ones who plied their trade out on the street. They were vulnerable to beatings and disease. They were often on drugs. And forget proper nutrition.

He noted that the woman's hair was a tangle of bleached blond ringlets around her head, and her tight dress barely covered the intimate parts of her body. She gave Olivia a casual glance, then switched her total attention back to Max.

"Long time no see," she drawled.

"I've been busy."

"What are you doin' slumming now?"

"I *was* shot. After I recovered, I switched from the force to a PI agency. I'm on a case." He gestured toward Olivia. "Ms. Winters hired us."

Tonya gave Olivia a second look. "Don't I know you?"

Max had told Olivia he'd do the talking, but when she gave him a quick look, he nodded.

"I do some modeling," she said in a low voice.

"Yeah, that's right. And now you want to find out how the other half lives?"

Olivia shook her head. "No. My best friend was murdered, and I need Max to figure out who did it." It wasn't exactly true. She and Angela had grown apart since high school, but she figured the best friend part would have some impact.

Tonya snorted. "And I'll bet the cops are useless."

Olivia nodded in agreement. "It looks like it."

Max had let the women talk for a few moments. Now he jumped back into the conversation. "Honey, you're not saying I was useless when I used to work down here, are you?"

"Not you, baby. But most of 'em, you know."

"I'm hoping you can help me solve a puzzle we've run into."

"Like what?"

"Let's sit down, and I'll buy you a drink."

She flicked a glance at Olivia. "And then we can have a hot threesome?"

When Olivia drew in a quick breath, Tonya cackled. "Relax, darling, I know Max is too much of a straight arrow for anything like that. He had plenty of opportunities to get into trouble down here, but he never took advantage of them."

"Thanks for the vote of confidence," he murmured. "Why don't we go back to your table, if that's okay?"

"Sure."

She threaded her way through the crowd, and Max

reached for Olivia's hand as they followed. She held on to him with a tight grip, and he was pretty sure she was rethinking her decision to come slumming with him, especially since several rough-looking guys were eyeing her with interest.

Back at the table, Tonya plopped into a seat, and Max and Olivia followed suit. He knew some of the other people in the bar remembered him from his days on the vice squad, but they also knew he'd disappeared from the force. And they would follow the unspoken rule of minding their own business, unless their self-interest was involved.

"How about that drink?" Tonya said.

"Sure."

"Champagne."

He laughed. "Nice try. How about your old favorite, a shot of Jack Daniels with a beer chaser."

"Fair enough."

He looked at Olivia. "You want your usual?"

She blinked, then nodded.

"Will you girls be okay alone for a few minutes?"

When they both said yes, he recrossed the room, standing half turned away from the bar so he could keep an eye on them while he ordered the bourbon and a beer chaser for Tonya and soda water with ice for himself and Olivia. Asking for a tray, he carried the drinks back to the table and discovered that the women were talking about hair products. Good for Olivia.

Tonya downed her Jack Daniels, then sipped the beer while he and Olivia both took a sip of the soda water.

When Tonya had drunk half her beer, Max said, "Olivia told you her best friend was murdered. But it wasn't just her. There are others who also bought the farm. Most of those people were at a certain party. It broke up because one of the guys got reckless and shot off a gun."

The working girl winced. "He killed someone?"

"Actually, no," Max said. "But he screwed up the party scene, and two of the guys weren't ready to call it a night. We've heard that they came down here and that something bad happened."

"When was this?" Tonya asked.

"In the spring." Max named the date.

The informant laughed. "Oh come on. And you expect me to remember something that happened down here ten years ago?"

"Not under ordinary circumstances," Max agreed. "But in this case, I think it was something memorable. Something people were talking about. Something that would stick in your mind—if you knew about it."

Tonya leaned back in her chair, thinking, and he was pretty sure she did have some information—which she wasn't going to give up for free. "Something very bad," she mused.

"Yeah."

"Like murder?"

Max let the words hang in the air.

She looked around, like the people at the other tables might be listening to the conversation. As far as Max could see, they were all absorbed in their own business.

When he didn't say more, she filled the silence. "I can't give out information like that for free."

"I understand." He got out his wallet and pulled out two fifties, which he passed across the table.

She took the money and tucked it into the purse that hung from her shoulder. "You want me to tell you about a murder for a hundred dollars," she said.

He added another fifty. "You know something. Tell us what it is."

"I did hear something, but secondhand, you know. It's Julie who'll be able to tell you more."

"Who is Julie?"

"The gal who didn't get killed, you know."

"What does that mean?"

"You'll have to ask her about it."

"Can she come here?"

"Not likely. She's in a bad way, but I can take you to her," Tonya said.

"A bad way?"

"She's sick. With some lung thing."

Max weighed his options. Likely he was going to have to pay this Julie, too. It might turn out to be a wild-goose chase, but if the woman really did know what had happened after the party, this could be their big break.

"Let's go," he said.

Tonya stood. "Sure. It's quicker if we go the back way."

They followed her down the hall, past the kitchen and the restrooms, through a door, and into an alley that smelled of cheap whiskey and garbage. Max drew his gun and held it down by his side as they proceeded along the uneven pavement, then crossed a narrow street and continued up the alley. The trash was thicker here, and the backyards of the row houses were walled off by board or chain-link fences, many of which looked like they could have been pushed over by a strong wind.

Olivia glanced at him, and he gave her a reassuring look. Tonya might seem like she would do anything for money, but she'd always been straight with him. Besides, she hadn't known he was going to step back into her life, and she hadn't gone off to make a phone call before leading them out of the bar. Still, he wished again that Olivia were tucked safely away.

Tonya paused at one of the backyard gates, pushed it open, and led the way into a narrow yard with patches of scraggly grass lining a sidewalk leading to a back stoop. When she knocked at the door, there was a pause before the blinds were pulled aside.

When the person inside saw Tonya, the door swung open. An older woman in a dressing gown looked from Tonya to Max and Olivia.

"Who's this?"

"People who want to talk to Julie."

"About what?"

"That night ten years ago."

The way she said it clued Max in that something significant had happened back then.

"This is Marge," Tonya said.

"Max and Olivia."

Nobody said nice to meet you, because it was clear the circumstances were far from nice.

"She's been sleeping a lot. She may not be awake," Marge said.

"It's important," Max said.

Marge gave them a long look. "Nobody cares about a broken-down old whore."

"We do."

"A lot of good it's going to do her now."

"This has to do with some recent murders. And it may go back to Julie."

The woman at the door thought about that, then stepped aside.

They walked into a small, dimly lit kitchen, and he was surprised to see that it was neat and clean, although the linoleum on the floor was worn and the appliances looked like they were thirty years out of date. Turning, he saw that Tonya had not come in with them. In fact, when he looked out the back window, he saw her hurrying away.

"This way."

They followed the woman through the kitchen, along the end of a small, shabby sitting room to a stairway, then up to a second floor landing. There were four doors, all closed, and she led them to the one on the right.

"Just a minute."

Marge went inside and was gone for several moments. Then she opened the door again and motioned them inside, where Max caught the odor of sickness and saw a woman lying on a narrow bed. A low light on a bedside table gave a small amount of illumination, and Max could see the woman in the bed was small and shrunken, with paper-white skin and thinning dark hair hanging around her shoulders. She looked up when she saw the people in the doorway.

"Who are you?" she asked.

"We're hoping you can give us some information," Max said.

"I don't know nothin'."

"About the two boys who came down here ten years ago. I think it's something you remember."

She winced, and he gathered from her reaction that she knew exactly what he was talking about, even after all these years.

"Please," Olivia said. "My best friend was murdered a few weeks ago. And there are other murders, too. We're trying to find out how it's related. We're hoping you can piece it together for us."

"Let me sit up." The woman on the bed tried and failed to push herself up. Marge came forward, lifted her narrow shoulders up, and propped the pillows behind her.

Just moving that much seemed to exhaust Julie, and she leaned back with her eyes closed.

Finally she opened them and focused on Olivia. "I don't know who they were," she said. "I never knew."

"Just tell us what happened."

"It was two boys. From the suburbs, I think. They had a flashy car and a lot of money."

"What kind of car?" Max asked.

"I don't know much about cars. I just know it was red and sporty." She stopped talking and started to cough, and it was several moments before Max could ask her another question.

"How old were they?"

"Late teens, probably. School boys."

"High school or college?"

"I'd say high school."

"Why? There are a lot of colleges in town."

"Yeah, and the college guys are more sophisticated."

"Okay."

He and Olivia exchanged glances. So far, it fit, but it could have been any two boys.

"Troy had a sporty red car," Olivia said, sotto voce.

He nodded, then turned back to the woman on the
bed. "Okay. And what did they do?"

"Pammy and me was on the corner with some of the
other girls. The two boys in the car stopped and asked
who wanted to party. They looked like they were okay,
and a lot of the girls said they did, but they picked me
and Pammy." She paused, closed her eyes and rested for
a moment before going on. "They took us to a motel out
near Security Square. You know where that is?"

"Yes," Olivia answered.

"It was a double room with two beds." She turned her
head away. "We thought they were nice suburban kids,
but they wanted to play rough. They wanted to tie us up,
and we didn't like that idea, but they offered us a lot of
money, so we agreed.

"They tied each of us to one of the beds, and they
started doing stuff to us. And one of them got too rough.
He had his hands around Pammy's throat, choking her.
And he did it too hard." She said the last part with a little
sob. "He choked her to death while he was fucking her."

Olivia gasped. Max reached for her hand.

"How did you get away?" he asked.

"The one who strangled her was upset. Not because
he had killed her, but because he thought he was going
to get caught. He told the other guy he had to help get
rid of the evidence. He said she was just a whore and
nobody would be looking for her. They wrapped her in
the bedspread and took her outside, and they left me tied
to the bed."

She stopped and gave Olivia a pleading look. "And
I knew that if they came back and I was still there, they
were going to kill me, too, because I was a witness. So

I struggled and I tugged like a mad woman, and I got one hand free, then the other. They had said they'd pay us big, and they'd left five hundred dollars beside the TV. I pulled on my clothes, took the money, and climbed out the bathroom window. Then I ran like the devil to a truck stop. I got a trucker to give me a ride back into the city, and I hid out. My friends helped me keep under cover, and I stayed out of sight for a long time. I think those boys was looking for me. But nobody told where I was, even when one of them waved money around."

"So a lot of people knew about it?" Max said.

"Yes. But nobody told," she said again, and lapsed into another coughing fit.

"Like the gunshot at the party," Olivia whispered when the room was quiet again.

"What?" Julie asked.

"Somebody shot off a gun at the party where they started out," Olivia said. "The party broke up, and that's why they came into town."

"Just my luck." She laughed and started to cough again.

"You're wearing her out," Marge said in a stern voice, then turned to Julie. "You need to lie down again, honey."

"No, it's okay. Resting ain't gonna do me much good, and we both know it."

Marge sat on the side of the bed and took Julie's hand.

"Why didn't you go to the police?" Olivia asked.

"You think they'd believe the word of a whore over two fine upstanding kids from the suburbs?" she answered. "Besides, I didn't even know who they was."

Max wanted to say there would have been DNA evidence in the room, but there was no point in going back over it now. It was in the past, and nobody was going to convict Troy. Or was it Tommy Larson?

"Can you tell us what they looked like?" he asked.

"Like I said, they were both young. Good bodies. Dark hair."

"Anything that would identify them?"

"I didn't think so. And all I wanted was to get myself out of there." She started coughing again. "For all the good that did. Look at me now. I never had a good life after that. I was always looking over my shoulder. I should have got out of town, but where would I have gone? The only friends I knew were here, and they were good to me." She looked at Marge. "They're still good to me."

"You just rest up, honey," Marge said, then looked at the visitors. "I think you've asked her enough questions."

"I'm sorry. Just a few more," Max said. "Can you tell me if there was anything special about that night? About the date, maybe."

Max's breath was shallow as he waited to see if she'd give him the clue he wanted to hear.

"The date," she mused, and her expression changed. "One of them told us it was Cinco de Mayo."

Olivia and Max exchanged glances.

Julie was still speaking. "And we didn't know what that meant. They told us it was May fifth, a big celebration day in Mexico. Does that help?"

"Yes it does," Max said.

When Marge gave them a pointed look, they stepped into the hall.

"Is this your home?" Max asked.

"Yes. And I take in friends who need a place to stay."

Max dug out his wallet again and pulled out five hundred dollar bills. "This isn't much, but I hope it will help," he said.

"Thank you. Yes it does," the other woman said, then added, "I should have told you, you can't talk about Julie or about this house. I could get busted for operating a nursing home without a license. Julie isn't the only sick woman here."

"We understand," Max said.

When Julie started coughing again, Max said, "Go back in. There's one more thing I need to ask her, but it will take me a minute to set it up."

Marge gave him a questioning look. "I can show her their pictures. From the Donley yearbook. It's online."

When Marge went back into the room, Olivia looked at Max. "The yearbook is online?"

"Yes. A lot of them are these days. Even real old ones. Sometimes the school does it, or someone in the class scans it in and makes it available to anyone who's curious."

He got out his phone and began scrolling through material.

"We're just going to show them Troy and Tommy's pictures?"

"No. We're going to do it the right way." He began downloading yearbook pictures, and she saw Brian, Gary, Patrick, Tommy, Troy, Joe Gibson, and several other boys, some of whom hadn't been at the party.

Olivia looked at them. "Like a time machine," she murmured.

"Yeah. We don't have to worry about their looking different. These pictures were probably taken a few months before the party."

When Marge came back into the hall, Max showed her the phone. "We're hoping it's two of them. Can we have a few more minutes with her?"

"If you're quick."

Max and Olivia went back into the room. Julie was propped up in bed, looking expectantly at them.

Max squatted beside the bed. "These are some boys who could be the ones. I'm going to show them to you one at a time, and you tell me if it's one of them."

As he began scrolling through the pictures, Olivia waited with her breath frozen in her lungs.

When Julie gasped, every muscle in Olivia's body tensed.

"Him," she whispered.

"You're sure?" He glanced at Olivia. "Troy."

"I couldn't forget that sickening smirk. He thought he had it made, that he could do any damn thing he wanted to anyone he wanted."

Max began scrolling through the pictures again, and once again Julie stopped him.

"That one."

It was Tommy.

"And you're sure about him, too?"

"Not as sure," she conceded. "But I think so."

"I know this was hard for you, but you've been a tremendous help," Olivia said. "Thank you so much."

"It wasn't hard. I hope you can make them pay—after all these years."

They thanked her again and stepped back into the hall.

"I hope you won't tell anyone about Julie or this place," Marge said.

"Of course not," Olivia answered.

"Then she can't be a witness."

"We don't need her for that. One of these guys is still murdering people. We just have to figure out which one," Max said.

―――∽∽∽―――

Downstairs, Marge went into the kitchen, and Olivia whispered to Max, "We can't prove it was Troy or Tommy. And we promised that Julie wouldn't have to get officially involved."

"But we've got some pretty good evidence. She identified them. She confirmed the party date. I think we need to proceed on the assumption that the murderer is one of them."

"And what—get a confession?"

"It may be too late to tie him to Pammy's murder, but there will be evidence at his house connecting him to the current murders."

"There's still the question of a motive," she said. "I could see killing Gary because in a twisted killer's mind, he could somehow blame Gary for breaking up Brian's party and therefore 'causing' the hooker's murder. But why Angela and Claire? And why is he after me?"

"It's all speculation at this point," Max answered. "I mean there's no way to know for sure yet. But we have to assume this guy is into cleaning up messes by eliminating witnesses. He wants anyone who could testify to what happened after the party out of the picture. And if he was raping classmates up at the cabin, he wants all those witnesses gone, too."

"But why now? Why ten years later?"

"Because he's afraid that the reunion is stirring up memories—like it did for you." Max gave her a direct look. "Maybe Patrick tried to blackmail him. Maybe Gary did, and he got rid of those threats early on. But I can't get into the mind of a twisted killer. Let's hope we take him alive, and he can tell us."

"You think the police might not take him alive?"

"The way he's acting, he might force the cops to take him out, if he's desperate enough. Or if his plans aren't working out."

The conversation was cut short when Max's cell phone rang, and he saw that it was Shane on the other end of the line.

"Yeah?" he asked.

"We got a DNA match on that blood sample," his friend said.

"You mean the name?"

The confirmation, Olivia thought. Then she heard Shane say, "Right. But it's not who you think."

Chapter 23

TODAY THE MAN WHO HAD KILLED CLAIRE LOWDEN was calling himself the Masked Avenger because the name amused him. He'd always given himself clever names. In high school and college, he'd been the Wonder Boy. Sometimes he was the Bondage Master. Other times he was the Business Whiz. For this mission the Masked Avenger worked best. Not that he was avenging wrongs against society like Spider-Man or some dumb superhero from a comic book. This was his own private vengeance. Only it hadn't gone the way he'd planned. He had come to Olivia Winters's house thinking he would leave a dead woman behind and take Olivia with him. He'd killed Claire, the weak one. But she was only a means to an end.

He slapped his hand against the steering wheel. "Fuck," he muttered. "Fuck, fuck, fuck."

Olivia and that son of a bitch of a private detective had vanished. They could have left the area, but he didn't think so. They were too hot to track him down. But they couldn't go back to Olivia's house because it was a crime scene. He laughed. And also a wreck, what with that broken window and the stink from the smoke bomb all over the place. Which probably meant that they were staying in a hotel or motel in the county.

He'd cruised the parking lots of all the likely places, and he hadn't seen the bastard's SUV.

He wanted to scream, but he had to keep himself under control. When he realized his hands were shaking, he gripped the wheel, centering himself. Forcing the panic down, he took a couple of deep breaths. Everything was under control again. He'd hit upon a better approach—using the cops.

He'd started by calling the police station on a burner phone and saying he had some important information about the murder at the Winters' farm. He'd been in the vicinity, and he needed to talk to the police about what he'd seen. They'd put him through to the detective investigating the case who had answered the phone, "Archie Hamilton." As soon as the guy had identified himself, the Masked Avenger had hung up.

He smiled to himself. Once he'd gotten the guy's name, he'd gotten his picture too. Then he'd parked down the street from the police station with the local and national reporters staking out the place.

When Hamilton left, he would follow him, hoping for a lead on Winters and Lyon. And if not, he'd find out what the fat guy knew.

Meanwhile, he pulled his cap lower over his eyes, eased back the seat of his car, and relaxed as he thought about the string of murders he'd pulled off—starting with that dumb prostitute down in Baltimore. It always helped him relax to think about his successes. The misfire at the Winters' farm was only a temporary setback.

He'd get Olivia. And Brian Cannon would be next.

His mind drifted back to the Baltimore whore. When he'd taken her and her friend to that cheap motel, he'd been the Bondage Master. He wasn't even sure now that he'd intended to kill her. Maybe he'd only wanted to see how far he could go. But once he'd gotten his hands around her throat, he hadn't been able to stop himself from squeezing harder and harder.

The guy who'd gone to Baltimore with him had been scared—especially after the other girl had gotten away and stolen their money, to boot. The Masked Avenger had assured his partner the girl wouldn't tell on them. And he'd been right about that. There had been absolutely no blowback. It was his first murder success. And the whore must have left town, because he'd never seen or heard of her again—even though he'd tried to hunt her down.

He hadn't worried that his friend would tell anyone what had happened that night. The guy had been just as guilty as the Avenger—at least according to the law, and he wasn't going to screw himself up for something another guy had done.

Knowing he could kill without getting caught had energized the Avenger. But he hadn't done it again for a few years, not until after college. Then finally he'd gotten tired of paying off Patrick Morris. Patrick was blackmailing him, not because he knew about the Baltimore murders but because he knew about the stuff that had gone on at the cabin near the dam. He'd threatened to talk, and the Avenger had fixed his furnace so it would dump carbon monoxide into the guy's house.

A year later, he'd gone after Gary Anderson to settle an old score. Gary had ruined the party that night at Brian's. It was appropriate to make him pay for that.

He'd lain low for a few years, enjoying his cushy lifestyle and thinking that what had happened in high school would stay in high school. And then he'd been jolted by an email about the ten-year reunion. It had brought back memories.

And if it did that for him, what about the people from the reunion class who could be a threat? Like Angela Dawson.

She'd kept quiet about the rapes up at the cabin. And so had Olivia and Claire. But what if they got together at the reunion, compared notes, and decided to talk?

His hands were damp now, and he wiped them on his pants legs.

"That's not gonna happen now," he muttered. "You've already stopped the bitches from talking to each other."

Doggedly, he focused on his biggest success again. Not money. Murder. If you had an issue with someone, there was an easy way to settle the beef. There were subtle ways to eliminate people who were in the way, but he'd strangled Angela because it was like a repetition of his first success. And he'd figured it was safe to do it that way because what did it matter—nobody was going to suspect him. After that, he'd started having some fun with Claire. Like why not drive her crazy before he killed her?

Then he'd realized she was the perfect tool to use when he needed to get to Olivia after she'd hired that bastard detective to solve the murders.

There was no chance of that, of course. The guy was too stupid to finger the Masked Avenger. Look how easy it had been to lure Lyon away from the Winters' farm. And it was probably dumb luck that he'd figured out the ploy and come racing back.

His mind was spinning with plans now. It would be safer to kill Lyon, too. Either before or after he did Olivia. However it worked out.

And then there was the Avenger's friend. The guy who'd gone to Baltimore with him. Maybe Angela's murder and the incident at the Winters' farm had made him nervous. Maybe he could guess who had done those bitches. And maybe he had to be eliminated, too. Just in case.

A lot of dead people were piling up. That might have worried the Avenger. But now he knew he was invincible. He'd gotten away every time—even from the farmhouse. And he was going to keep getting away.

Except that suddenly he felt the edge of panic creeping in on him. Gritting his teeth, he pushed it away. He would stay calm. And focused. And he would win—because he always had.

Olivia heard Max swear.

"What?" she asked.

"The DNA," Max answered, then turned on the speaker so she could hear better.

"Who is it?"

"Either of you know someone named Damon Davidson?"

Confused, Olivia shook her head.

"Oh Christ," Max swore, and she knew from his reaction that the name meant something to him— something bad.

"Who is he?" she and Shane both said at the same time.

"He's a drug dealer I put away six years ago. He swore he was going to get even with me. He must have been released from Jessup, and I didn't even know it." He glanced at Olivia, his expression grim. "He must have started checking up on me, found out I'd be at your house, and booby-trapped the woods. "

"So it wasn't connected with the murders," Olivia breathed.

"Right. And before anything else happens, I'm taking you to…"

"The Rockfort Security safe house," Shane finished. "Do you want me to come down there and pick Olivia up?"

"That would just take more time," Max answered. "I want her out of Baltimore right now. We'll meet you at the safe house. But if he's following me, it may take some time to lose him."

"Okay," Shane answered and clicked off.

Max paused in the living room, looking to the front of the house, then the rear, and back again.

"I said it looked like whoever was at the farm the night of the reunion meeting was after me, but I thought it was connected with the case. I didn't think I was actually the target."

"You couldn't know."

"Maybe I should have kept tabs on Davidson."

"Oh come on. How many guys who said they were going to get you followed through?"

"None until now," he bit out. "Just your luck it had to be this guy."

He cursed under his breath as he looked toward the front door, then the back. "And for all we know, he could have followed us here."

Marge came back from the kitchen, taking in the tension crackling between them. "Trouble?" she asked.

"Sorry," Max said. "A guy I put away when I was

with the Baltimore PD is after me. And he could show up here." He looked at the older woman. "Do you have a gun?"

"Yes."

She walked to an end table, pulled out a revolver, and gave it to Max.

He checked to see that the weapon was loaded, then gave it to Olivia. "I'm going to get the car. You wait here. I'll go out the front and come back to the rear."

"Okay," she answered, and he knew she was struggling to keep her voice steady. They'd been making certain assumptions, and they'd thought they knew the identity of the killer—or at least one of two guys. Now it turned out that someone else entirely had come to the farm the other night.

"Stay inside until I pull up in the alley," he said.

She reached for him and tugged him toward her, and they clung together for a long moment.

Finally he eased away. "The sooner we get out of here, the better."

"Be careful."

"I will," Max answered as he stepped to the window and inspected the street. It was dark now, and everything was quiet. All he had to do was make it to his car and come back for Olivia.

He was angry with himself for letting her talk him into bringing her into this part of the city. But he was going to get her to safety. He'd leave one of the other guys with her at the safe house.

Then he and Jack or Shane would split up. One would stay with Olivia. One would go after Troy Masters, and the other would pay a call on Tommy Larson. The reunion killer was one of them, he was sure, even if he didn't know why the killing had continued over the years and sped up recently. His best guess was that the guy was coming unglued, but there was no way to know for sure until they caught him.

He saw Olivia's anxious gaze on him as he eased the door open and stepped into the dark. He stayed close to the house for several moments, then started down the block, intending to circle around to where he'd left his SUV.

He made it about twenty yards down the sidewalk when a figure leaped out from the darkened passageway between two row houses.

Max caught only a flash of movement, then someone was on him. A hot pain slashed into his arm through his shirt and jacket, and he knew he had been cut.

"You son of a bitch," his assailant called as he tried for another strike. But Max twisted to the side and grabbed the man's knife hand, forcing it back toward him. The man gasped as the blade dug into his side.

He'd cut the bastard, but he didn't know how badly.

It must be Davidson. The ex-con had been following them, then hid out in a passageway between two row houses, ready to move to the back or the front as soon as Max came out. Thank God Olivia was still inside.

His arm was on fire, but his own stab at the guy must have done some damage too because Davidson was less enthusiastic about the attack now. Max managed to knock him to the ground. Too bad he didn't carry handcuffs anymore.

The guy struggled up, looking like was going to run instead of fight, just as a shot rang out. Both men went rigid. Then Davidson wrenched away and ran, and Max fell back against a lamppost. Looking up, he saw Olivia charge down the steps toward him, Marge's revolver in her hand.

"Get back in the house," he called out, but she ignored him and hurried toward him.

"You shot…"

"Into the air," she finished. Craning her neck, she looked in the direction where the man had disappeared. "Was that Davidson or a mugger?"

"Davidson."

"Too bad I couldn't shoot at him," she answered, "but he was too close to you."

Max stayed where he was, leaning against the lamppost, glad of the support. He knew he was going into shock, and he hated having Olivia see him that way.

"Max?" she asked softly.

"Um."

"You're hurt."

She knelt beside him on the sidewalk. When she looked at his arm, she gasped.

This time he wasn't going to argue that it was "nothing," because he felt the blood soaking his shirt and jacket.

Olivia eased the jacket off. It was made of light material, and she used it to make a tourniquet above the cut.

Marge had rushed out onto the sidewalk. She was carrying a blanket, which Olivia tucked around Max.

"I called 911," the older woman said. "An ambulance should be here soon."

"Thank you," Olivia breathed.

She sat beside him, and he closed his eyes. He should stay alert, but it was too much effort.

"Call Rockfort," he told Olivia.

"Yes." She grabbed his cell phone and called back the last number.

Shane answered. "Max?"

"No. It's Olivia," she said.

"Where's Max?" his partner asked, an edge in his voice.

Her hand tightened on the cell phone. "That Davidson guy was waiting for him with a knife. Max was cut. An ambulance is coming."

"You're still in Baltimore?"

"Yes."

"We're on our way. Do you know what hospital?"

"Not yet. I'll have to call you back," she answered, hearing the wail of a siren in the distance. As it grew louder, she was aware that people were coming down the street, curious about what had happened.

"Stay back," Marge cautioned. "Give him air."

The ambulance pulled up, and two paramedics jumped out, a man and a woman. They rolled a stretcher toward Max and got him onto the horizontal surface.

"He was cut in a knife fight," Olivia told them.

The man tended to his arm. The woman took his vital signs, then started an IV drip of clear liquid.

"What hospital are we going to?"

"Memorial," the woman answered.

"And I can go with him?"

"Yes."

While they got Max into the ambulance, she called the Rockfort men. "We're going to Memorial Hospital."

"Okay. We'll be there as soon as we can."

She climbed into the vehicle after the woman medic and sat down on one of the benches, reaching for Max's hand as they sped off toward the hospital.

He lay with his eyes closed, and she knew he was barely conscious.

"Cold," he whispered.

"Because you've lost a lot of blood. But you're going to be all right," she told him, praying it was true, because the alternative gave her cold chills.

The ride with the siren blaring couldn't have been long, but seemed to take forever. Finally, the ambulance pulled up at the emergency room door, and the medics wheeled Max inside.

"They've taken him right back because his condition is serious, but we need you to fill out some paperwork," the woman at the desk told Olivia.

"Like what?"

"The usual." She pushed a form toward Olivia, and she stared at the questions. She'd filled out many similar forms for herself, but never for anyone else. And as she read the boxes, she felt lost. She knew Max's name. She knew his occupation. And that was it. She didn't know his date of birth, his social security number, his medical insurance, or any of the other things this form wanted her to provide.

"Sorry," she told the receptionist, hating her ignorance on the subject of Max Lyon. "I don't know him well enough. You have to wait until his partners arrive."

The woman nodded. "Okay."

Olivia was too restless to sit down, and she was still pacing back and forth in the waiting room when Shane barreled through the door, spotted her, and hurried over. He gave her a quick hug, and she clung to him for a moment, then stepped away.

"How is he?" he asked.

"They haven't told me anything. He was cut, and he was pretty weak when they brought him in."

Shane waited while an elderly man in a wheelchair was checked in, then stepped up to the counter. "I want to know how Max Lyon is doing," he said.

"After you give us the insurance and personal information on him."

Olivia knew Shane was about to yell at the woman and put a hand on his arm.

He glanced at her, then sighed, and she saw him making an effort to get control of himself. "Okay."

Jack Brandt came in, and the two men worked on the form together, then turned it in.

Olivia didn't know what Shane said to the woman, but a few minutes later, a nurse came out to speak to them.

"He's doing much better," she said. "But we're keeping him for a few days. He's being transferred to the third floor in a while."

"Can we see him now?" Jack asked.

"Only two of you at a time."

"You of course," Shane said to Olivia.

"Thank you."

The two men glanced at each other.

"You go in," Jack said to his partner.

"Are you sure?" Shane asked.

"Go on. I'll have my turn later," Jack answered.

The nurse ushered her and Shane through the door to the working part of the emergency facility, where some patients were lying on beds in the wide hallway. On the far side of the nurses' station, Max was in a brightly lit treatment room.

Next to his bed was an IV stand with liquid running

into his right arm, only now the bag held blood instead of a clear liquid. And his left arm was bandaged where he'd been cut. The lower half of his body was covered by a sheet and blanket, but Olivia saw he was wearing one of those hospital gowns that opened in the back.

He looked up and smiled when he saw them, and she considered that a good sign.

"Looks like I'm going to make it," Max said.

Olivia crossed to him, bent down, and pressed her cheek against his. He moved his left arm, gripping her elbow, but she could tell it took a big effort.

"How do you feel?" she asked.

"Not too bad, considering."

"You get better," she murmured. "Jack's here too. But only two of us could come in."

He nodded.

"Davidson attacked you?" Shane asked.

"Yeah. And he got away, unfortunately."

"They're keeping you for a few days," Shane said.

"I want out of here," he said immediately. "We have two suspects, and we have to follow up."

"As soon as you're better," Shane answered.

They were interrupted as someone else strode into the room. It was Archie Hamilton, looking like he'd discovered them robbing a bank instead of gathering around a sickbed.

Max gave him a questioning look. "What are you doing here? This isn't your territory."

"But you're involved in my case. What happened to you?"

"I was cut."

"You mean because you were investigating the

Howard County murders when I told you to stay out of my way?"

"It didn't have anything to do with that," Olivia answered. "He was attacked by Damon Davidson."

"Who?"

"A drug dealer he put in prison. Davidson was released, and he came after Max," Shane replied.

The Howard County detective looked from one of them to the other. "And this happened in North Baltimore?" he said.

"Yeah," Max answered.

"And what were you doing there?"

Chapter 24

WHEN NEITHER MAX NOR OLIVIA ANSWERED, Hamilton made a snorting sound.

Olivia watched Max's eyes narrow as he focused on the detective. "Davidson got away. Maybe you and the Baltimore PD can cooperate on finding him."

"They probably don't want me interfering," Hamilton responded.

Switching the subject, Olivia asked, "Any progress on the reunion murders?"

"What do you mean, the reunion murders?"

"That's what we call them, because everyone who's been killed was in the Donley High School ten-year reunion class. What do you call them?"

"There is no 'them.'"

"It's just a coincidence that someone went after three women from the class? Only I escaped."

"Maybe not," Hamilton snapped, as he swung toward her. "Maybe it would help if you tell me what you know." My God, was he conceding that the murders were connected?

Olivia glanced at Max, who gave a small nod.

She dragged in a breath and let it out. "Okay, we think that the murderer is either Troy Masters or Tommy Larson—both of whom were in my class."

"And what makes you think so?" Hamilton asked.

"Because we talked to a working girl who says one

of them murdered her friend at a motel near Security Square ten years ago."

The detective kept his gaze fixed on her. "That's what you've got? Information on a ten-year-old murder that might not have even happened? I mean, do you really think that's credible?"

Olivia struggled for calm. When he put it that way, it didn't sound very convincing, but she couldn't tell Hamilton about the yearbook pictures because she'd given her word that she wouldn't drag Julie or Marge into this. "You could check it out," she said.

"What working girl?" Hamilton demanded.

Again Olivia was prevented from answering because of the promise to Margie.

"Well," Hamilton pressed.

"We can't tell you."

"Because you're just guessing," the detective snapped.

"No."

"If you want to help, give me some information I can use to solve this murder case."

"Check out Masters and Larson," Max said in a weary voice.

"You've just named two upstanding citizens—with no proof they're involved."

"Everyone who's died has been an upstanding citizen. Let's assume the killer fits right in," Olivia answered.

Hamilton turned to Max. "I guess this will keep you out of the action for a while," he said, then exited the room.

"Nice guy," Shane muttered sarcastically, then said, "We should let Jack have a turn visiting."

"Yes," Olivia agreed. She bent and kissed Max on the

cheek. "I'll be up to your room as soon as they tell me where they're taking you."

"You should let the guys take you to the safe house," he answered.

She shook her head. "You know I can't do that. I'd be climbing the walls."

He sighed. "I didn't think you'd agree."

She and Shane stepped into the hall and started back to the waiting room.

"Getting out of here would be the safest thing for you," Shane said.

"Not an option."

"Then one of us will be here while you are."

"Thanks."

In the waiting room, they met up with Jack and told him about Hamilton's visit.

"Yeah, I saw him come sailing in like he owned the place," he said. "Did he have any information on the murders?"

"No, he wanted to harass Max," Shane answered.

"How did Hamilton know we were here?" Olivia asked.

"I guess he's keeping tabs on you."

"I wish he'd keep tabs on Troy Masters and Tommy Larson."

"Maybe he will, but he's not going to share that information with you," Jack said.

"We can hope."

Jack went back to visit with Max, and Shane and Olivia took chairs in the waiting room.

"So you were down here looking for a witness to an old murder?" Shane asked.

Olivia told him about the visit to Julie and her

encounter with the two high school or college boys.

"And what hard evidence do you have that it was them?" Shane asked.

"Are you trying to outdo Hamilton?" she asked.

"I'm trying to find out why you're so sure it was one of those guys," Shane answered.

"Because the party was on Cinco de Mayo. And the murder was on Cinco de Mayo."

"That wouldn't stand up in court."

"Max also showed Julie pictures of some boys from the Donley class. She picked out Troy and Tommy," Olivia said.

"That's more like it."

"We promised not to involve her, but now that we've got something solid, we think we can figure out which one it is. And why. We still don't know what triggered this killing spree."

Shane nodded. "He's a good investigator."

She was grateful for the chance to talk about Max.

"I didn't know what to expect from him at first. Now I know he's good—in so many ways. Ways he doesn't even realize."

"You're good for him," Shane said, switching subjects abruptly.

"Am I?"

"Yes. He's been pretty closed up as far as women were concerned, but it's obvious he cares a lot about you."

She flushed. "You can tell?"

"Yeah."

"Well, I care a lot about him, too. The question is, can we work things out?"

"You mean, can he deal with your celebrity status?"

"I may be giving that up," she answered.

Shane looked shocked. "Why?"

"Because I've figured out that life is short, and if I don't grab some of the good stuff, I'll wake up one day and find out I've missed my chance."

"I came to a similar conclusion," he said.

"Really?"

"Yeah. I found the right woman, and I've never been happier."

They were interrupted when Jack returned with the news that Max was being moved to room 321.

While they were sitting in the third-floor waiting area, they saw Max wheeled out of the elevator, then down the hall to his room. All of them watched the attendants come out, then gave Max a few more minutes before going down the hall. He was lying with his eyes closed, but they blinked open as soon as he realized he wasn't alone.

"We didn't mean to wake you," Olivia said.

"I wasn't sleeping."

"We'll check in on you after a while," Olivia said.

Max looked at his friends. "Want to help me to the bathroom?"

"Are you sure it's okay?" Jack asked.

"Better than peeing in bed."

"Hospitals have ways to take care of that."

"I'd rather get up," Max answered.

Olivia withdrew from the room and went back to the waiting area. It was several minutes before the two Rockfort men came back.

"You were discussing the case?" she asked.

"Briefly," Max replied.

The two men sat down without elaborating. Olivia wanted to press them for information, but she was pretty sure they would have given it to her if they thought it was important.

"One of us will be with you all the time in case Masters or Larson shows up," Jack said.

She nodded, knowing the precaution made sense.

"Plus, we're keeping an eye on Max, in case that Davidson guy figures out where he is," Jack added.

Olivia clenched her fists. "I didn't think about that."

"Max told us he cut Davidson, so maybe he's not in the best shape to attack again," Shane said.

"Or not yet," Jack added.

"You think the Baltimore PD is looking for him?" Olivia asked, not expecting much after their experience with Hamilton.

"Max said that before we talked to him, a Baltimore city detective showed up in the ER and took a report from him. It was someone named Will Ryker, a guy Max knew from his time on the force, and he was a lot friendlier than Hamilton. I think that if Davidson is in Baltimore, Ryker will get a lead on him."

"But since Davidson knows Max worked with the Baltimore PD, maybe Davidson realizes this is a dangerous place to hang around.

"We can hope."

Shane left the waiting area, and Olivia and Jack stayed where they had a view of Max's room. A couple of times she got up and went down the hall to see how he was doing, but he was sleeping, and she returned to Jack.

—ᴟᴟ—

The Masked Avenger lurked in the hallway, thinking that the hospital was a perfect place for death. People here were sick or injured. You could kill them and nobody would know it hadn't been God's plan.

He laughed. He didn't believe in God, of course. Or the devil, or anything metaphysical beyond the fact of human existence. This was a one-way trip—from birth to death. You weren't going anywhere but into the ground after you died, and you'd better make the most of your life while you were here. Get all the money you could. Live well. Eliminate people who got in your way. Never regret your decisions. Tip the odds in your favor.

He'd started learning those lessons back in nursery school, playing in the sandbox of all places. His dad had gotten him a little dump truck, and he'd been happily scooping up sand and dumping it out when another kid named Sammy had asked if he could play with the truck. The Avenger had refused, and the kid had gone away. Then a half hour later, a teacher had marched out and hauled him into the office. Sammy had been there, with a scrape on his cheek and a triumphant expression in his eyes. He'd told the teacher that the Avenger had hit him with the dump truck.

It wasn't true, but when the Avenger had protested, the teacher had said Sammy had the mark on his cheek from the attack.

There had been no way for the Avenger to convince the teacher of his innocence. She'd taken away the truck and barred him from the sandbox for a week. He'd been humiliated and sad and furious. But he'd bided his time.

And when he'd had a chance to surreptitiously push Sammy into the path of a kid who was swinging, without getting caught, he'd done it. Sammy had gotten hit in the head and gotten a much bigger injury than the one he'd claimed from the truck attack. And the Avenger had gotten a lesson in justice.

At the age of five, he hadn't killed the other kid, of course. But he'd understood that hurting people could be an effective policy—as long as you didn't get caught.

He'd hit the jackpot when he'd seen Archie Hamilton rush out of the police station and jump into his car. The Avenger had followed him down to Memorial Hospital in Baltimore. It seemed that Max Lyon had gotten cut in a knife fight down in the city.

What was he doing in Baltimore?

The Avenger had sneaked into the emergency room and stolen a scrub suit. With one of those caps over his head and a sterile mask over his face when he needed it, it had been easy to blend into the hospital scenery. All you had to do was stride around like you knew where you were going.

Still, the emergency room staff was small. And it hadn't been possible to get close enough to find out what Lyon was doing in Baltimore. But this gave him a perfect opportunity to kill Lyon.

He'd determined that the guy was staying overnight, then found out what floor he'd be on. But it hadn't been so easy to get close enough to kill him. Olivia was hanging around, and one of his PI friends was on duty with her.

Fuck.

But maybe he could change plans again. If he couldn't get Lyon, maybe he could get Olivia.

He hadn't been thinking this was the best place to abduct her. But it looked like she was settling in for the long haul, which gave him time to leave, make some preparations, and come back.

—◦◦◦—

The next time Olivia went down the hall to check on Max, his eyes opened when she walked in, and he smiled at her.

"How are you?" she asked as she came into the room, feeling a little awkward.

"Much better."

"Are you just saying that because you think it's what I want to hear?"

"No. The blood transfusion and the sleep did me a lot of good," Max said.

"What about the pain?"

"Nothing I can't handle. I think I can get out of here tomorrow."

"Maybe your doctor should make that decision."

"We'll see." He was staring at her. "I know what would make me feel a lot better."

"What?"

"Come lie down with me."

"You can't be serious."

"I'm not dangerous."

"I didn't think you were. But it must be against hospital rules," Olivia protested.

"Let's stop playing by the rules."

She wasn't sure if he meant now or in general, but she longed to be close to him.

Kicking off her shoes, she moved to the side of the

bed. "You've got a bandage on one arm and an IV in the other. How am I supposed to get in with you?"

He considered his options. "I guess the bandaged side is better."

"You're sure?"

"Yeah." He moved over a little, and she eased onto the bed beside him, being careful of the knife wound.

"Get under the covers so I can hold your hand," he said in a husky voice.

Because she was already in pretty deep, she pulled the covers aside, seeing that the short gown he wore barely preserved his modesty.

Slipping in beside him, she pulled the covers back into place.

He found her hand and clasped it, and they lay together in the narrow bed.

For long moments, he didn't speak. Finally he said, "Almost bleeding out makes you think about your life."

She winced at the way he'd put it.

"Like I told you, I never considered myself good marriage material."

"And now?" she asked, her breath stilling.

"Would you take a chance on me?"

The question took her completely by surprise. "What are you asking exactly?"

"Like, would you consider being in a relationship with me?"

Her thoughts had also traveled in that direction, but she'd had no idea how he felt. Well, she'd had some idea when they'd made love, and afterward, but she hadn't expected him to come right out and say anything. Or maybe he was having the same reaction as she was.

That life was short, and if you didn't go after what you wanted, you wouldn't get it.

She could feel the tension radiating through him and realized it had been several moments since he'd spoken.

"Yes," she answered.

"We'd have to work it out. I mean, I'm not moving to New York."

"I don't have to stay there."

"If you left New York, what would you do?"

"One thing I didn't do was spend all my money, like a lot of people who suddenly start making big bucks. I've got a lot saved up—and I had a good investment counselor. And, of course, I'm sitting on a very valuable piece of Howard County property. I have time to think about work."

"You'd sell your family farm?"

"Well, not to just anyone. It would have to be to the right person. Someone who wouldn't throw up a cheap development where the houses were packed together. And I wouldn't have to sell all of it. I could preserve some of it as farmland—if Yeager or someone else wants to work it."

"Olivia." He turned his head, brushing his lips against her cheek. "Look this way."

She did and their mouths met. He kissed her tenderly, then with more passion. She loved the way his lips moved against hers, the way his tongue teased hers.

But finally, she forced herself to be sensible and pulled back. "You shouldn't."

"Kissing you is doing me a world of good. I'd like to do a lot more."

"Yes. When you're out of here."

It was hard not to go back to what they'd been doing, but she had more to say. "There's something I haven't liked about my life—that my looks have been so important."

"You're beautiful."

"And you like that."

"Of course, but it's certainly not the most important thing about you."

Relieved, she answered, "And it's only skin deep, as they say. Plus I'd like the option of being ordinary. I hate always having to be fixed up, even when I'm just going to the grocery store. This is an opportunity to change direction."

"Like what?"

"The best would be finding a job where I could use my mind. Maybe, you know…" She laughed. "I could even go to college and get a degree in something useful."

"If that's what you want."

"I can give myself time to figure it out."

A throat-clearing sound from the doorway made her look up. A nurse was looking at them with a quizzical expression on her face.

Olivia was glad they hadn't been doing anything besides talking at the moment. The woman cleared her throat again, and Olivia slipped out of the bed, turning away as she pulled on her shoes.

"I asked for special therapy," Max said.

The woman laughed, then began to take his vital signs. "BP is elevated," she informed him.

"Shows I'm not dead yet," Max quipped.

"I'll see you later," Olivia said.

When she came back to the waiting area, Shane had left and Jack had come in—with sandwiches and tea for her.

"How's Max?" he asked.

"Better," she said without elaborating. She hadn't been hungry, but the visit to Max had lifted her spirits, and she settled back into the lounge chair to eat.

There wasn't much sense of night and day in the hospital, although maybe there were fewer staffers on the night shift. But finally she looked at her watch and saw that it was early in the morning. She'd been at the hospital all night, wearing the same clothes she'd had on the day before.

She glanced over at Jack, who was dozing with his long legs stretched out in front of him. Trying not to wake him, she got up quietly, but he was instantly alert. The way Max would be, she thought, her heart squeezing as she thought about him lying in the hospital room down the hall. She needed to see him, but she felt pretty grungy after her night in the chair.

"You need something?" Jack asked.

"I have to freshen up."

"Okay." He cleared his throat and said, "Before you go, we should talk."

"About what?"

"When we were down in Max's room right after they brought him in, he said he'd like to know you're in a safe place."

"I will be—when he can come with me."

"He can't stay with you," Jack answered. "You know he's getting back on the case as soon as he can, because that's the best way to protect you."

"I don't want him doing anything… foolish," she answered.

"He thinks the same about you."

Her eyes narrowed. "I can't leave here until he does."

"You'd ease his mind if he knew you were safe."

"Let me think about it," she conceded. "I'll be back in a few minutes—and I'll give you an answer."

"Okay."

She stopped at the nurses' station and asked if there were any toiletry articles for relatives who had come to the hospital on short notice to be with a patient.

One of the nurses brought a plastic bag with some soap, a toothbrush, toothpaste, and a disposable washcloth. She went down the hall to the ladies room, which she was glad to find was empty. After using the facilities, she brushed her teeth, then washed her face. While she was making herself presentable, she thought about what Jack had said and also about her conversation with Max while she'd lain in bed with him. Maybe she'd communicated with him more honestly than she ever had with anyone else in her life.

Then something else struck her. Earlier, when she'd talked to Jerry, she'd remembered how she'd felt after she'd first met him—like Superman had taken her hand and was flying her over New York City. Oh Lord, and now...

She hadn't felt that warm glow in years—until she'd made love with Max. Once again Superman had grabbed her hand and taken her flying with the wind streaking through her hair and the ground rushing past below them. Only this was different. It had nothing to do with making it as a model. It had everything to do with her and Max—and the joy they brought each other. He'd said he wanted a relationship, and she wanted that too. More than anything else. And she knew that they could make it happen because they were both as determined as a conquering army.

Or Max would be when he got better. Her heart squeezed as she pictured him lying in that hospital bed. She didn't want to leave him now, but she knew that if she stayed here, she'd give him something to worry about. And the less stressed he was, the faster he'd heal.

It was a heart-wrenching choice to make, but she felt better both emotionally and physically after she'd made her decision and cleaned up. Turning to leave, she saw the door swing open, and a man dressed like a hospital staffer in a green uniform walked in. At first she thought he had come to clean up the bathroom. Then she saw his face and gasped.

Chapter 25

OLIVIA WENT RIGID AS SHE TOOK IN THE SIGHT OF TROY Masters. "What…what are you doing here?"

"Guess." His voice sounded nasty. And the look on his face conveyed the same impression. Nasty or angry? Probably a combination of both.

The expression and his mere presence here gave her a terrible jolt. The last time she'd seen him, he'd been wearing a gas mask to hide his identity and keep the smoke from choking him and burning his eyes.

He was blocking half the doorway. She thought about pushing past him. She thought about screaming. But he was a step ahead of her.

"Don't do anything foolish," he said, raising his arm to show her the gun he was holding. Probably the same gun he'd brought to the farm. Then she'd been armed too. Not now. She didn't even have a canister of Mace in her purse, and that was a mistake. But she'd felt safe with Max. Then with Shane or Jack, and she'd honestly thought she was protected. Unfortunately, she'd stepped out of their protective zone when she'd gone to the ladies' room.

She'd told Jack a few minutes ago that she didn't want Max doing anything foolish. Now she was thinking that she should have taken Shane's advice and left while she still could.

Would he come looking for her if she didn't reappear

in a reasonable time? Probably not, since she'd told him she'd be a while.

"Come on. We're leaving," he said.

"Let me go to the bathroom first."

"Nice try. You already did that."

"How do you know?"

"I was outside the door. I heard the toilet flush, and I looked in and saw you washing."

She winced, hating the idea of his watching her take care of intimate personal details.

"Stop stalling," he said. "Or I could just kill you here."

Her gasp brought a smile to his face. "I guess you don't like that idea. Probably you want to stay alive a little longer."

The offhand comment was like his fingers tightening around her neck, but maybe she still could get away. Maybe she could somehow signal Jack.

"Quit wasting time. I don't want that guy you're with coming looking for you."

"What guy?"

"The one in the lounge. Jack Brandt. The other hot-shot Rockfort PI. Not the one whose cell phone I stole to trick your boyfriend."

"He's not my boyfriend."

Troy snorted. "What is he?"

"I don't have to talk about him to you."

"Not now, anyway. Come on before I do something you're really not going to like. We're going to walk out of here together. I'm going to be right in back of you with the gun. Don't try to go back to the lounge area where you spent the night. Turn the other way. You'll come to an exit. Walk through the door and into the stairway.

His directions were very explicit. He must have been here for a while, planning his moves.

"How long have you been here?" she asked.

"Stop wasting time. Get into the hall and turn right."

She did as he asked, praying that a nurse or someone would come along as they took a couple of awkward steps down the corridor. Then she canceled that prayer. If they did encounter someone, she could get them killed by asking for help.

Just as she had that thought, a nurse came down the hall toward the ladies' room.

Olivia's heart stopped, then started up in double time as she felt Troy's gun pressing into the middle of her back.

She raised her eyes, and for a moment, she met the other woman's gaze. But probably the nurse had been on duty all night and she didn't catch the urgency that Olivia was trying to convey.

Feeling like she was on her way to her execution, she headed for the exit. As she walked, she eased her shoulder purse to the front and dipped her hand inside. At the exit, she pulled the door open and stepped into the stairs — where she scuffed her foot against the raised doorsill and stumbled.

Troy cursed and grabbed for her, holding her upright, but in the moments when he was holding her up, she managed to pull out the credit card she'd extracted from her wallet and drop it on the floor. In the scuffle, he didn't notice, and he pushed her ahead of himself as they headed downward.

"We're coming out at the side of the building," he told her. "Turn right to the parking lot. And keep your head down."

"Okay," she whispered. She didn't want to leave the hospital. She kept hoping that there was some way to run from Troy Masters. On the ground floor, the door had one of those horizontal bars instead of a knob.

"Push the bar," he ordered, and she caught the tension in his voice. This was a dangerous time for her—and anybody who got in the way.

With no alternative, she did as he asked, and they were outside in the morning grayness.

"My car is in the lot. The red Beemer near the exit. I got a good space."

She'd seen that red car before, she realized, but she hadn't paid attention to it. Then she remembered he'd been driving a red car ten years ago too.

There were people out here, either walking toward the hospital or away, but she didn't dare involve them. She and Troy made it to the car, and he opened the back door.

"Get in."

Was he going to just leave her loose? Could she jump out when he stopped at a red light or something?

That hope was dashed when he slapped something wet and cold over her face. She coughed, then felt blackness closing in on her.

Jack glanced at his watch, thinking Olivia had been gone a long time. Trying to tell himself not to worry, he walked down toward the nurses' station.

"Did the woman who was with me come this way to the ladies' room?" he asked.

"Yes. I gave her one of our packages of personal articles."

He looked at his watch, thinking that she might still

be in there brushing her teeth. But he didn't think she would have taken this long. She'd want to get back so she could see Max.

Another nurse came from the direction of the ladies' room.

"Did you see the woman who was with me?" he asked.

"Why yes. She was with another man."

"Who?"

"Someone on the hospital staff."

"Someone you knew?"

"No. But he had on an orderly's uniform."

Which meant it wasn't Shane. And he hadn't come back yet, anyway.

"Which way did they go?"

The nurse pointed in the other direction, and Jack sprinted off. When he came to the stairs, he stopped short and pushed the door open. A credit card was lying on the floor, and when he picked it up, he saw Olivia's name on the front.

"Oh Jesus." She'd said she was just going to the ladies' room. Apparently she'd taken an unexpected detour.

Cursing, he sprinted down the steps and out onto the sidewalk. But he didn't see Olivia outside—or anyone else he recognized. And when he tried to get back into the hospital through the exit door, he found it was locked from the outside.

Cursing again, he ran back to the hospital entrance, where Shane was just coming in. His partner took in his wild-eyed look.

"What happened?"

"Olivia said she was going to the ladies' room to freshen up. When she didn't come back, I went looking for her. She dropped her credit card in the stairwell," Jack said.

"To tell us where she'd gone," Shane finished.

They both stepped into the lobby, bypassed the desk, and strode to the elevator. When they arrived on Max's floor, they hurried to his room. The IV had been taken out of his arm, and he was sitting up with a breakfast tray in front of him.

When he saw the expressions on their faces, he went rigid.

"What happened?"

Jack closed his eyes for a moment, then forced himself to speak. "I was with Olivia. She said she wanted to freshen up. She stopped at the nurses' station, then went around the corner to the ladies' room. When she didn't come back after ten minutes, I went down there. A nurse saw her with a man in an orderly's uniform. I went to the nearest stairwell where I found her credit card lying on the floor."

Max's face had taken on a look of horror. "The killer's got her. And we don't even know who the hell he is."

"I should have gone down the hall to the bathroom with her," Jack said, sounding miserable.

Max saw the stricken look on his partner's face. "He would have found some other way to get her," he said, not sure if it was true. But he wasn't going to yell at Jack, not when he'd made his own mistakes in this case.

He pushed the breakfast tray aside and climbed out of bed, then had to grab the rail to steady himself. When he turned back to his friends, he saw them watching him.

"You should be in bed," Shane said.

"Right. But I can't be." He took several breaths and tested his footing, then said, "It has to be one of the two suspects. Masters or Larson. That woman, Julie, picked out their pictures from the classmates I showed her."

"We'll do it," Jack said.

"It's going to take three guys."

"The cops?" Jack said.

Max laughed. "You think Hamilton is even going to believe us? If we're going to get Olivia back, it's got to be us."

"But you lost a lot of blood yesterday," Shane argued.

"And they replaced it. I'm okay."

"The hell you are. You almost fell down when you got out of bed."

"Because I'd just gotten up. I'm better now."

Before Shane could put forth another objection, a nurse walked into the room and looked at the three men facing each other. "What's going on?" she demanded.

Max swung toward her. "What's happening is that I'm leaving."

"You haven't been discharged. You can't simply leave."

"Watch me."

"It will be against medical advice."

"Screw medical advice."

She turned on her heel, probably on her way to report him. But Max was already thinking about his current problem. "Christ, I don't even have a shirt and pants."

"Not to worry," Jack said. "I brought clothes for you. I just didn't know you'd need them today."

"Bless you, my brother." Max grabbed the bag Jack held out, tore off the hospital gown, and dressed as fast as he could, considering that he was still a little unsteady on his feet.

"We've got to be quick," he told his partners as he dressed. "This guy has killed at least five or six people."

"If he wanted to kill Olivia right away, he could have done it here," Shane pointed out.

"Yeah, but why don't I find that reassuring?" Max snapped as he thought about what the bastard might want with her. He knew what had already happened to her at that damn cabin.

He started for the door, then stopped. "Oh shit. Something else I forgot. They took away my wallet, phone, and car keys when they admitted me, not to mention my gun."

"I have them too," Jack said, hefting a briefcase.

"Thank God."

Max took back his belongings, and the three men exited the room. As they approached the nurses' station, a dark-haired man wearing a white coat stepped into their path, his gaze fixed on Max.

"Mr. Lyon?"

"Yeah."

"I am Dr. Applebaum," he said. "I looked at your chart, and I do not advise your leaving the hospital at this time."

"I have business to attend to," Max snapped.

"And you have fifteen stitches in your arm, which could pull out if you don't take it easy."

"Okay, I heard your warning," Max answered. "Now I have to leave."

"At least let me…"

Max stepped around him. "No time. We're trying to save a life."

Jack looked back. "Sorry. Wild horses couldn't keep him here."

Shane had already pressed the elevator button. When the car arrived, they all stepped in, Max feeling the disapproving looks of the doctor and nurses on his back. In some corner of his mind, he knew they were right. He could end up doing himself serious damage. Yet he simply couldn't stay here and let others look for Olivia.

Another thought struck him. "Shit."

"Now what?" Shane asked.

"My damn car. It's about a block from where I was cut." He looked hopefully toward Jack. "You didn't bring it over, did you?"

"Um, I figured you'd get a ride back to the hotel with one of us. We've got two cars here," Jack said. "Either Shane or I can take you over to where you left yours."

"Which means we're going to have to separate," Max said, letting the implications sink in and realizing that they couldn't simply rush off. "We'd better do some planning before we leave."

The three of them found a quiet corner in the waiting room.

"The reason this is going to take three of us is that there are three likely locations where Olivia might be held," Max said, focusing on the logic of this mess as they stood facing each other. "Larson's house. Masters's house, and that cabin up by the dam. I'm betting that's going to turn out to be it, but we have to check the other two places, in case one of them had plans to hole up at home."

"I'll take Larson's house," Jack said.

"I'll go to the cabin," Shane said.

"No. I'm going there. You check out Masters's."

Shane gave him a doubtful look. "You're not exactly in fighting shape."

"Unfortunately," he conceded. "If you don't find Olivia at either suspect's house, you can join me at the cabin."

He could see his friends didn't love the arrangement, but he wasn't going to budge. He was pretty sure Olivia would be at the cabin, and he wasn't going to waste time getting there.

Outside, he and Shane went to the latter's car. Jack climbed into his own vehicle, and they went in separate directions.

Shane glanced at Max's pale face. "Listen, I was thinking about what that Dr. Applebaum said."

"Don't tell me to go back to the hospital," Max shot back.

"I'm not. But he talked about the stitches in your arm. If you drive, you could start bleeding again before you get to the damn cabin. And if you pass out, you're not going to do Olivia any good."

"I'm not going to fucking pass out."

"Yeah, but why don't we both take a quick trip to Masters's house. If he's not there, we go to the cabin. Unless Jack calls us with better information."

Max clenched his fists. That could be wasting precious time, but he knew his friend was right. If he got to the cabin and passed out or started bleeding, he'd be putting Olivia in even more danger.

Chapter 26

OLIVIA WOKE FEELING COLD AND CONFUSED. IT TOOK A moment for her to remember what had happened to her, and when she did, she shuddered. Smelling dampness, she opened her eyes and found herself in a small room lit by an electric lantern on the floor in one corner. It had a floor made of plywood strips. The walls were the same material. When she looked up, she saw the ceiling was just dirt. Below her was a bare mattress that was dirty and stained. It looked like it could have been here for years.

She clenched her teeth, fighting a surge of panic. She was in the underground room Max had described to her.

Had she been in this place before? She couldn't be sure, but Max's account was vivid in her mind. This was the room under the cabin that he had inspected the other day.

She fought terror—and tears. If she'd tried to imagine the worst thing that could have happened to her, this was it. That is, the worst thing besides losing Max. And at least she could comfort herself that he was safe. Troy had gone after her—not him.

She closed her eyes, desperately wanting to shut out reality. It was tempting to withdraw into herself. Maybe that was the way she had coped when…

She cut off that thought. How she'd coped in the past wasn't important. Right now, she knew that if she shut down, she would end up dead, like Angela and Claire. Clenching her fists, she willed herself to coherence. But the last things she remembered sent a shudder through her. Troy had been dressed like a hospital staffer, and he'd come into the ladies room with a gun. He'd taken her down the stairs and outside. Then he'd put something wet over her nose and mouth, and then she had woken up here.

When she shivered and tried to wrap her arms around her shoulders, she found her wrists were tied together. So were her ankles. And the wrists were linked to a chain that was fastened to a stake pounded through the floor to her right. It gave her enough room to sit up, which she did. Leaning over, she pulled at the stake with her bound hands. It didn't budge, and she wondered if it was cemented into the ground below the wood floor. Max hadn't mentioned it. Which must mean it was newly planted—for her.

A sound a few feet away made her focus on the entrance to the room, which was nothing more than a large, dark rectangle.

As she watched, Troy Masters came in and sat down on a plump red cushion across from her.

"What are you doing, Troy?" she asked.

"What do you think?"

"You're going to kill me, like you killed Claire."

"No. Do you think I wanted to kill you at the farm?"

She answered with a small nod.

"You're wrong. I was using her to get to you. I was going to take you away then."

"But you shot at me," she blurted.

"Because you had a gun. You were shooting at me."

"I was defending myself."

He made a dismissive sound. "You don't have a gun now. And now we can spend some quality time together. Like we did ten years ago."

The words or the tone of his voice made her heart start to clunk inside her chest, but she wasn't going to ask what he had planned. She remembered him hustling her out of the hospital, and she remembered dropping her credit card. Had Jack found it? And even if he hadn't, the men would have to know she was missing by now. But would Max think to look for her *here*? She prayed that he would. Otherwise she was on her own.

Then another thought intruded and made her go cold. Max would come looking for her, all right, but he was in the hospital—in no shape to confront anyone—especially a crazed killer with a gun.

Troy Masters.

He'd already talked to her a little. Would he answer questions? Or was questioning him dangerous? He'd already killed a lot of people. There was no reason to keep her alive unless he wanted to. And for how long?

Jack had looked up the location of Larson's house. For a suburban property, it was on a fairly large, wooded plot of land. He made the turn into the driveway and stopped well away from the house. Drawing his gun, he started for the building, staying in the trees.

When he reached the side of the driveway, he hurried across and looked in one of the garage windows. There were two cars inside. One was a late model Lexus that looked like the owner kept it washed and polished. The other was a cheap Chevy. But outside the garage was something even more interesting — an unmarked cop car. So the police were here? Which meant that he'd better put away his gun if he didn't want to get shot.

He holstered the weapon and moved toward the house, wondering what to do next. Again, because he didn't want to get shot, he rang the doorbell and waited. When nobody answered, he tried the knob and found it was locked.

The setup gave him a bad feeling. It was too quiet here, like nobody was home. But he knew that couldn't be true. Using his shirttail, he wiped off the knob, then started around the house, looking in the windows.

When he got to the rear of the property, he stopped. A sliding glass door was half open. But this was an expensive house, and the owner was unlikely to just leave the place unlocked.

Was this some sort of trap? Were the cops lying in wait for someone to show up?

If he were with the PD, he'd call for backup. But he didn't have that option. He was the only guy here, and he knew that every moment he delayed was a moment when something very bad could happen to Olivia Winters.

Again he kept his gun in its holster as he pushed the door open farther with his shoulder and stepped inside. He walked cautiously into the kitchen, hearing nothing, but he was pretty sure from the odor coming from the front of the house that he wasn't going to like what he found.

He made his way from the kitchen into a short hall, toward the living room, he assumed. Ten yards from the entry door, he stopped short and quietly drew his gun when he saw two men lying on the floor, each in a pool of blood that spread across the expensive travertine marble, soaking into the natural depressions.

Having seen Tommy Larson's picture, he knew one of them was him. The other was Archie Hamilton. Son of a bitch.

What the hell had happened here? From the looks of the victims, this could be a murder-suicide, but he didn't think so. More likely a double murder. And the killer must be the other suspect—Troy Masters. Had he come over to eliminate Larson and found the detective here? Or had Hamilton's presence on the scene triggered the murders? There was no way to know.

Jack didn't go over and check for a pulse in either man. It was clear from the amount of blood and the condition of the bodies that both of them had been dead for several hours, presumably before Masters had showed up at the hospital to snatch Olivia.

He backed away, retraced his steps, and exited through the sliding glass door. Glad of the wooded lot, he hurried down the driveway and climbed into his car. After driving a couple of blocks away, he reached into the glove compartment and pulled out the burner phone he kept in case he needed to make a call without using his own number. His first call was to the Howard County 911 operator.

"There's been a double homicide at 223 Stanhope Way," he said in an artificially low voice when the operator asked him the nature of his emergency.

"Who is calling?"

"A concerned citizen," he answered, then hung up before they got a fix on him.

Max leaned back against the car seat and closed his eyes, conserving his energy.

When a phone rang, he jerked awake, blinking as he realized he'd been asleep.

Jesus! He couldn't even stay awake for more than an hour, and he thought he was going to rescue Olivia?

"Is it Jack?" he asked.

"Not his regular number. But he could be using the burner he keeps in the car." Clicking the phone connection on the steering column, Shane said, "Hello," then switched to the speaker.

"Jack?"

"Well, it's not the guy you sent me to check out," their partner said in a hard voice.

The roundabout way he gave the information alerted Max that something significant had happened.

"Because?" Shane asked.

"I'll have to tell you when I see you. I'm heading toward the cabin."

"Go to the other house," Max instructed.

Jack hesitated. "I'll do it. But I don't think he's gonna be home."

Max wanted to shout—just spit it out, but he knew Jack wasn't being evasive because he wanted to play stupid games. Something had happened. Something he thought better than to spell out in a phone conversation.

"If you end up meeting us at the cabin, Olivia said the kids parked down the road in the woods and walked back."

"Okay." They heard Jack hesitate again. "Someone

was with the guy you sent me to meet," he said. "Someone we didn't expect."

"What the hell is that supposed to mean?" Max demanded.

"Sorry, it's got to wait until I see you," Jack answered and clicked off.

Max and Shane exchanged glances.

"Sounds like something bad happened at Larson's house," Max said.

"Yeah. Like maybe he's dead. And somebody else is there—dead. But who?"

"Another member of the class?" Max speculated, suddenly unsure of what had seemed so clear a few hours ago.

"It can't be both Larson and Masters. Or if it is, we're all screwed up. Shit!"

Shane put a calming hand on his arm. "I think we have to assume from Jack's call that Larson is dead. And if he is, then the murderer is Masters—from what you've been saying."

Max struggled to bring his roiling emotions under control. "Yeah. They went down to Baltimore together to score some pussy. And one of the women they picked up was killed during violent sex play. We talked to the woman who got away. That's what Olivia and I were doing right before you called and said Davidson was on the loose."

"Sounds like it's the best we've got," Shane agreed.

"But what if we're wrong?" Max asked, arguing against his own conclusions because he knew that if he made a mistake, he was risking Olivia's life.

"Maybe we should call the cops," Shane said.

The statement firmed Max's resolve. "Unfortunately, given the way things have played out, that's more dangerous for Olivia. The more people involved, the more chance she gets killed in a ham-handed rescue attempt. We're only calling the boys in blue if she's not at the cabin."

He glanced at Shane, then opened the glove compartment and took out the medical kit they always carried. Pawing through the contents, he found what he was looking for and opened a small bottle.

"You think taking an amphetamine is a good idea in your condition?"

"That's what they're here for," Max said. "For when we need them."

Reaching in the backseat, he grabbed a bottle of water, unscrewed the top, and took the pill.

Chapter 27

OLIVIA PRESSED HER BACK AGAINST THE WALL, thankful that the chain gave her some room.

Raising her head, she looked at Troy. She'd seen him at the reunion meeting, and he had looked pretty normal. Apparently he had the ability to seem nonthreatening. Now she saw from his eyes that he was losing it. Silently she cursed herself for not seeing that before, but there had been a lot of people at the meeting, and she'd had to pay attention to all of them.

"You're studying me," he said.

"No."

"Don't lie to me."

She should talk to him, but should she mention the murders? Maybe that was a bad idea, under the circumstances. But then, she'd already talked about Claire.

He was the one who brought up the subject.

"You should have stayed in New York. But you came down here because Angela was murdered, didn't you?"

"Yes."

"She was your best friend."

"Yes."

"But she wasn't all that good a friend," he said with an edge in his voice, and she knew he was waiting for her to ask what he meant.

"Why?" she managed to ask.

"You thought the two of you were raped up here."

"Yes."

"But, see, it was only you. She wanted to fuck me. Then she helped hold you down."

Olivia gasped. "No."

"She was very cooperative. And I'll bet the two of you comforted each other afterward. And assured each other that it was better not to tell anyone."

"Yes," Olivia breathed. He was making her see the past in terms she didn't want to admit. But was he telling her the real truth? What if Angela had agreed to make love with Troy because she'd had no alternative? And had she really helped hold Olivia down? There was no way of knowing for sure. And even if Troy thought he was telling the truth, he might not be remembering it the way it had happened.

He began speaking again, and she focused on every word.

"Back then I made sure she was going to keep you quiet. But when I saw that notice about the reunion, I was afraid she was going to fess up to you if you came down for the big weekend. So I had to get rid of her."

Olivia had gone cold all over.

"I never let anyone stand in my way," he said. "Like Patrick. He was blackmailing me, you know. And I kind of let him do it because I liked him." Troy laughed. "But it got to be too much, and I finally said—fuck this."

She pressed her back more firmly against the wall, her mind racing as she tried to think how she was going to get out of this. Troy had killed a lot of people, and she was going to be next, if she didn't figure out how to stop him.

"Of course, there were all the people at the party that

night. You know, the one at Brian's. He's on my list too. Now. What happens, I think, is that people make a pact to keep quiet. Then after years pass, they think it's okay to talk. Like the ones who were still there when we went down to Baltimore. Claire. And Craig Pendergast. And of course, it's the same with the people who came up here. Everybody kept quiet about the rapes. But I'll bet you and Angela were going to talk about it. Victim to victim."

He'd said Angela wasn't really raped. Which was it? She thought it was better not to ask.

Instead, she said, "You've figured everything out."

"Don't try to patronize me."

"Why didn't you go after Brian?" she heard herself ask.

"Because I thought he was too much of a pussy to cause me any trouble. Now I think I was wrong, with his talking to you and Lyon and all. He's next on my list. Of course, Tommy was more of an immediate problem, but I took care of him already."

––––––––––

As Shane's SUV reached a wooded area along Wilkins Dam Road, Max said, "Slow down." He pointed up the hill into the forest. "The cabin's up the hill. You can't see it from here."

They passed the chained driveway and the parking spot where he and Olivia had been when the truck driver had interrupted their frantic grappling. Then he'd still thought she was hiding something from him. Now he knew what it was, and pain and guilt ripped through him like whirling knife blades when he thought about leaving her alone at the farm.

"She said they parked in the woods," he related, "but maybe it's better to pull up on the other side of the highway."

Shane kept going, saw a gravel road on the other side that led into the trees and waited for a car to pass before turning. Shane pulled up far enough so that they couldn't be seen from the road.

Max got out, relieved that he was a lot steadier on his feet than he had been at the hospital. He was in for a major crash later. But he'd worry about that when he had the time.

As they hurried up the hill, Max filled his friend in.

"When Olivia and I were here, a security guard was waiting for us when we came out of the cabin."

"Nice. I guess one of us can hold him at gunpoint."

"Yeah. Hopefully, we won't meet up with any guards." Max dragged in a breath and let it out. "The cabin's probably an old maintenance facility. Olivia and I got inside by pulling up some loose siding in the back. Inside there's a trapdoor that leads to a tunnel and an underground room. I'm thinking he'd be down there with her because it's a good defensive position."

"And you're going to get in there *how*?" Shane asked.

"I'm going to have to rush him."

"Hard to do if you're in a tunnel on your hands and knees."

Max made a sound that was part agreement and part anger. "You have a better suggestion?"

"Flush him out."

Troy's words and his tone made Olivia realize how dangerous this game was. But did she have a choice? Was there any other way to get out of this underground room alive?

And what was he thinking? He'd been on a killing rampage that had started small and built over the years. He'd just as good as told her he'd killed Tommy Larson. Did he think he was going to get away with that? Maybe it made sense to him—but they'd already talked to that detective, Archie Hamilton, about the two of them going down to Baltimore. Maybe Hamilton would figure it out.

But that wasn't going to help her now. She had to make a decision, and quickly.

"You know I've been looking for a long time for a strong man who could protect me."

"Are you trying to say I'm it?"

She kept her gaze on him, trying not to look calculating. On the face of it, there was no logic to her wanting to hook up with him. But she thought he was egotistical enough to eat up her praise of him.

"You know you are. Look at how you've managed your life all these years—making sure you were always on top. I want to be there with you."

He laughed, and she didn't know if he was agreeing with her or laughing at her attempt to convince him that she was on his side.

"You're on top of your profession," he said.

"Yes, I make a lot of money. With your talent, we'd make a great team. The guy who manages me is an idiot. I'm sure you can do better."

"I'll bet I could. But I don't want to move to New York. I like it here."

"I could come back and forth."

"Yeah." He tipped his head to the side. "You're being very cooperative."

She raised one shoulder. "You drugged me last time I was here," she said. "That's why I didn't know what had happened. But really you don't have to do that. I've wanted to make love to you for a long time."

"Then why didn't you let me take you and Angela home after the party?" he shot back.

"You know why. Because I was afraid of my father. He was really strict with me. If he found out where I'd been, he would have gone ballistic."

"That does make sense," he agreed.

"But he's dead, so he has no control over me now. Why don't you make love with me, and we can both find out what we missed all those years ago. I mean, was it really fun fucking a woman who was half unconscious?"

"It had its points," he murmured.

"Well, I'm an experienced woman, now, and I think you'll like me better awake," she answered, forcing herself to keep up the seductive conversation because it was the only way she could see to save her life. And maybe it wasn't even going to work.

She saw he was on the edge of a decision, and whispered, "Please."

Long seconds stretched before he said, "I'm not going to unchain you, if that's what this is all about."

She raised one shoulder in a compliant gesture. "I'm not asking you to do that. But, of course, you'll have to free my ankles so I can open my legs."

Her own plans amazed her. It was almost like some-one else were sitting here facing Troy Masters, and she was somewhere else, watching the performance. But then her acting ability was what had gotten her choice jobs in commercials that other models had failed to win.

Putting on the performance of her life, she brought her hands to the front of her blouse and began to open the buttons one by one, working awkwardly because of the binding and because she kept her gaze fixed on Troy. And maybe slower was better, because she was definitely holding his attention as she revealed more and more skin.

———∿∿∿———

"And how do we flush the bastard out?" Max asked.

"What if he thinks there's an earthquake in the area, and he's gonna get buried?"

"We can arrange an earthquake?"

"Not a real one. But we have some C4 in the trunk."

"But that could really collapse the tunnel."

"I guess we'll have to place it carefully. Close enough to shake the place but not close enough to do any damage down there. And I'll bring the portable siren. We can turn it on so he'll think it's some kind of warning."

Max nodded, thinking that he'd make the decision when they got to the cabin. Getting out his cell phone, he called Jack.

"We're at the woods at the location I told you about."

"Then I'm about five minutes away."

"You'll see a chained access road on the right. Don't park near it. We're parked across the highway. You'll see a gravel road going uphill into the woods. The cabin's on the other side, not far from the access road. Watch out for security guards. We're going up, and you can follow."

Max clicked off, and Shane took a canvas gym bag out of the trunk.

There were also assault rifles in the trunk, and Max eyed them.

"I think Troy's only carrying a sidearm," he said. "And an assault rifle is going to be kind of conspicuous if we're caught here."

Shane nodded. "Of course, so is the C4, if anyone looks in the bag."

"We're just here for an exercise routine," Max quipped.

"Right."

They made their way down the hill to the highway, then waited for traffic to pass before crossing.

Instead of taking the access road, they moved through the trees as silently as possible, heading for the cabin, circling around so that they wouldn't approach from the road.

"He could have booby traps or sensors," Shane whispered.

Max kept his own voice low. "He could. But that would mean he put them in place earlier."

"He did a lot of planning for that assault on the farmhouse."

"But he had the time for it. Let's hope he's improvising now."

They came in toward the back of the cabin, and Max saw a flash of red through the trees. Stopping behind a tree, he peered out and realized he was looking at a red Beemer.

"His car," Max said. "He drove right up here like he owned the place."

They cautiously approached the vehicle and looked

inside. The odor of chloroform wafted out from a rag lying on the floor of the backseat, and Olivia's purse was lying beside it.

Max's heart thumped. Masters had drugged her and driven her here. But was she alive?

Turning from the car, he and Shane crept toward the building.

A few feet away a man in a green uniform was lying on the ground.

Max hurried over and saw that it was the same guard who had stopped him and Olivia a few days earlier. Then, he'd taken them by surprise. This time, it looked like the other way around. And the encounter hadn't gone so well for the security man.

He was dead, the back of his head blown off by a bullet that had gone through the center of his forehead.

Chapter 28

"OH SHIT," MAX MUTTERED. "POOR GUY, HE WAS IN the wrong place at the wrong time."

"Another body," a voice behind them said.

They both whirled to find Jack, breathing hard after running up the hill. "Lucky it's not Masters who snuck up on you."

Max made a sound of agreement. "When you called, were you telling us that Larson is dead?" he asked.

"Yeah."

"And who else?"

"Hamilton."

"Jesus," Max responded. "I guess he decided there was a chance we weren't full of shit after all."

"And going over to Larson's place got his ass killed," Shane added.

"Probably he thought he was on a wild-goose chase, and he wasn't being careful," Max said.

"Probably," Jack agreed. "I called it in anonymously. The cops know about the bodies by now, but they won't know I was there."

Max looked from him to the man on the ground. "And then there's this poor bastard. When are they going to miss him, and what's going to happen when they do?"

"We'd better get on with it," Shane said.

"Yeah." Max turned toward the cabin. "The interior is empty, but it's not very secure. I'm betting Masters is under the cabin with Olivia. There's a tunnel with an underground room at the end. A good place to hold someone. And there's only one way in or out." He swallowed hard. "And going down there could get Olivia killed."

Shane told Jack about their blasting plans.

"Risky," he concluded.

"We can't just stand around talking," Max said as he moved quietly toward the back of the building. He could see the spot where he and Olivia had climbed inside. They'd put the siding back into place. Now it was pulled away again, with no attempt to disguise the fact that someone had gone inside.

Max stepped back. The others followed, and they spoke in whispers.

"I'm going in," he said.

"What about the explosives?" Shane asked.

"They could be risky. Suppose he panics and kills her?" Max said.

Shane winced.

"They may be our last resort. But I'm going to see if I can get down there without his knowing it—and try to hear what's going on."

"How?" Jack asked.

He wanted to tell them to stop asking questions, but maybe they were giving him time to think.

"If I were Olivia, I'd be trying to hold his attention. Because she knows I'm coming," he added, praying that it was true. And praying that she was alive and conscious and able to deal with Masters.

"We're coming with you," Jack said.

Max shook his head. "The tunnel's too small for that.

It's a one-man operation. Stay out here." He thought for a moment. "If I think we need the explosives, I'll phone."

"And if you're disabled?"

"If you haven't heard from me in half an hour, go ahead with the explosives. And if the cops come, you can tell them you didn't kill the guard."

Jack snorted. "Why should they believe us?"

"Yeah, well it could start out like that night when Masters came to the farm. But your guns haven't been fired. And if they had, the bullet wouldn't match."

"But we'd have to do a lot of fast talking."

"Which will give me time to get in there and get Olivia out," he said, still praying he could do it.

—⁓—

A little smile flickered on Olivia's lips as she watched Troy's face. It was a real smile, celebrating her success. When she'd first awakened, he'd looked at her with evil intent. Then he'd bragged about his kills. Now she knew his thoughts were swinging toward the sexual. Apparently what she'd said made sense to him.

She finished unbuttoning her shirt, then moved her shoulders, shrugging the garment back. With her hands bound, she couldn't reach around to unhook her bra, but she could tug it up so that it rode above her breasts. They weren't large, but the band of the bra thrust them invitingly toward Troy. Her nipples were rigid, not because this was turning her on, but because it was cold in this underground room. Although the cold helped her play her part, she was sure the man watching her with such lust wouldn't know the difference.

As quietly as he could, Max crawled inside the cabin. With the windows boarded up, the interior was dark, and he didn't dare use a flashlight, lest the light show in the underground room and give him away. If he had ever needed to be steady, it was now, he thought as he waited for his eyes to adjust to the darkness.

When he could see a little, he inched forward, stopping when the toe of one running shoe hit open air. The trapdoor to the tunnel was open, a big clue that Masters was down there with Olivia and had left it open for ventilation.

Max stretched out on the ground, leaning over the opening and listening. He didn't hear voices, but he thought maybe he heard rustling from down the tunnel. Or was that what he wanted to hear?

Olivia saw her breasts attracted Troy's riveted gaze. She saw his breath catch as she swiped a finger across her nipple and accompanied the provocative gesture with a small, moaning sound as though she were making herself hot.

She knew she was making *him* hot, because she could see the bulge at the front of his slacks.

Fine. Hopefully that would affect his thinking processes.

He moved suddenly, surging forward. Grabbing her ankle, he pulled her toward him, so that she ended up sprawled on her back on the mattress. He caressed her ankle, then he pulled a penknife from his pocket. Fear leaped inside her, and she thought she had made a terrible mistake—until he began to saw at the duct tape that held her ankles together. Still, she eyed the knife. She hadn't counted on that.

He freed her legs, and she squirmed on the mattress, returning the circulation to her feet and moving provocatively as she inched a little closer to the stake that tethered her to the ground.

"What are you doing?"

"Getting comfortable."

"Let me help."

He reached to open the button at the top of her slacks and then her zipper. When the top was open, he pulled the pants down her legs. She was wearing only panties now, and he hooked his fingers around the waistband, pulling them down her legs and tossing them away so that her sex was exposed to him. She wanted to scream for someone to save her. Instead she smiled at him, then stroked her tongue across her top lip.

His eyes never leaving her, he unzipped his own pants and pulled his penis out. It was red and swollen, but it wasn't all that large, thank God, because she felt as shriveled inside as if she'd used a vinegar douche.

From his pocket he pulled a condom. Again she thanked God when she saw it was lubricated. So he'd been thinking about having sex with her all along.

After holding the condom up for her to see, he tore the wrapper, then rolled the tube onto his penis.

"Ready, honey?" he asked in a thick voice.

With no preliminaries, he came down on top of her, using his hand to shove his cock inside her. Knowing she had to endure this awful invasion for a few moments, she gritted her teeth and raised her hips meeting his thrust as she reached out her hands and pulled at the chain that tethered her to the ground.

Praying there was enough slack in it, she pulled her arms up, then brought the heavy links crashing down as hard as she could on Troy's back.

She couldn't tell where she'd hit him, but he screamed and leaped away from her—which gave her leverage to pull back her legs and kick him in the face.

"You bitch," Troy shouted, and she knew he was fumbling on the ground for the knife he'd dropped.

She moved to block him, kicking out again, this time landing only a glancing blow as he dodged to the side.

"You're dead," he shouted.

—◆◆◆—

Max heard a shout of pain, then of anger, and knew it was Troy. Olivia had done something to him, but Max didn't know what it was or what was happening now.

Without waiting for a further clue, he threw himself down the access to the tunnel.

He could hear the sounds of a struggle and harsh breathing from the room at the end of the tunnel.

Unable to stand upright because of the low ceiling, he bent over, running at full tilt down the tunnel, and into the room.

Troy had a knife in his hand, and he was swinging it down toward Olivia.

With only a split second to act, Max pulled his gun and fired into the man's back, then fired again. Troy toppled toward Olivia, and Max surged forward, knocking him to the side and kicking the weapon out of his hand.

Max reached for the man's shoulder and turned him

over. Masters lay breathing shallowly, his gaze fixed on Max. His lips moved. No words came out, but a trickle of blood escaped.

"You killed your last victim," Max grated.

Again Troy tried to speak. Instead his breathing stopped.

Max leaned over to feel for a pulse in his neck and detected nothing.

"He's gone. He can't hurt you anymore." It was then that he saw the man's pants were open and a condom covered his cock.

Max wanted to spit on the bastard. Instead he turned toward Olivia. She lay on the mattress, staring at him. He saw her pants were off, her blouse was unbuttoned.

When she took in the look on his face, he saw her eyes glaze with tears.

"I'm sorry," she whispered. "It was awful, but I knew I had to distract him."

He came down quickly beside her, closing the distance between them. "Of course you did. You have nothing to be sorry about."

"But I do. I had to make him think I wanted to make love with him."

"You did what you had to. You were very brave to carry out a plan like that."

"But he...." She gestured toward her lower body. "You see what I let him do."

Max gathered her close. Leaning back against the wall, he cradled her on his lap, stroking his hands over her back and into her lush hair. "Shush. It's all right." He kept repeating reassuring words, meaning them. "You did what you had to do. You knew how to distract him until I could get here. Because you knew I'd come for you."

"Yes," she managed to say before she began to sob.

He wrapped his arms more tightly around her, stroking her and rocking her, feeling her shoulders shake and feeling his own relief like a burst of sunlight after a terrible storm. "It's okay. Everything's okay now. You're safe."

"Yes, safe."

When she raised her hand and tried to clasp him, he realized that her wrists were still tied together.

"Christ. Sorry."

He also had a knife in his pocket, and he pulled it out. Opening the blade, he carefully cut away the bonds. Then he leaned back against the wall again, wanting to hold her forever but knowing that they had to get out of there. She snuggled against him for a few moments, then lifted her head and gave him a critical look.

"Max. Are you all right?"

"Yeah."

"We need to get you out of here," she murmured.

He laughed. "I was about to say the same thing."

She swung her head toward Masters. "What about him?"

"I'm not sure. Let me call Shane and Jack. They're waiting to hear from me." She nodded, still looking at him with concern. "Did you talk them into discharging you from the hospital?"

"That would have taken too long."

"Then…"

"I'll get checked out," he said, glancing at his arm, glad to see no blood seeping through the bandage, partly because he didn't want to leave any evidence that he'd been here.

Olivia still looked dazed.

"You'd better put on your pants before we go up."

"Pants. Yeah, right. And my front."

She pulled her bra down over her breasts and seated them in the cups, then reached for her panties and slacks, pulled them on and then put on her shoes.

While she was putting herself back together, Max turned to the dead man, who was lying with his pants open and a condom on his cock. Max looked around, found an old hamburger wrapper on the floor, and used it to pull off the condom. Then he wrapped it up and shoved it into his pocket before stuffing Masters's dick back into his pants, closing the zipper, and fastening the button.

When he looked up, Olivia was watching him. She made a disgusted face, and he shrugged.

"Are we going to tell them what I let him do?" she asked.

"Not if you don't want to."

"I knew that if I let him fuck me, he'd be too distracted to know I was going to whack him with the chain."

"Yeah. But nobody needs to know about it."

"Thanks."

He reached for her and pulled her close. "What matters is that you're alive, and he's dead. And he was counting on it being the other way around—when he finished with you."

He had put that in stark terms to make sure she didn't forget how high the stakes had been. She answered with a grimace.

As Max got to his feet, the top of his head scraped the ceiling, and Olivia was in almost the same boat.

"Do you remember coming down here?" he asked.

"I was unconscious. He used chloroform or something like it in the hospital parking lot."

"Yeah, we smelled it in his car." Pulling out his phone, he called the surface. "We're coming up."

"Olivia's okay?" Jack asked.

"Yeah. I'll fill you in when we get there."

"Okay," Jack said before his voice turned strange and muffled as though he had shoved the phone into his pocket. "Trouble."

"Huh?"

Through the muffled effect, Max heard a harsh voice saying, "I'm tired of chasing around all over Maryland. Tell me where to find Lyon, or I'll kill you."

Chapter 29

Max cursed under his breath, then put a finger to his lips.

Olivia nodded.

He left the phone line open, and they made their way as quietly as possible down the tunnel.

"I said, where's Lyon?" the other man demanded.

"He's in the hospital," Jack answered. "You cut him, remember?"

Which told Max that Jack was talking to Damon Davidson, the bastard who had been stalking him. Just what they needed at the moment. Or any moment, come to that. Max remembered cutting Davidson as well. Apparently it hadn't been bad enough to put him out of action.

The lowlife laughed. "I cut him, yeah. But he's not in the hospital now. I know he discharged his ass out of there."

"Maybe," Jack conceded. "But what makes you think he's here?"

"Because I hung around, and I knew where the ambulance took him, so I could watch the hospital. I saw you and your friend go in and out, and I put a tracker on both your cars. You went somewhere else first. Then you came here."

"Clever of you," Jack said.

"Yeah, I'll bet you hate that I'm so smart."

Max reached the mouth of the tunnel and motioned for Olivia to wait.

"Is he in that cabin?" Davidson demanded.

"I don't know. We went separate ways."

"Well, suppose I spray the place with bullets?" Davidson said.

Max looked down at Olivia and gave her a look that warned her to stay below ground. Then he clicked off the phone because he didn't need it to hear what was going on outside.

As Jack kept the guy talking, Max climbed the ladder to ground level and moved to the corner where the siding was loose. Gently he pushed at it and looked out, seeing two sets of men's legs and wondering if he could get out before Davidson shot him. And also wondering why he wasn't seeing Shane.

"Hard to shoot the cabin and keep me covered," Jack said.

"I can kill you first."

"You could, and go to jail for life. Did you like it in the slammer so much that you want to die there?"

"I won't get caught this time."

"The Baltimore cops already know you're after Max. They'll get you."

"And you'll be dead."

Jack raised his voice. "This is kind of an explosive situation."

Max knew what that meant. Shane must have gone into the woods to carry out the emergency plan they'd previously discussed. Although they hadn't needed it for Masters, they needed it now.

Max glanced back to make sure Olivia was still in the

tunnel. He wanted to tell her to lie down, but he'd give himself away.

Outside, Davidson asked Jack, "What the hell do you mean by that?"

For answer, an explosion shook the ground, and Max was hurled against the wall. Assuming the men outside were similarly thrown off balance, he righted himself and dived through the hole in the siding in time to see Davidson bring his gun hand up, aiming at Jack, who shot first, and the ex-con went down.

He saw Shane running out of the woods.

"Everything all right?" he called.

"Yeah," both Max and Jack answered.

"And Olivia?" Shane asked.

"Right here."

She crawled out of the back of the cabin and looked at the man lying on the ground.

"Davidson? The man who cut you?"

"Yeah. He's not going to bother anyone again," Jack answered, then turned to Max.

"What about Masters?"

"The same. He had Olivia down in that hole. She whacked him with the chain he'd used to tether her. When he went after her with a knife, I shot him."

Jack and Shane nodded. Maybe they could tell they weren't getting the whole story, but they didn't push for more.

"And now?" Jack asked.

Before he could answer, uniformed cops swarmed out of the woods, surrounding them.

Chapter 30

"CHRIST, NOT AGAIN," MAX MUTTERED, RAISING HIS hands. He wasn't sure what had brought the cops. Maybe the guard hadn't checked in.

As he put down his gun and raised his hands, the other men did the same, and Olivia raised hers as well.

Max had been hoping they could get the hell out of there before they were discovered. He understood now that that had been wishful thinking, born of his desire to protect Olivia from any more trauma.

He glanced at her and mouthed, "Hang in there."

She gave a little nod.

Behind the uniformed officers was a slim, blond man in a sports jacket and crisp white shirt who came striding forward. Max breathed out a little sigh, partly from relief and partly from weariness. It was a Howard County detective, a guy named Fisher, and Max had also worked with him. Unlike Hamilton, he was one of the good guys. Which didn't mean he was just going to let them walk away from three dead bodies without a lot of explanations. Hopefully he wouldn't know that Jack had been at Larson's house, where there were two more.

Fisher started by inquiring, "Weren't the four of you at that murder scene a few days ago?" Before anyone could answer, he added, "What the hell is going on now? We got a call about a gunshot up here."

So that was how they had gotten here so fast, Max

thought as he watched the detective looking at the men on the ground.

Before Max could answer, Olivia spoke. "Like at my house, this is about the murders of people in my Donley High reunion class."

The detective swung to her, taking in her bedraggled appearance. "Do I know you?"

"I'm Olivia Winters, a member of the ten-year reunion class."

"And that famous model."

"Is that relevant?"

"Maybe it's more relevant that trouble is following you around."

Max jumped into the conversation. "The man who killed Claire Lowden kidnapped Ms. Winters and brought her here. It was Troy Masters. We figured it out and came to rescue her. When we got here, the security guard was already dead."

Fisher looked at the two dead men on the ground. "Neither one of these is Masters."

"The guard must have discovered Masters dragging Ms. Winters here. The other guy is Damon Davidson—the ex-con who cut me up yesterday in Baltimore," Max supplied.

"The guy who put you in the hospital?" Fisher clarified.

"Yeah."

"And you left against doctor's orders."

"How do you know that?"

"We've kept you on our radar."

Max sighed. "Okay. I found out Ms. Winters had been kidnapped—presumably by Masters," he said, leaving out the other suspect.

"And you didn't call the police for help?"

"Not after the help I was getting from Hamilton," Max snapped.

Fisher gave him a long look. "Hamilton is dead."

The information drew a gasp from Olivia, who hadn't known about the two previous murders. "How?" she asked.

"He and Tommy Larson were found dead at Larson's home."

The blood had drained from Olivia's face. "Oh no."

Max saw Fisher take in her reaction.

"So the next question is, where's Troy Masters?" he asked.

"In an underground room beneath the cabin." Max gestured behind himself and decided that the only way they were going to get out of this was to tell the truth—or most of it. "He was holding Ms. Winters there. When he came at her with a knife, I shot him."

"He's dead?" Fisher asked.

"Yeah."

"I think we're going down to headquarters," Fisher said.

"Good idea. I think I need to sit down," Max answered. He could feel the stimulant he'd taken wearing off.

Olivia gave him a worried look.

"I'm okay," he said.

He was still thinking their best chance of getting out of this was to tell the truth. But he was sure there was one thing Olivia wanted to leave out.

"I got to Ms. Winters as Masters was trying to rape her," he said.

The detective's gaze swung to her, and she nodded. Then her bottom lip began to tremble.

Max looked at the cops who were still surrounding them. "She needs to sit down, too."

Once again they were taken to Howard County police headquarters in separate cars, although under friendlier circumstances.

This time Olivia went in first. Then Max, followed by Shane and Jack. As Max told his story to Fisher, he gathered that the detective didn't think much of the way Hamilton had handled the case.

Max was running on fumes, and he'd hoped they could go right back to the hotel, but when they stepped outside, a crowd of reporters was waiting for them.

"The reunion killer is dead?" a man from one of the local television stations shouted.

"Yes," Shane answered.

"And Ms. Winters was a target?"

"Yes," she said.

"He kidnapped you?" someone else asked.

"Yes."

"Can you tell us what that was like?"

Max glanced at her, seeing the rigid set of her jaw. "Ms. Winters needs to rest," he said. "Get the rest of the story from the cops."

"I'll have something to say later," she told the crowd.

"Were you trying to throw them a bone?" Max asked when they'd climbed into the back of Shane's SUV.

"Actually I was thinking about something I want to say, but not now," she said wearily.

"So we're going back to the hotel?" Shane asked.

"Yeah. I need some sleep," Max said.

When Olivia finally unlocked the door, Max was swaying on his feet.

"You need to get back in bed," she told him.

"I know. After a shower," he answered, hearing the exhausted sound of his own voice.

He knew that he and Olivia had to talk, and that the three Rockfort men needed to compare notes about the lead-up to the scene at the cabin, but he couldn't do either one right now.

He threw off his clothes, took a quick shower, and pulled on shorts before climbing under the covers, and he didn't wake until hours later, when he realized Olivia wasn't with him.

He lay still for a few minutes, testing his body. He seemed to be in pretty good shape, all things considered. But where was Olivia? After their conversation in the hospital, he'd hoped the two of them would stay together. Now he wondered if her experience in the underground room had changed things. And what had she told Fisher?

Max had only been with her and Masters at the end of the ordeal, which left her free to tell the detective any version of the facts she wanted.

Hoping he would find her in the living room, he pushed himself up, pulled on a T-shirt and jeans that were still in his carry bag, and went into the next room. To his relief, Olivia was there with the TV turned low, listening to an account of "the reunion murders."

"You want to watch?" she asked.

"I've had enough of it."

She clicked the remote and he sat down next to her, slid closer, and waited.

"Shane stopped by and brought me some breakfast."

"I slept all night?"

"Right. I left some sticky buns for you. And there's a coffeepot in the room."

"Good." He was still speaking in sentences of one syllable as he reached for the tray and picked up a bun, munching on it. Olivia brought him coffee, and he drank some, wondering when the conversation would turn serious.

When he was finished with the bun, he licked his fingers and wiped them on a paper napkin.

"That was good."

She gave him a little smile. "You're not too talkative this morning."

"Neither are you."

"You're up for a serious discussion?"

"Yeah."

He thought she might say something personal, instead she went back to the case.

"When Shane was here, he had some stuff to say about Troy Masters."

"Such as?"

"He never did really well in any of the businesses he started. There was a cleaning service and a restaurant that both went bust. He put on a show of being successful, but mostly he was living on investments he inherited from his family."

Max nodded. They hadn't dug into his background at that level because he had simply been one of several suspects until the past few days.

"Maybe his rampage was triggered by some recent financial failures. Up until the past year, he had been doing pretty well with the investment income. It seems he'd lost a lot of money in the stock market—partly from the market downturn and partly because of some wrong decisions. Probably he couldn't cope with the failure."

"That could have contributed," Max agreed. "But most people who fail in business or investments don't need to start killing."

He heard Olivia swallow. "I'd like to forget about Troy Masters, but he's always going to be part of my past." She looked at Max, then away. "On the way over to police headquarters, I thought about what I was going to say to Fisher. But I didn't decide until I was in the interview room."

He waited for her to continue.

"I told Fisher I was raped in high school by Masters and raped again yesterday."

His breath caught. "I didn't know if you were going to say anything about that."

She gave him a direct look. "And I told Fisher you took away the condom so I wouldn't have to talk about the rape if I didn't want to."

"What did he say?"

"He said nobody else had to know the details. Troy is dead, and nobody's going to prosecute him."

She laid her head on Max's shoulder, and he put his arm around her. "I also decided Fisher had to know that Troy was killing people to hide what he'd done in high school. Not just to me, but to that girl in Baltimore."

"Yeah."

"It could have just been about her, but I realized his raping me was part of it."

"How did Fisher react to all that?"

"I think it helped him understand."

"Good."

She swallowed hard. "Something you don't know. Troy told me that Angela wasn't really raped at all. That she just said she was so we'd keep quiet together."

Anger flashed through him. "Nice of him. It might or might not be true."

"I know. I hope he was lying."

"Yeah." He dragged in a breath and exhaled. "Don't let what he said mess with your head—or interfere with your life."

"I'm trying not to."

"Good. Because you have better things to do." He brought his mouth to hers, moving his lips, showing her the depth of his feelings for her.

When they broke apart, he said in a husky voice, "We both need to get him out of our minds, and I know how we can do it."

"I think we're on the same wavelength."

He stood and took her hand and led her back to the bedroom. He needed to love her, and he ached to make it good for her, to wipe out the awful things that had happened—and to show her how much she meant to him.

His tongue played with the seam of her lips, and she opened for him so that he could explore the line of her teeth, then stroke the sensitive tissue on the inside of her lips.

When his tongue dipped farther into her mouth, tasting her, he felt hot, needy sensations curling through him.

She moved her hands over his back, and he stroked her, too, his fingers gliding over her ribs, then the sides of her breasts.

When he found her nipples, they were rigid, poking out against her shirt.

But he saw her eyes were squeezed tightly closed.

"Did he touch you there?" he whispered.

"No. I did it. To get his attention."

"Good thinking."

"But…"

"Let's get that out of your mind."

He kissed her again, trying to show her how much he loved her, how much he wanted her.

And when she tangled her hands in his hair, holding his mouth to hers, he smiled against her lips.

Still kissing him, she eased a little away so that she could slip her hands under his T-shirt and stroke his chest, finding his nipples, circling them with her fingers, making them tighten.

"Why did you put your clothes on when you got up?" she whispered.

"In case someone knocked at the door. My mistake." He pulled the shirt over his head and reached for the button at the top of his jeans. But he left on his briefs as he kicked the pants away.

She was wearing a knit top and twill pants. He pulled the top over her head, waiting to see her reaction. When she smiled at him, he reached around to unsnap her bra and get it out of the way so that he could lower his mouth to one of her breasts.

Her breath caught as he licked at her nipple, then sucked it into his mouth, loving the pebbled texture.

"Yes," she murmured as she clasped her palms around his head.

He was burning with the need for her, but he went slowly, making sure she was with him every step of the way. He removed her slacks but left on her panties for the time being as he took her down to the surface of the bed, then gathered her close, still a little worried that he might be going too fast after what had happened with Masters.

"Okay?" he asked.

"Good. Really good."

He continued to stroke her and kiss her, thrilled as he sensed her passion rising to meet his.

They both got rid of their remaining clothing, and when she whispered, "Do it now," he parted her legs and eased inside her.

Her eyes met his, and neither of them moved for a long moment. Then she raised her hips, and he responded, losing himself in the joy of making love with her. He held back, waiting for her to climax. And when he felt her contract around him, he let go, coming in a burst of intense feeling and emotion.

Shifting to the side, he held her close.

"Thank you," she whispered.

"A pleasure."

They drifted in each other's arms for a while, until he said, "I'd like to stay in bed with you all day, but the guys are going to want to talk about yesterday. And probably Shane wants to share more of his research."

"I know."

"We'll make it quick," he promised.

They got dressed, and Max was about to call his partners when he heard a knock at the door.

"Who is it?" he called out.

"Jerry Ellison."

"Who?"

Olivia stepped up beside him, a stunned look on her face. "My agent. The guy you talked to on the phone."

"What do you want?" Max demanded.

"I want to talk to Olivia."

Max glanced at her. When she nodded, he opened the door and a short, balding man wearing a gray turtleneck and dark slacks stepped into the room.

This was the famous Jerry Ellison? The guy who had been so important in Olivia's career for ten years? If you passed him on the street, you wouldn't give him a second look.

Still, Max felt his nerves twang like banjo strings as he waited to find out what Ellison and Olivia were going to say to each other. The man was looking at her, taking in her mussed hair. He probably had a pretty good idea of what they'd been doing a little while ago.

"How did you find me?" Olivia asked.

"Not too hard. There's a crowd of reporters down there chomping for red meat."

She made a sound of distress. "I thought they hadn't figured out where we were."

"Think again."

"What do you want?" Olivia asked.

"You can take a few days off, but this kidnapping thing is huge. We can use this, baby. Top model abducted. You can sell that story for big bucks, and you can name your price for any job you want."

"Can I?"

"Yeah."

She glanced at Max, who was now standing with his breath frozen in his lungs.

"You had a lot of power over me because you knew how to influence a naive girl. But you don't have that kind of power over me now. If I come back to New York, it's on my own terms," she said.

Max saw the other guy's jaw drop. "What do you mean?" Ellison asked.

"I can see the advantage of using my current notoriety. But I'm not going to work the schedule I've been on."

"Okay," Ellison said cautiously. "What would you want?"

"I'd want to work only two weeks a month. And I'd want at least two months a year when I didn't work at all."

Ellison swallowed. "We could do that."

Olivia looked surprised, like she hadn't expected him to agree, but apparently he could see that getting Olivia Winters on any terms was better than not getting her at all.

"Let's talk in a few days," she said. "I think everybody will understand that I've been through a terrible ordeal, and I need some time off."

"Yes. Okay. Fine," he said quickly.

"I'll call you late next week," she said.

"Sure. That's fine." He backed out of the room, and Max shut the door and put on the security chain.

"You really only want to work two weeks a month?" Max asked.

"Yes."

"Why?"

"Two reasons. I hope. I'd like to be an advocate for rape victims. If that's okay with you."

"You don't need my permission."

"A lot of guys wouldn't like people to know their wife was raped."

"Their wife," he said.

She flushed. "Am I getting ahead of myself?

He felt joy swell inside him. "No. It was what I was hoping when I asked if you wanted to be in a relationship."

"I was hoping that, too. When I woke up with Troy in that underground room, I wanted to live—so I could spend the rest of my life with you."

He reached for her, hugging her to him. They stayed locked together until she said, "We should have that meeting with Shane and Jack and get it over with."

"And after they leave, we can…"

She gave him a wicked smile, then finished the sentence differently than he'd expected, "Go up to the courthouse and get a marriage license. If we know it's what we really want."

"Love to," he answered, "But I guess you'll have to wear a disguise if the hotel is full of reporters like Jerry said."

"I'll just go without makeup, and they won't know it's me."

"It will take more than that. Maybe a Groucho Marx nose and glasses."

She grinned at him, and he grinned back, thinking of the astonishing way his life had turned out. First he'd found good friends he could depend on like no others. And he'd found an amazing woman who wanted to spend her life with him. It was more than he'd ever dared hope for, and he was going to make the most of it.

About the Author

New York Times and *USA Today* bestselling author Rebecca York's writing has been compared to Dick Francis, Sherrilyn Kenyon, and Maggie Shayne. Her award-winning books have been translated into twenty-two languages and optioned for film. A recipient of the RWA Centennial Award, she lives in Maryland, near Washington, D.C., which is often the setting of her romantic suspense novels.

Bad Nights

Rockfort Security

by Rebecca York

New York Times Bestselling Author

You only get a second chance...

Private operative and former Navy SEAL Jack Brandt barely escapes a disastrous undercover assignment, thanks to the most intriguing woman he's ever met. When his enemies track him to her doorstep, he'll do anything to protect Morgan from the danger closing in on them both...

If you stay alive...

Since her husband's death, Morgan Rains has only been going through the motions. She didn't think anything could shock her—until she finds a gorgeous man stumbling naked and injured through the woods behind her house. He's mysterious, intimidating—and undeniably compelling.

Thrown together into a pressure cooker of danger and intrigue, Jack and Morgan are finding in each other a reason to live—if they can survive.

"Rebecca York's writing is fast-paced, suspenseful,
and loaded with tension."—Jayne Ann Krentz

For more Rebecca York, visit:

www.sourcebooks.com

Betrayed

Rockfort Security

by Rebecca York

New York Times and *USA Today* Bestselling Author

To trust

Rockfort Security operative Shane Gallagher has been brought into S&D Systems to find a security leak. Confidential information has been stolen, and Shane suspects Elena Reyes, a systems analyst with the access and know-how to pull it off. As he finds excuses to get close to her, their attraction is too strong to ignore, but how can Shane trust the very woman he's investigating?

Or not to trust

Elena has spent her life proving herself, but now she's risking it all: everything she's worked for, and her growing feelings for Shane. Much as she wants to trust the devastatingly sexy, hard-as-nails investigator, she can't let herself fall for him…the stakes are too high.

"Rebecca York delivers page-turning suspense." —Nora Roberts

"Rebecca York's writing is fast paced, suspenseful, and loaded with tension." —Jayne Ann Krentz

For more Rebecca York, visit:

www.sourcebooks.com

I Own the Dawn

The Night Stalkers

by M. L. Buchman

—⁓—

NAME: Archibald Jeffrey Stevenson III

RANK: First Lieutenant, DAP Hawk copilot

MISSION: Strategy and execution of special ops maneuvers

NAME: Kee Smith

RANK: Sergeant, Night Stalker gunner and sharpshooter

MISSION: Whatever it takes to get the job done

You wouldn't think it could get worse, until it does…

When a special mission slowly unravels, it is up to Kee and Archie to get their team out of an impossible situation with international implications. With her weaponry knowledge and his strategic thinking, plus the explosive attraction that puts them into exact synchrony, together they might just have a fighting chance…

—⁓—

"The first novel in Buchman's new military suspense series is an action-packed adventure. With a super-stud hero, a strong heroine, and a backdrop of 1600 Pennsylvania Avenue and the world of the Washington elite, it will grab readers from the first page." — *RT Book Reviews* (4 stars)

For more M.L. Buchman, visit:

www.sourcebooks.com

Wait Until Dark

The Night Stalkers

by M.L. Buchman

NAME: Big John Wallace

RANK: Staff Sergeant, chief mechanic and gunner

MISSION: To serve and protect his crew and country

NAME: Connie Davis

RANK: Sergeant, flight engineer, mechanical wizard

MISSION: To be the best… and survive

Two crack mechanics, one impossible mission

Being in the Night Stalkers is Connie Davis's way of facing her demons head-on, but mountain-strong Big John Wallace is a threat on all fronts. Their passion is explosive but their conflicts are insurmountable. When duty calls them to a mission no one else could survive, they'll fly into the night together—ready or not.

"Filled with action, adventure, and danger… Buchman's novels will appeal to readers who like romances as well as fans of military fiction." —*Booklist* Starred Review of *I Own the Dawn*

For more M.L. Buchman, visit:

www.sourcebooks.com

Take Over at Midnight

The Night Stalkers
by M.L. Buchman

NAME: Lola LaRue

RANK: Chief Warrant Officer 3

MISSION: Copilot deadly choppers on the world's most dangerous missions

NAME: Tim Maloney

RANK: Sergeant

MISSION: Man the guns and charm the ladies

The past doesn't matter, when their future is doomed

Nothing sticks to "Crazy" Tim Maloney, until he falls hard for a tall Creole beauty with a haunted past and a penchant for reckless flying. Lola LaRue never thought she'd be susceptible to a man's desire, but even with Tim igniting her deepest passions, it may be too late now…With the nation under an imminent threat of biological warfare, Tim and Lola are the only ones who can stop the madness—and to do that, they're going to have to trust each other way beyond their limits…

"Quite simply a great read. Once again Buchman takes the military romance to a new standard of excellence."—*Booklist*

For more M.L. Buchman, visit:

www.sourcebooks.com

Pure Heat

The Firehawks

by M.L. Buchman

―――――

These daredevil smokejumpers fight more than fires

The elite fire experts of Mount Hood Aviation fly into places even the CIA can't penetrate.

She lives to fight fires

Carly Thomas could read burn patterns before she knew the alphabet. A third-generation forest fire specialist who lost both her father and her fiancé to the flames, she's learned to live life like she fights fires: with emotions shut down.

But he's lit an inferno she can't quench

Former smokejumper Steve "Merks" Mercer can no longer fight fires up close and personal, but he can still use his intimate knowledge of wildland burns as a spotter and drone specialist. Assigned to copilot a Firehawk with Carly, they take to the skies to battle the worst wildfire in decades and discover a terrorist threat hidden deep in the Oregon wilderness—but it's the heat between them that really sizzles.

―――――

"A wonderful love story…seamlessly woven in
among technical details. Poignant and touching."
—*RT Book Reviews* Top Pick, 4.5 Stars

For more M.L. Buchman, visit:

www.sourcebooks.com

Light Up the Night
The Night Stalkers
by M.L. Buchman

—᷍᷍—

NAME: Trisha O'Malley
RANK: Second Lieutenant and AH-6M "Little Bird" Pilot
MISSION: Take down Somali pirates, and deny her past
NAME: William Bruce
RANK: Navy SEAL Lieutenant
MISSION: Rescue hostages, and protect his past—against all comers

They both have something to hide

When hotshot SOAR helicopter pilot Trisha O'Malley rescues Navy SEAL Bill Bruce from his undercover mission in Somalia, it ignites his fury. Everything about Trisha triggers his mistrust: her elusive past, her wild energy, and her habit of flying past safety's edge. Even as the heat between them turns into passion's fire, Bill and Trisha must team up to confront their pasts and survive Somalia's pirate lords.

—᷍᷍—

"The perfect blend of riveting, high-octane military action interspersed with tender, heartfelt moments. With a sigh-worthy scarred hero and a strong Irish redhead heroine, Buchman might just be at the top of the game in terms of relationship development." —*RT Book Reviews*

For more M.L. Buchman, visit:

www.sourcebooks.com

Thrill Ride

Black Knights Inc.

by Julie Ann Walker

New York Times and *USA Today* bestselling author

He's gone rogue

Ex-Navy SEAL Rock Babineaux's job is to get information, and he's one of the best in the business. Until something goes horribly wrong and he's being hunted by his own government. Even his best friends at the covert special-ops organization Black Knights Inc. aren't sure they can trust him. He thinks he can outrun them all, but his former partner—a curvy bombshell who knows just how to drive him wild—refuses to cut him loose.

She won't back down

Vanessa Cordera hasn't been the team's communication specialist very long, but she knows how to read people—no way is Rock guilty of murder. And she'll go to hell and back to help him prove it. Sure, the sexy Cajun has his secrets, but there's no one in the world she'd rather have by her side in a tight spot. Which is good, because they're about to get very tight...

"Walker is ready to join the ranks of great romantic suspense writers." —*RT Book Reviews*

For more Black Knights Inc., visit:

www.sourcebooks.com

Born Wild

Black Knights Inc.

by Julie Ann Walker

New York Times and *USA Today* bestselling author

Tick...Tick...

"Wild" Bill Reichert knows a thing or two about explosives. The ex-Navy SEAL can practically rig a bomb blindfolded. But there's no way to diffuse the inevitable fireworks the day Eve Edens walks back into his life, asking for help.

Boom!

Eve doesn't know what to do when the Chicago police won't believe someone is out to hurt her. The only place to turn is Black Knights Inc.—after all, no one is better at protection that the covert special-ops team. Yet there's also no one better at getting her all turned on than Bill Reichert. She has a feeling this is one blast from the past that could backfire big-time.

"Drama, danger, and sexual tension... Romantic suspense at its best." —*Night Owl Reviews* Reviewer Top Pick, 5 Stars

For more Julie Ann Walker, visit:

www.sourcebooks.com

Hell for Leather

Black Knights Inc.

by Julie Ann Walker

New York Times and *USA Today* bestselling author

Unlimited Drive

Only a crisis could persuade Delilah Fairchild to abandon her beloved biker bar, let alone ask Black Knights Inc. operator Bryan "Mac" McMillan for help. But her uncle has vanished into thin air, and sexy, surly Mac has the connections to help her find him. What the big, blue-eyed Texan has against her is a mystery… but when the bullets start to fly, Mac becomes her only hope of survival, and her only chance of finding her uncle alive.

Unstoppable Passion

Mac knows a thing or two about beautiful women—mainly that they can't be trusted. Throw in a ticking clock, a deadly terrorist, and some missing nuclear weapons, and a man just might find himself on the wrong end of the gun. But facing down danger with Delilah is one passion-filled thrill ride…

"The heat between the hero and heroine is hotter than a firecracker lit on both ends… Readers are in for one hell of ride!" —*RT Book Reviews*, 4.5 Stars

For more Julie Ann Walker, visit:

www.sourcebooks.com

Full Throttle

Black Knights Inc.

by Julie Ann Walker

New York Times and *USA Today* bestselling author

Steady hands, cool head…

Carlos "Steady" Soto's nerves of steel have served him well at the covert government defense firm of Black Knights Inc. But nothing has prepared him for the emotional roller coaster of guarding the woman he once loved and lost.

Will all he's got be enough?

Abby Thompson is content to leave politics and international intrigue to her father—the president of the United States—until she's taken hostage half a world away, and she fears her father's policy of not negotiating with terrorists will be her death sentence. There's one glimmer of hope: the man whose heart she broke, but she can never tell him why…

As they race through the jungle in a bid for safety, the heat simmering between Steady and Abby could mean a second chance for them—*if* they make it out alive…

Praise for Julie Ann Walker:

"Drama, danger, and sexual tension… Romantic suspense at its best." —*Night Owl Reviews*, 5 Stars, Reviewer Top Pick, *Born Wild*

For more Julie Ann Walker, visit:

www.sourcebooks.com

Cover Me

Elite Force

by Catherine Mann

It should have been a simple mission...

Pararescueman Wade Rocha fast ropes from the back of a helicopter into a blizzard to save a climber stranded on an Aleutian Island, but Sunny Foster insists she can take care of herself just fine...

But when it comes to passion, nothing is ever simple...

With the snowstorm kicking into overdrive, Sunny and Wade hunker down in a cave and barely resist the urge to keep each other warm...until they discover the frozen remains of a horrific crime...

Unable to trust the local police force, Sunny and Wade investigate, while their irresistible passion for each other gets them more and more dangerously entangled...

Praise for Catherine Mann:

"Catherine Mann weaves deep emotion with intense suspense for an all-night read." —#1 New York Times *bestseller Sherrilyn Kenyon*

For more Catherine Mann, visit:

www.sourcebooks.com

Hot Zone

Elite Force

by Catherine Mann

—⁓—

He'll take any mission, the riskier the better…

The haunted eyes of pararescueman Hugh Franco should have been her first clue that deep pain roiled beneath the surface. But if Amelia couldn't see the damage, how could she be expected to know he'd break her heart?

She'll prove to be his biggest risk yet…

Amelia Bailey's not the kind of girl who usually needs rescuing…but these are anything but usual circumstances.

—⁓—

Praise for Catherine Mann:

"Nobody writes military romance like Catherine Mann!"
—*Suzanne Brockmann*, New York Times *bestselling author of* Tall, Dark and Deadly

"A powerful, passionate read not to be missed!"
—*Lori Foster*, New York Times *bestselling author of* When You Dare

For more Catherine Mann, visit:

www.sourcebooks.com

Under Fire

Elite Force

by Catherine Mann

—◦◦◦—

No holds barred, in love or war…

A decorated hero, pararescueman Liam McCabe lives to serve. Six months ago, he and Rachel Flores met in the horrific aftermath of an earthquake in the Bahamas. They were tempted by an explosive attraction, but then they parted ways. Still, Liam has thought about Rachel every day—and night—since.

Now, after ignoring all his phone calls for six months, Rachel has turned up on base with a wild story about a high-ranking military traitor. She claims no one but Liam can help her—and she won't trust anyone else.

With nothing but her word and the testimony of a discharged military cop to go on, Liam would be insane to risk his career—even his life—to help this woman who left him in the dust.

—◦◦◦—

"Absolutely wonderful, a thrilling ride of ups and downs that will have readers hanging onto the edge of their seats."
—*RT Book Reviews* Top Pick of the Month, 4 1/2 stars

For more Catherine Mann, visit:

www.sourcebooks.com

Free Fall

by Catherine Mann

USA Today Bestselling Author

On this mission, there are no accidents...

Pararescueman Jose "Cuervo" James is the guy they call for the most dangerous assignments. He lives for his job.

On a high-risk rescue deep in the African jungle, Jose encounters sexy, smart Interpol agent Stella Carson. They'd once had an affair that burned hot and fast, but family is everything to Stella, and Jose just can't go there.

Fate has thrown them into the deadly hot zone together, and sparks will fly...but only if they can live to tell about it.

"Mann sweeps readers along with pulse-pounding
suspense, passion, and a full-out frontal assault
of the senses that will keep readers gripping
their seats."—*RT Book Review*, 4.5 Stars

"Mann's novel of romantic suspense has everything
she's known for—engaging protagonists, a solid
military background, great sex and sexual tension, and
a ripped-from-the-headlines immediacy."—*Booklist*

For more Catherine Mann, visit:

www.sourcebooks.com